Wrong Score

Kenna King

Copyright © 2024 by Kenna King

All rights reserved.

This book is a work of fiction.

No part of this publication may be reproduced, distributed, or transmitted in any form or by any means, including photocopying, recording, or other electronic or mechanical methods, without the prior written permission of the publisher, except as permitted by U.S. copyright law. For permission requests, contact Bridgetown Publishing Inc at info@bridgetownpublishing.com

The story, all names, characters, and incidents portrayed in this production are fictitious. No identification with actual persons (living or deceased), places, buildings, and products is intended or should be inferred.

1st edition 2024

Contents

Dedication	1
Chapter One	5
Chapter Two	20
Chapter Three	36
Chapter Four	45
Chapter Five	58
Chapter Six	75
Chapter Seven	84
Chapter Eight	92
Chapter Nine	102
Chapter Ten	113
Chapter Eleven	125
Chapter Twelve	145
Chapter Thirteen	161
Chapter Fourteen	167
Chapter Fifteen	173

Chapter Sixteen	183
Chapter Seventeen	191
Chapter Eighteen	199
Chapter Nineteen	210
Chapter Twenty	215
Chapter Twenty-One	227
Chapter Twenty-Two	235
Chapter Twenty-Three	242
Chapter Twenty-Four	250
Chapter Twenty-Five	260
Chapter Twenty-Six	268
Chapter Twenty-Seven	272
Chapter Twenty-Eight	277
Chapter Twenty-Nine	283
Chapter Thirty	288
Chapter Thirty-One	296
Chapter Thirty-Two	303
Chapter Thirty-Three	310
Epilogue	317

Dedication

I want to take a moment to thank every single one of you who have taken this journey with me and have loved the Hawkeyes boys as I do. I appreciate each and every one of you! Your sweet Insta DMs, emails and getting to know you on my Facebook reader group has been the highlight of this entire experience. Keep them coming, I love hearing from you!

I also want to acknowledge the amazing people who have put up with me and my crazy ideas, helping me bring my characters to life. My amazing editors, Michelle, Erin, Julie and Madeline. Thank you for steering me in the right direction and for taking my last-minute emails. And to my insanely talented PR guru Mikaela who has been with me since the beginning, believing in me and taking over so much so that I can focus on writing. I couldn't do this without any of you.

I want to thank the amazing beta readers who have gone through and helped me with all those left over errors. You all have saved me, and I appreciate you: Chelsea, Hosana, Julia, Caitlin, Taylor, Alicia, Stephen, and so many other amazing readers who have reached out!

And lastly, my husband and children who have been living on take-out for the last year while I have been writing my heart out

– Kidding... kind of. It has been a marathon not a sprint and I have to thank my husband for jumping in to make sure that everything on the family front is covered so that I could write these stories. You are my rock!

To Keep up with Kenna King, follow here:
Subscribe to my email: https://www.kennaking.com/
Join the Facebook Reader Group: Kenna King's MVPs
Check out the Instagram: @kennakingbooks

The Hawkeyes Hockey Series

1. Cocky Score

2. Filthy Score

3. Brutal Score

4. Rough Score

5. Dirty Score

6. Lucky Score

7. Tough Score

8. Perfect Score

9. Wrong Score

Check out **www.kennakingbooks.com** for more books and information.

SCAN ME

Chapter One

Bex

The sharp slap of a hockey stick echoes through the stadium pulling me back to the present. Briggs Conley, our right wing, sends the puck rocketing toward the net, a streak of black against white ice, and barrels past Reeve Aisa, our goalie. He dives for it, fully committed—but it's no use. The puck slams into the back of the net with a dull thud, followed by the shrill sound of Ezra's whistle cutting through the cold air like a warning shot.

Aisa sprawls out on the ice, punching at it with his padded glove, his frustration clear from every angle of the rink.

He glances up, catching my eye, already bracing himself. He knows damn well that I won't be pleased, but there's a tight line between what I can expect out of him, and what might push his knee too far, so soon out of rehab.

It's been two months since Aisa was cleared to return to the ice after his injury, just in time for Thanksgiving. Although he's allowed to practice with the team, he's not yet approved for games. His progress has been steady—at least until this week.

Something's been off with him the last few days–I can feel it.

This isn't his usual energy on the ice that I've come to expect from him.

The rest of the team, scattered all around the rink, turn back, looking in my direction expectantly for instruction or critique.

"Oi!" I yell out toward Aisa, tossing up my hands. "What the bloody hell was that? You know this play better than anyone. How did you miss the shot?" I call out, my voice echoing through the Hawkeyes stadium.

"Sorry, Coach!" I hear Aisa yell, dressed in full goalie gear, his facemask blocking most of my ability to see any facial expression from here. "I got it now–I'm good. Let's run it again. I won't miss this time."

I shoot a look at my assistant Coach, Ezra.

He's been my assistant coach since I started six years ago. We've worked together long enough that we don't have to exchange a word. He knows I'm not happy with the play and he also knows that I've been considering changing out Reeve for Seven this entire week. But with Seven retiring after this season, I need Reeve to get stronger and to get as much practice time as possible. Because unless I can convince Seven to stay on as the special team's goalie coach next year, Seven plans to move him and his girlfriend Brynn down to Mexico permanently.

Ezra gives me a nod, in agreement with Aisa to run the play again.

"You heard the lad, let's run the play again," I say with a deep sigh, knowing well enough that I've got a soft spot for Aisa, especially after I spent an entire night in the OR waiting for him to get out of surgery after a hit and run took him out one rainy night in Seattle. Ezra knows I worry about favoritism—letting my concern for a player personally cloud my judgment that could cost us the playoffs. "This time, I want to see sharper passes and quicker transitions. And Aisa?" I call out, his eyes locked on mine. "You'd better guard that net with your life."

He gives a curt nod. He knows what I expect.

All of my players do.

Lake Powers, our team captain and our left wing takes the lead, calling out the play again.

As the team repositions themselves, I inexplicably glance up at the rows of stadium seats behind me, not surprised in the least to see the same woman sitting in the third row, seat seven, and directly behind where I stand in the home box. The same seat she's always sitting in during practice.

Rowan Summers.

A reporter for *The Seattle Sunrise* by day, but I'm fairly certain she spends every other waking hour plotting new ways to piss me the fuck off.

I watch as her eyes skim over the rink from right to left, taking in the players on the ice, undoubtedly scrutinizing every move, probably jotting down notes for her next riveting article, that's sure to include what Ninja Turtle Briggs' most relates with and if Kaenan ever wished for a pony on his third birthday.

I should be watching my players instead of wasting a second wondering what she writes in that notebook of hers. And why the hell doesn't she bring a tablet or laptop like all the other reporters do? And for Christ's sake, why the hell is she determined to catch her death of cold out dressed like it's game day in trousers, a thin blouse and a suit jacket. I shouldn't give a shit that she's shivering half the time behind me or rubbing her hands together to keep her fingers from freezing solid.

It's entirely inconvenient the way her golden blonde hair catches the overhead lights, making her hair look as soft as spun silk. And how utterly distracting the way her full pink lips demand my attention whenever she speaks, even when she's spouting complete nonsense in my direction.

And her laugh. Fuck... her laugh echoes through the rink when a player says something funny during their interview that has her amused. My head whips in her direction no matter where she is in the stadium, whether I like it or not. It's as if I don't have any control over my body's reaction when it comes to her.

Any misguided interest in her can easily be stifled due to the increasing marks against her. For one, she's still a reporter that I don't trust and she's also eighteen years younger than me, which is reason enough for me to keep my distance. Her eyes shoot from the rink down to me, locking with mine. I turn quickly, breaking the connection and try to focus back on the players out on the ice.

Ezra moves closer to me, his eyes still on the team running the play. There's a whistle between his fingers, ready to end the practice run if needed, and a clipboard in his hand. His breath forms small clouds in the cold air. "I know you didn't want to make that call but you're not going easy on Aisa by keeping him in."

I don't take my eyes off the players either. "We need the team ready for the upcoming away game. Making the call to keep him in could cost us the playoffs."

Ezra nods. "He's come a long way. I honestly thought his career was over after the accident but he's been performing above what any of us thought he'd be able to. This week is an off week... so what? It'll get better."

I frown, my gaze zeroing in on Aisa as he skates back and forth between the front of the net, waiting. He's right, Aisa's been through a lot. My memory flashes back to four months ago when I burst out of Oakley's Bar the second I heard commotion inside the bar that Reeve had gotten hit by a car.

I remember sprinting full force toward Reeve lying lifeless on the asphalt with Keely kneeling over him screaming for someone to call 911. I remember the feeling of his weight on the gurney as I helped the EMTs hoist him into the back of the ambulance. I thought I might never speak to him again. And then I spent the entire night in the OR with Keely and Sam Roberts, the Hawkeyes GM, while he was in surgery.

Ezra's right. It's a miracle that Reeve's back out on the ice at all, let alone practicing at the capacity that he is. But Aisa is a force to be reckoned with. Ever since he joined the team, he's been the first to show up and the last to leave. He puts in more time on the ice than any other player, and bribes players with pizza and beer to come out and huck some pucks at him on their days off.

He still has a heart for this game, and he reminds me a lot of myself in my earlier years when I was playing professionally, but he should be improving this week, not missing a shot from our own team on a play he already knows.

Powers shoots to Conley, and then Conley shoots it to Slade Matthews, our center, who shoots the puck back to Powers.

Aisa dives down, stopping the puck with his pads but the puck gets away from him and Matthews recovers it, shooting it back at Aisa and making it past him and into the net.

Score for Matthews.

Ezra blows the whistle again at the end of the play.

"Aisa!" I call out, waving him over. He looks up from the net, his eyes meeting mine through the cage of his helmet.

He skates over while Ezra motions for Seven Wrenley, another goalie for the team, to jump out onto the ice and take Aisa's spot in the huddle with Powers and the rest of the team. Aisa comes to a stop at the boards in front of me. "Coach... I...I" he stammers, a flicker of something in his eyes. Guilt? Uncertainty? Disappointment?

He's never distracted. That's one of his best qualities. Just like me, he uses the ice to escape.

I lean in closer, lowering my voice. "What's going on out there? Is your knee acting up? Do you need Keely to look at it–"

Reeve hesitates, glancing around at his teammates. "No, no, It's not my knee. It's sore but it's fine–stronger every day."

"Okay, then what's going on up here?" I say, knocking lightly on his helmet.

"It's nothing, coach... really. Just some personal stuff with Keely. But I'll get it together, I promise."

"Keely? What's wrong with Keely? Is she okay?" I ask, unable to keep the sound of concern out of my voice.

Ever since the night of Reeve's accident, and spending the evening in the OR with her, I feel especially protective over Keely, the Hawkeyes' in-house PT.

Yesterday morning, I had an appointment with her for my shoulder. Her stretching techniques have been helping a lot with the pain from the bucket of pucks I shoot every morning between the time slot when Penelope, the Hawkeyes Assistant GM, comes in for morning warm-up and the team comes in for practice.

Keely seemed off, but it's not as if she and I are in the habit of sharing war stories over afternoon tea and biscuits.

"Yeah, she will be. Or at least I think so. Rowan got involved..." he looks up at me and something flashes in his eyes—like he shouldn't have said anything.

"Rowan got involved? Does this have anything to do with the conversation you two were having right before Thanksgiving when she left my office?" I glance back at Rowan's usual spot to find she's not sitting there anymore.

I'd told Rowan to lay off the team. During our first run-in right before Thanksgiving in my office, I warned her off my players. She left, stomping out of my office and leaving the door wide open. I saw her stop in front of Reeve. I couldn't hear what she was telling him, but whatever it was, Reeve didn't look happy.

I can see Reeve bite down on the inside of his lip. He wants to tell me something, but he thinks he shouldn't.

"Aisa, if Rowan has something on you or Keely—"

"Never mind," he blurts out. "It's not important."

It's one thing if Rowan is asking my players trivial questions like, *"Did you leave a cookie for Father Christmas as a kid, and if so, were they chocolate chip or oatmeal raisin?"* but if she's collecting dirt on my players, I need to know about it.

The thought makes my blood boil.

"Take a break, go see Keely about your knee," I tell him.

He nods, practice is almost over anyway and whatever is going on, he needs to work it out so that he comes back to practice ready to play at his best. He skates over towards the player tunnel and heads for the locker room.

The rest of practice passes in a blur of drills and strategy discussions. By the end, I'm more frustrated than ever with my own inability to focus.

"Alright, team," I call out. "Let's wrap it up for today. Good work out there but remember—we're a team. We rise together, we fall together. I want to see that unity on the ice tomorrow."

As the players file off the ice and down the player's tunnel, I make my way to my office, my mind a whirlwind of thoughts.

I leave my office door open. A policy I started when I first started coaching here years ago to allow players, coaches, and any other Hawkeyes employee access to me whenever they need.

I settle into my chair, leaning back and glance around the bland beige walls of my office, Rowan's voice echoing in my head about the lackluster state of my office.

She wasn't wrong in suggesting that my office lacks a personal touch. Besides the large whiteboard that takes up most of the wall to the right of my desk, covered in blue and red marker from working out a play this morning with Powers, everything else was here when I took over for Coach Lennox after he retired. The man who coached me for the years I played for the Hawkeyes, until my injury.

He took with him all of his lifetime achievements he'd accrued over his long career in the NHL. His awards, plaques and signed memorabilia from all the players he coached through the years.

He boxed up the pictures of his wife and kids in Saint Barts for Christmas and the ones of them wearing Mickey Mouse ears in Disney World. The kind of photos I've never had since I chose hockey over a family life. There's no wife and kids waiting at home for me at the end of a long day—a tough game—or a championship loss like last year. Which means, no framed pictures of a family I don't have.

And now at forty-six years, I've stopped looking for 'the one'. The one woman who could knock hockey into second place, giving her the top spot. If anyone had a shot at it, it would have been my ex-wife, Lily. Lily was my college girlfriend and the only woman I thought would have me racing home after practice and away games. But it didn't happen.

I'd stay late to practice to get in more time on the ice. I used my days off to watch replays, pouring over where I could be faster or more accurate. She got tired of being alone and homesick for London. She blindsided me with divorce papers, though if I hadn't been consumed with my rookie year maybe I would have seen the signs.

I barely felt a thing as I signed the divorce papers all while wondering if I could still make it back that night to the stadium to get in more skate time before the janitor locked the doors. When I looked up after signing in the last spot where her lawyer had put bright yellow tabs for me, I saw the tears in her eyes. I knew at that moment that I was the man responsible for breaking her spirit.

I didn't contest the alimony that her lawyer fought for, though she refused it stating that she didn't want a penny from the career that ended us.

I did, however, deposit a large sum into her bank account to help her start a new life, paying to get her into a nice flat on the good side of London. She didn't fight me on that. It was the least I could do after I stole two years of her life... and I guess more if you count the years we were together at university.

I made a pact with myself that day, after she closed the door with the divorce papers in hand, and the movers driving away with the boxes of her things they would ship off to her. I made a pact that I would never break another woman like I broke her. That I'd never settle down with someone again unless I found someone worth giving hockey up for.

Since then, I've dated my fair share of women, but it's only worked to reaffirm that 'the one' doesn't exist. Not for me anyway.

Coach Lennox clapped me on the back on his last day, and my first.

"Now this old girl is ready for new memories," he said, referring to the office space that only held an empty desk, a leather chair, a couch and a coffee table in it. "If the walls could talk about the conversations held here," he reminisced.

I knew a few of them since I used to play for him before I got injured and had to give up playing. Then, when Coach Lennox decided to retire, Phil Carlton called me up, offering me the position.

It took me all of five minutes to decide.

I wasn't done with hockey. Or maybe hockey wasn't done with me.

I didn't have a wife and kids to consider, just two brothers and our mum anxiously waiting for me to move back home and take my spot within the family business. An art printing business that I don't know the first thing about.

My lack of personal mementos in the head coach office mirrors the same lack of personality and family that my penthouse in The Commons has.

The penthouse came fully furnished, and so did this office—both were given to me by the Hawkeyes. I didn't see a reason to change anything. After all, nothing is permanent. Not my first wife, not the team who signed me my rookie year and played me for three more years before trading me, and not the two other teams who would play me long enough to boost their rankings and then trade me, their best player, for two to three mediocre ones.

I was the golden ticket—the wild card in a game of billionaire hockey owners. I was hockey currency, but my contract was expensive, and once they thought their ranking would hold with the players they had, they'd unload me, thinking their team could sustain it, but they never did. Within a year or two, the team would suck again. Eventually, the Hawkeyes made a trade for me and those eight years I played for Phil Carlton were the golden days of the Hawkeyes, before Sam Roberts retired as our team captain and I tore a tendon in my shoulder and it was never the same.

I knew eventually I'd vacate both that penthouse and the office that I've used for the last several years.

A flash of blonde hair streaks across my open office door, causing me to straighten up.

Rowan.

Before I can process what I'm doing, I'm on my feet, moving towards the door. I shouldn't care if she's here. I shouldn't be curious about her whereabouts. Yet, here I am, following the path where I thought I saw that familiar blonde hair move in the corner of my eye.

As I step into the hallway, a faint scent wafts through the air—vanilla and citrus. I inwardly curse myself for recognizing her scent. When the hell did that happen?

I round the corner and stop short. There, at the end of the corridor, stands Reeve and Rowan. Deja vu from Thanksgiving. Their body language is tense, Reeve's face a mask of frustration while Rowan seems to be trying to calm him down. My eyes narrow as I watch their interaction.

What the fuck is going on here? If she's screwing with my players, Phil and Sam will have to see it my way. They'll have to demand a cease to the story with *The Seattle Sunrise*, or at least demand that they have another journalist take over for her.

I take a step closer, straining to hear their conversation, but they're speaking in hushed tones. Reeve crosses his arms over his chest, a gesture to show he doesn't like the conversation they're having.

Before I can get close enough to hear anything, Reeve's phone rings. He glances at the screen, then back at Rowan, saying something I can't catch before answering the call and walking away, leaving Rowan standing alone in the hallway.

This is my chance. I stride towards her, my jaw clenched.

"Summers," I call out, my voice harsh and demanding.

She turns, surprise flashing across her face before it's replaced by a guarded expression. "Coach Bex," she says, her tone neutral, but the frown on her face says she isn't eager for another run-in with me.

Good.

I stop a few feet away from her. Now I'm the one crossing my arms over my chest. "Care to explain what that was all about?"

She raises an eyebrow. "I'm not sure what you mean."

"Don't play dumb, Summers. You and Reeve. He played piss-poor out there today. He's one of my most solid players, right up until today. What were you two discussing?"

Her eyes narrow. "That's between Reeve and me. It's not my place to share personal conversations."

"You're affecting my player's performance on the ice," I growl. "So whatever you're doing, whatever angle you're working, back off Summers."

Rowan's eyes flare with anger. "It's not what you think."

"Then enlighten me," I challenge.

She shakes her head, a bitter laugh escaping her lips. "Maybe if you were more approachable, Reeve would have already told you himself."

Her words hit me like a slap to the face. Before I can respond, she turns on her heels and storms off, leaving me fuming in the middle of the hallway.

If I didn't like her before, I really don't like her now. The nerve of that woman implying that I'm unapproachable to my own players. And what the hell is she up to with Reeve? Is she digging up dirt? Trying to stir up drama for her next article?

Frustration is coursing through me. This is exactly why I didn't want her around my team. She's causing problems, distracting my players, and now she's got secrets about them or with them—I'm not sure which.

I turn and stalk back to my office, slamming the door behind me —a rare occurrence with my open-door policy, but I'm doing a favor to anyone who unknowingly ventures into my office after the heated conversation I just had with Rowan.

I drop to my chair and rest the back of my neck against the headrest, staring up at the ceiling.

My phone dings with an incoming text from my oldest brother Leo who still lives in the same city we grew up in–Liverpool.

> Leo: Camille keeps asking if Uncle Bexley is coming to her sixth birthday party this summer.

I haven't been home in two years and it would be good to go back but I don't want to promise anything unless I can make good on it.

> Bex: I'll get back to you on that. Tell my favorite girl that I miss her.

> Leo: Come home and tell her yourself.

Camille Townsend

Five years old, missing her two front teeth and the only female that holds my heart. Though I'd never admit that to my mum.

I flop my phone onto my desk with a loud clunk. I know what will happen if I go home. My brothers Leo and Archie will spend every day hassling me to retire at the end of my contract terms next season and move back home.

Our mum is getting older and with our dad passing away years ago, I need to make family a priority.

I need to go home but can I walk away from hockey for good?

The one thing I am sure of, I need to talk to Sam about the issue with Rowan. I've worked too hard as the head coach of this team to let a reporter walk in and ruin our chances at a Stanley Cup victory this season. Sam will surely see my side.

Chapter Two

Rowan

Before walking through the halls of the Hawkeyes corporate office only a few moments ago, I spent my morning staring at the email I received from my boss, feeling the weight of the words pressing against my chest.

"Rowan, we need an interview from Coach Bex ASAP. He's a key figure in this season's story, and you've got the best chance at getting him to talk. Make it happen."

Best regards,

Charles Albright

He makes it sound so easy. As if the grumpy arrogant head coach hasn't made it his life's mission to avoid me, dodge interviews, and treat me like I'm planning to load antifreeze in the Zamboni water tank.

Now I'm standing in Sam Roberts' office, watching the Hawkeyes' GM across his desk. Despite Coach Bex's agitated reaction to Sam's news, Sam stands relaxed, hands on his hips, calmly waiting for Bex to finish his rant.

Bex is clearly unhappy that I'll be joining the team on away games starting in two weeks, but Sam is one of the most unshakeable GMs I've met in my years as a reporter—almost nothing ruffles him.

"Absolutely not, Sam. We only have eight more weeks to make it to the playoffs and you want to send a reporter with us for out of town games starting in two weeks? We can't afford any distractions," Bex says, leaning over Sam's desk.

Bexley Townsend.

Six foot two, two-time Stanley Cup winner, NHL Hall of Famer, and a former player for the Hawkeyes. Not that you could tell that the man was ever injured if you saw him out there on the ice during practice with the guys or in the gym lifting weights. You'd think he still plays professionally. He's in just as good of a shape as when he was playing, maybe even better, and he must have some kind of Benjamin Button disease because as much as I want his face to match his personality, he's inexplicably better looking with age.

And to add more to the man's bolstered ego, the gossip around the water cooler is that over his long career, he's turned down a full spread in Playgirl—twice. Not to mention that his sexy British accent could incinerate a woman's panties. Bex is eighteen years older than me but has the grumpy disposition of my eighty-year-old neighbor Hans, who lives three doors down and gripes at me regularly every time I work from home while listening to true crime murder mysteries.

Each time I pass Hans in the halls these days, he tells me in a huff, "People should work in an office. Why is everyone now working from home? It's screwing with my nap schedule."

Get with the times Hans, it's a new age. No one wants to go outside anymore.

I'd like to respond with something similar, but I can't bring myself to do it. Hans has the cutest Boston Terrier that absolutely loves me, and when Hans has a doctor's appointment or needs someone to let Sherlock out for a tinkle midday, he calls me. Once a year Hans heads down to Portland to visit his daughter overnight, and I always volunteer to keep Sherlock for a sleepover.

We snuggle under a blanket on my couch and watch CSI Las Vegas together. I can usually guess who the killer is within the first ten minutes, but Sherlock doesn't mind... or at least he's never mentioned that it bothers him.

I'm too busy to have a dog of my own. The long hours, the travel—it wouldn't be fair to the dog. So I borrow Sherlock when the very real ache to get my own fur baby arises, and I need to snuff it out. It's a temporary Band-Aid on a deeper wound that refuses to heal, but it's the best I can do for now.

The truth is, the ache goes deeper than just wanting a pet. It's tied to something I can't have, something I've had to accept over the years. The doctors have all but confirmed that I'll never have children of my own. Drew, my ex and I, tried everything, and now, with that chapter firmly closed, I've told myself to stop hoping for something I can't have. No kids, no fur babies—just me, focusing on what I can control.

Sports journalism wasn't my first dream. I wanted to write about art, about things that inspire people. But after everything that's happened, I'm determined to make this work. It's all I have left to build, and I won't let it crumble. At least here, I can prove myself, show everyone what I'm capable of. And if I can secure this interview with Coach Bex, I'll secure my position as a top sports reporter for *The Seattle Sunrise*.

For now, that's enough. It has to be.

It dawns on me that maybe Bex and Hans share the same problem. Team practices are messing with Bex's nap schedule. That must be it.

Lack of sleep makes Bexley a grumpy boy.

Oh, how I wish it were that easy, but I suspect Bex's mood is his unfortunate default setting. And as far as I know, Bex doesn't have a cute puppy to force me to be nice to him for future play dates.

Instead, he'd like to see me sidelined from attending any away games, but neither my boss at *The Seattle Sunrise* nor his boss will allow such a thing to happen. Though if I'm wrong and Coach Bex has a bigger pull with Sam than I know, getting kicked off the Hawkeyes jet could threaten my ability to do my job and prove to Charles that I deserve the head sports journalist position.

With every game, the Hawkeyes get closer and closer to the playoffs. The official NHL playoffs are within sight, and as long as the Hawkeyes boys can pull off eight more weeks of game wins, they'll have earned their spot in the Western Conference.

"Bex," Sam says evenly, "this arrangement was approved months ago. Rowan's presence isn't negotiable. The deal was that she will start to travel with the team as we get closer to the payoffs."

Sam Roberts' phone, dings and lights up on his desk. I catch the name *WIFE* on the incoming text. Wife?

He types a quick reply, a small smile tugging at his lips, then sets the phone down. I thought he was divorced.

A glance at his ring finger shows it's bare—no indent or tan line. Not all men wear wedding bands, but for some reason, I'd expect Sam to if he were married. Could he be rekindling something with Penelope's mom? With Penelope now firmly established as Assistant GM for the Hawkeyes, maybe Sam's considering life after hockey.

I glance at Bex's left hand, finding it clenched and also ringless. I know he has an ex-wife—his rookie-year marriage that ended quickly. The official "irreconcilable differences" didn't reveal much, and while gossip columns hinted at infidelity, neither side confirmed it.

Spending so much time around Bex lately, I can take a wild guess why she walked away.

Still, Sam's situation intrigues me. I make a mental note to dig into his future with the team. Penelope might know something about the *WIFE* contact on Sam's phone, but asking her outright risks tipping her off. For now, this stays a solo mission.

"Non-negotiable?" Bex scoffs, running a hand through his irritatingly full head of dark brown hair. "We're talking about the future of this team, Sam. Every second counts. We can't have some reporter poking around, disrupting our players' focus.

Asking what animal they most closely identify with or what they wanted to be when they were five years old."

"Hey!..." I interject. I've held my tongue for long enough. "I've never asked a question that the fans don't gobble up. The players like the questions, too. It lightens the mood during an interview, and the fans enjoy hearing about their favorite players."

I'm a professional, not some tabloid vulture, and I already know that Phil Carlton wants me on that jet in two weeks, which means that Bexley Townsend is going to have to deal with it.

I've had full access to the team since Thanksgiving, far beyond the typical media room privileges my press badge grants most reporters at the Hawkeyes stadium. Yet, over the past four months, I've kept my presence scarce, sticking to game highlights and brief interviews with one player a week to keep the fans engaged.

Bex acts as if I'm hounding his players daily for sit-down interviews—it's not like that. He should know since he lives, eats, and breathes this place. I don't think I've ever stepped into the Hawkeyes stadium without Coach Bex being in the building. If I hadn't already seen his office and saw for myself that there isn't any evidence that he has a cot stashed in the corner and lives here full-time, I'd wonder.

He should be happy that I'm doing my job so efficiently. The ticket and jersey sales have increased since *The Seattle Sunrise* has created a special segment each week for just the Hawkeyes team. Meaning that his attitude towards me is completely unprovoked.

Okay, maybe not completely. There is the matter of the article I wrote about him earlier this year, before I knew I would land this huge opportunity and have to work side by side with him.

As a reporter, I don't usually worry about hurting a player or coach's feelings, especially since I report what is factual or observed firsthand. If I had known that the most senior sports reporter at *The Seattle Sunrise* was going to have his appendix rupture out of nowhere and my boss would choose me to fill in for him, I would have rethought writing an article about the versatility of Bex's resting asshole face. Maybe then he wouldn't be attempting to block my access to the team and effectively making it look like I can't do my job.

The article wasn't untrue, but it didn't paint him in the best light.

And I might have made a reference to the similarities between Coach Bex and a very large bridge troll.

The thing is, I'm not even close to the first reporter to write spot-on observations about Coach Bex's prickly disposition, and I doubt I'll be the last. In the column, I also wrote that despite his personality shortcomings, he's still arguably one of the best coaches ever to lead an NHL team.

Sam clears his throat, stepping in. "This isn't just about the team, Bex. It's about the franchise. The publicity from this coverage could be invaluable. Tessa is already seeing a rise in social media following and Autumn is getting more requests for product placement within the stadium. Not to mention that sales are up."

"Publicity?" Bex practically spits out the word. "We're here to win championships, not gain followers."

Sam looks to me and then back to Bex. "And we can do both," he counters, his tone patient but firm. "Phil Carlton himself signed off on this. The Hawkeyes have a chance to connect with our fans on a deeper level. Let them see the human side of our players as they fight for the cup."

Bex's jaw clenches, and I can almost hear his teeth grinding. "The human side? These are professional athletes, not reality TV stars. They need to focus on their game, not chit chat about their zodiac sign with a reporter who will turn around as soon as she gets her promotion and return to labeling us all as..." he turns his head to glare at me with a lifted brow. "What was it that you called me in that article? Oh right, a bumbling bridge troll with the approachability of a rabid porcupine and the social graces of a feral cat at Sunday brunch." Bex's eyes narrow as he finishes the quote, his voice dripping with disdain.

I knew it!

I knew this is why he's had it out for me since the minute I stepped on the Hawkeyes property with a shiny new full-access badge.

It's a grudge.

Sure, I know that Bex doesn't like reporters. I've been in the press box long enough and in the after-game media frenzy where Bex barely sits for his allotted time to take questions from reporters. I could see it in his eyes the second I walked into the stadium four months ago with Sam, a shiny new badge around my neck that gives me more clearance to this place than any other reporter has ever had, that he wasn't happy with the new arrangement.

It was a look of disdain across his sharp nose, strong jaw, and deep hazel-green eyes.

My boss expects an exclusive interview with every player on this team—including the head coach who hasn't taken a one-on-one interview with a reporter in over twenty-five years— not since his rookie year and subsequent divorce. Charles is practically foaming at the mouth to get this Coach Bex's story on paper.

"Make it juicy," Charles said, his tone dripping with anticipation when he first gave me the exclusive Hawkeyes story. *"Dig into the failed marriage, the divorce, his reputation on and off the ice. We're talking the inside scoop, Summers. The kind of story that makes headlines for weeks."*

This is where I should back down.

But I just can't.

I shrug, meeting his glare with a sweet smile. "For the record, I compared your leadership style to a bridge troll, not you personally. It wouldn't be fair for me to make an assumption about the man behind the coach since you refuse all my attempts to interview you. It would seem none of your fans know you personally either." I place my index finger on my chin in fake contemplation. "And although you recited that article beautifully, I have to correct you on one small error. I do believe the reference I made was "the social graces of a disgruntled honey badger at a garden party." It's an easy mistake, though; anyone could have made it. And you're welcome. That article was purely poetic and completely free of charge."

Sam coughs, trying to hide his smirk. Bex glares harder, his lip twitches and I half expect him to snarl. "You've got jokes. But it's hard to take you seriously when your biggest claim to fame is calling out athletes from behind a keyboard. Must be nice, throwing shade behind the safety of the plexiglass."

"Bex..." I hear Sam warn under his breath, but Bex's eyes stay glued to mine.

I resist the urge to flinch under Bex's narrow stare. Instead, I lift my chin slightly. "Well, it's great to know that you're an avid reader of *The Seattle Sunrise*. Didn't expect you to be such a fan of my work. Should I autograph the article for you? I could frame it, and you could hang it on the wall in your office. It would add some much-needed personality and humor to the otherwise charming bare beige walls. And just to be clear, staying safely behind the Plexiglas is the perk of my chosen profession."

Bex growls while fighting the urge to throttle me. "Don't flatter yourself, Summers. The last thing I want is anything from you, including your autograph. I'm relieved you plan to stay on the spectator side of the ice, though. You can also keep your opinions of my coaching style to yourself. If I want to hear a more half-baked take on my coaching style, I'll go to social media, where I can find all the insightful critiques from the knobheaded followers you've added for us. Thanks again for that, by the way."

The readers of *The Seattle Sunrise* are not knobheads. Or at least I don't think they are. I'm not British but I know an insult when I hear one and I'm assuming that's what he meant.

Sam clears his throat, preparing himself to diffuse the tension. "Okay, you two, it's time for a cease-fire. This conversation is getting out of hand, and I have stayed hopeful that you two could hash out your differences like grown adults, but it seems that you can't. The decision has already been made for this to happen," Bex turns back to Sam as if to make another plea, but Sam holds up his palm to Bex, indicating that he's not interested in hearing anymore. "Look, Bex, I understand your concerns. But I do think that your reasoning is unfounded. Everything that I have seen shows that Rowan is capable of doing her job, and I've only received positive reactions from players on the team at how she conducts her interviews. You're the only one with an issue of her presence around here. This is happening whether you two can get along or not, but I strongly suggest, for both of your careers," he says, glancing between us both, "that you two find a way to work together this season. Rowan will be joining the team for any home and away games that are required for her to keep *her* boss and *our* boss happy. That means that I expect everyone to cooperate fully. Her presence won't interfere with practices or game prep. She'll follow all team protocols."

Bex's nostrils flare as he takes a deep breath. For a moment, I think he might actually explode. But then his shoulders slump slightly in defeat.

"Fine," he growls. "But she stays out of the locker room, off the ice, and away from the players during warm-ups and cool-downs. And if I catch even a whiff of her disrupting my team during game days or knocking on their hotel room doors in the middle of the night—"

My eyes flare the second he insinuates that I would ever be unprofessional or blur the lines of personal ethics.

"Please tell me that you didn't just suggest that I would—"

"That's offensive," Sam says, coming to my aid. "Rowan is a professional, here to do her job--that's it. Don't make me get involved further."

Sam didn't need to step in like that. I would have put Bex in his place if I had to but it's nice to know that Sam has my back. I work in a predominantly male-driven workplace. It's not the first time a man has made comments about women in the locker rooms, or worse. I'm not saying that there aren't women who haven't taken advantage of a close proximity to a good-looking, well-paid athlete but working in the field of male sports, you realize how many of them are walking STDs.

And with the infidelity and divorce rate so high, I'm not the least bit interested.

The memory of Penelope's teasing voice at Keely's Hawkeyes Girl Club initiation comes back to me.

"Don't worry, we have plans for you next."

I shake the thought. She must have had too many sticky buns before I showed up and was tripping on a sugar rush.

"I didn't mean to offend you..." I hear Bex say under his breath like a spoiled brat who was just reprimanded by the principal.

Yes, he did mean it, but I doubt Bex is the kind to apologize for anything so I'll take it for what it is.

I clear my throat softly, drawing both men's attention. "I want the team to win just as much as you do—it makes for a better come-back story which is just as good for your career as it is for mine. I'm here to document, not disrupt."

Bex shakes his head, disagreeing with what I said. "With all due respect, Summers, you can't possibly understand the pressure these players are under. Every distraction, no matter how small, could cost us everything we've worked for."

Before I can respond, Sam's phone buzzes. He glances at the screen and holds up a hand. "It's Phil. I need to take this." He looks at us as if disappointed in us both. "We'll continue this discussion later. For now, the arrangement stands."

Bex lets out a deep sigh, but he gives a nod to Sam as Sam takes the call. As we turn to leave, he stops at the door and fixes me with a hard stare. "Keep your reporting on the game, Summers and we won't have a problem."

I meet his gaze, refusing to be intimidated. "Crystal clear, Coach. I'm here for the story, nothing else."

He grunts, seemingly unconvinced, and stalks out of the office. I follow, my mind racing with the meaning behind his words. Does he really think I'm here to mess with his players or their chances at winning the Stanley Cup? My ability to garner my boss's attention enough to throw me another big story like this, hinges on the Hawkeyes winning, which sadly, is one thing completely out of my control.

Yes, technically, my job is just to report on the story, but reporting on the Hawkeye's big comeback will gain me more favor than a loss for the team. And God help me if they lose before the playoffs. Then my story dies too soon for me to gain momentum at work.

I want the Hawkeyes to go all the way. Just as bad as Bex wants it.

As I step into the reception area, I hear a familiar voice. "Wow, that was intense. I could practically feel the testosterone radiating off Bex from all the way over here."

I turn to see Cammy, Sam's assistant, and Seven Wrenley's daughter, grinning at me from behind her desk. Her brown hair pulled up in a messy bun with a pencil through it as if she'd just walked out of an all-nighter study session for a college exam before coming in for work.

"You heard all that?" I ask, feeling a mix of embarrassment and frustration.

Cammy nods, her eyes twinkling with mischief. "Hard not to. It got a little heated in there, huh?" She asks.

I blow out a breath. "I know that the article I wrote last year isn't doing me any favors, but is he always like this? I mean, it can't be that he doesn't see how he's perceived out on the ice."

I watch as Cammy stuffs mailers in envelopes for Briggs Conley's Kids With Cancer Gala coming up in a couple of weeks.

"Don't let him get to you, Ro. He can be finicky, but it's nothing you can't handle."

I give a small smile at her attempt to lighten the mood. "Thanks, Cam. I just feel like I'm fighting against more than just his issues with me. I get the feeling I represent everything he hates."

Cammy shakes her head. "You're probably right. That man wouldn't give Mother Theresa herself a chance if she showed up wearing a press badge. It's not personal. Well, not entirely personal."

The article I wrote—I know. It's as personal as it gets.

I nod, grateful for her support anyway. "Thanks, Cam. I'll do my best."

As I walk out of the office and head down the long hallway of the Hawkeyes corporate offices, my eyes catch sight of Coach

Bex walking towards the lobby. Even from this distance, I can see the tension in his broad shoulders, the barely contained energy in his stride. I can't help but wonder what experiences have shaped him into the man he is today – a man who seems to view my presence as a threat to everything he's worked for.

Dread and anticipation fill my belly when I realize that he and I are about to ride the elevator down together, but just as he makes his way into the lobby, he glances over his shoulder to see me, and then turns the corner instead of heading straight for the elevator right in front of him.

I make it out of the hallway with just enough time to see the emergency stairwell door in the right corner of the lobby close shut.

I startle at the sound of Phil's assistant's voice coming from her desk, not realizing that she's back from lunch.

"He must have needed to work off some of that energy. I've never seen him so flustered," she says.

I turn to her, wanting to tell her what happened in Sam's office, but she was at lunch when I came up, and she probably didn't even know that Bex and I were in a meeting with Sam. It was an impromptu, last-minute meeting and not on Sam's agenda. It's better not to start gossip if she doesn't already know that Bex and I went toe-to-toe a minute ago.

Besides, even with Bex's prickly personality, everyone here still seems to love him and I'm just the new girl. I don't want to make any more enemies than the *one* I already have.

"Let's hope he pops out the bottom with a fresh new personality."

Adele must think I'm teasing because she gives a good throaty laugh.

"Oh, Ms. Summers, you are such a card."

I wish Coach Bex thought that I was a card too. Then maybe we wouldn't be foes.

"I'm heading out. Tomorrow's column won't write itself. Have a good day, Adele."

"You too, honey," she singsongs as I make my way to the elevator.

The elevator doors slide open, and I step inside, my mind already racing with potential strategies. How do I gain the trust of a man who seems determined to see me as the enemy?

Chapter Three

Bex

The final buzzer of the game sounds, sending a wave of relief rushing through me.

One more game down, forty-two still to go before the playoffs.

That was a close game–too close, a real nail-biter that had us clawing our way back in the third period, but it's still a win and worth celebrating.

Reeve played better than he did in practice, but I've seen him sharper on the ice and there was a goal that got past him that wouldn't have earlier in the season—before the injury and whatever's going on with Keely. It has me wondering if I'm making the right call putting him in with the Stanley Cup on the line. Still, he played a solid game and pulled off a win.

By the time I step into the locker room, the energy is all wrong. The chatter of excited players should be heard as far out as the players tunnel but instead, it's quiet. Too quiet.

I look around, expecting the usual scene: players pulling off their gear, celebrating, recalling outlandish plays and big hits, and icing down sore muscles. The sound of the team showers should serve as the background white noise to the dozens of conversations echoing throughout the locker room. But instead, half the team is still sitting on the benches, all eyes glued to their phones. Some of them are even chuckling to themselves as if whatever has their attention is amusing.

What the hell is going on? This isn't my team. Have they forgotten that we still have a job to do? Our night isn't over yet. We still have after-game interviews to get through.

Slade, our center, is hunched over his phone, a smirk tugging at the corner of his mouth. Even Lake, our left-wing and captain, who's usually the first to hit the showers after a game, is sitting there with his feet up on a bench, phone in hand, grinning at something on the screen. Not a single one of them has noticed I've walked in.

"Am I invisible, or have you all suddenly forgotten how to act like professional athletes?" My voice booms through the room.

There's a flurry of movement as the guys scramble to put their phones down. A few sheepish looks are exchanged, but no one's in a rush to make eye contact with me. I don't care if they're celebrating the win; they've got the press waiting for their interviews, and I expect my players to be ready for it, not sitting around like a bunch of teenagers in a group chat.

"What the hell's so funny, anyway?" I growl, stalking over to Brent who still has his phone open.

I swear to God if it turns out he's smirking at a dick pic he sent his new girlfriend Zoey, I'll be issuing a "no cell phones in the locker room" policy–effective immediately.

Brent, the team's left-defense, glances up, his grin faltering as he shows me the screen. "Uh, Coach... It's Summers' article. She posted this new piece about the team—"

The name *Summers* hits me like a punch in the gut. Of course. Of bloody course.

Now I wish it was a dick pic I'm having to deal with. Instead of having my team distracted by an article written by the pain-in-my-ass journalist running around this stadium with her "all access badge" like a free range chicken in a pantsuit and heels. I wish Sam was in here to witness the "Summers" effect on his team. Then he'd get what a liability she is in my locker room–physically, or otherwise.

"Summers?" I bark, snatching the phone from his hand. "You're all sitting around reading an article from *Summers* when you should be getting your ass ready for the press?"

The article is right there on the screen, bold and witty, the title alone making my blood boil: "Between the Pipes and the Pucks: Which Hawkeyes Player Reigns Supreme as the King of Trash Talk."

It's a post on the social media account that I've heard was Rowan's big idea–pushing the news outlet to go fully digital.

The likes and comments are blowing up on their page. No wonder it got the team's attention.

I skim the first few paragraphs, feeling my irritation grow with every word. It's classic Rowan—sharp, insightful, with just the right amount of humor to keep it light. The players love it, obviously, because she's playing to their strengths, calling out their quirks in a way that makes them sound like legends. But to me? It's a bloody distraction.

She might not be here in the flesh, but she's got these guys wrapped around her little finger even without stepping foot in the locker room. And now they're all too busy laughing at her clever little article to do their damn jobs.

I toss the phone back to Brent, my jaw clenched so tight I'm surprised my teeth don't crack. "Get dressed and get ready for the media. Now. All of you."

There's a chorus of "Yes, Coach," but I'm already halfway out the door, heading for the press area, my blood pumping with irritation. She's not even here in the locker room, and somehow, she's still managing to distract my players.

My mind starts spinning as I stalk through the stadium halls, searching for Rowan. I know she's here somewhere. She never misses a home game. Thank God Phil hasn't required her to start traveling with the team for away games yet.

I knew she'd be trouble the moment that Phil told us that the Hawkeyes and *The Seattle Sunrise* are partnering up for an exclusive to build excitement for this season, and this proves my point. Not to mention that riveting article she wrote about me at the end of last season–her take on the way I coach my team. She should have kept her opinions to herself.

I round a corner, and there she is, standing in the hallway near the press room, talking to Reeve.

Rowan nods profusely but Reeve is shaking his head, and his body looks tense and rigid as he talks wildly with his hands. This is the second time this week that I've seen them in the hallways of the stadium in a heated conversation.

What is going on? I've never seen Reeve act like this about anything. Which has me drawing one conclusion.

Rowan must have dirt on Reeve, and whatever it is, Reeve didn't want me to know about it a month ago. I doubt he'll be any more forthcoming with it now.

A visibly pregnant Tessa walks up, resting a hand on her belly as she leans toward Reeve with a playful smirk. "You're up, superstar. Press is waiting," she says, motioning to the media room.

Reeve groans, his shoulders sagging. "Can't they just skip me and focus on Conley? He's the one who scored the game-winner. Or Powers?... He loves talking about himself."

Tessa raises an unimpressed brow. "It's not optional, Reeve. The media is chopping at the bit to talk to you. It's your first game back since the accident. They want to hear from you."

Reeve reluctantly turns and follows Tessa.

Then I see Rowan grab her phone out of her pocket quickly and Charles Albriet flashes on her screen in a text message. Her fingers fly across her screen.

"Spilling secrets to your boss, Charles Albright, are we?"

Whatever Rowan and Reeve keep discussing alone in the hallway will have to wait. I'm still fuming about my players who are just now showing up from the locker room, dressed and ready.

I stop in front of her, towering over her small frame, my chest still heaving with frustration. "Summers."

She looks up, blinking in surprise, and I watch the realization dawn on her that I'm not here for a friendly chat. "Coach Bex," she greets me, her voice polite, but there's an edge there, like she knows something's coming.

"You think this is funny, don't you?" I snap, crossing my arms over my chest. "You've got half the locker room glued to their phones instead of doing their job."

Her brows knit in confusion, but there's a flicker in her eyes—somewhere between irritation and defiance. It's an expression I've come to recognize. She might play nice for the cameras, but behind that polished exterior, there's a sharpness she doesn't bother to hide around me. She locks her phone, slipping it into the front pocket of her black slacks that hug her toned legs, all the way down to her designer heels. Those heels should be impractical for a day at the rink, but she manages them effortlessly, like she was born to walk a tightrope in stilettos.

Her blonde hair is slicked back into a sleek ponytail, not a strand out of place, emphasizing her bright blue eyes, and full cherry red lips. Her press badge dangles around the delicate curve of her neck, almost taunting me, like a badge of honor for invading our space. Then she turns, squaring up to face me head-on. It's inconvenient the way the last button on her white blouse gapes open just enough that my six-foot two has a good vantage point. It takes all my willpower not to glance down her shirt.

Yet another distraction I can't afford.

"A distraction?" she repeats, her tone sharp, eyes narrowing. "What are you talking about?"

"You know damn well what I'm talking about." I point at her phone. "That article. They're all sitting around reading your little piece instead of doing their jobs. This is exactly what I warned Phil about when he told me he gave you full access to the team."

Should I have cursed? Maybe not, but the playoffs are on the line, and she needs to take this as seriously as I am. After all, the Hawkeyes fighting back from last year's loss of the Stanley Cup is the whole reason she's covering the team. But maybe she'd rather we failed. A dumpster fire of a season might make for better ratings.

Rowan's eyes widen, and for a second, I think I've caught her off guard. But then she recovers, her expression hardening as she straightens her posture to appear taller as if she's getting ready for battle.

"Oh, so now I'm responsible for your players being distracted? I didn't realize publishing a simple article has the power to derail an entire hockey team." Her voice drips with sarcasm, and she tilts her head, giving me a look that's equal parts challenge and exasperation. "Let me guess—next, you'll blame me if they lose a game."

I take a step closer. "That's not the point, and you know it," I growl. "This team needs to focus. They don't need you turning everything into a joke. King of trash talk might be a headline to get social media viewers but it's not helping this team make it to the playoffs."

She glances around to see if anyone is watching us but everyone else is around the corner and a good few hundred feet away.

Her eyes flash with anger when the coast is clear. "A joke? Is that what you think I'm doing? I wrote that article because I respect this team. Obviously, you didn't even read the post, or you would have seen that I wrote about the work they put in, highlighting the different attributions that each player brings to the team– and yes, that includes trash talking. But I shouldn't be surprised that you saw the headline and flew off the handle—per usual. If they're distracted, maybe that says more about you coaching your team and keeping your team engaged than it does about me being a problem."

I stare at her, caught off guard by the fire in her voice. She's standing her ground, meeting me head-on, and damn if it doesn't piss me off even more. Because part of me knows she's right. The article isn't the problem—the problem is how easily my players are distracted. If we want to win this season, everyone needs to buy in, and that includes Rowan.

"Look, Summers," I say, my voice low. "I don't care how witty you think you are. Keep your stories out of my locker room. I don't need my players treating you like some kind of celebrity. This team has one goal—winning—and I won't let anything get in the way of that. Not even you."

Rowan's lips part, and for a moment, I think she's going to tear into me again. But instead, she just stares at me, her eyes narrowing as if she's sizing me up. "You're right about one thing, Coach," she says, her voice calm but firm. "This team has one goal. But so do I. It's to tell the story of this team's journey—whether you like it or not."

With that, she turns on her heel and walks away, leaving me standing there, fists clenched at my sides, watching her long ponytail and hips sway side to side as she vacates our conversation.

Dammit.

Chapter Four

Rowan

The relaxing hum of the salon's pedicure massage chair vibrates through my body, easing away the tension from sitting on those stadium seats week in and week out. It's a welcome distraction, especially with my first away game with the team looming just a few days from now.

Strings of Valentine's Day twinkle lights and heart shaped cutouts fill the salon in every nook and cranny. The long rows of pedicure spa chairs are all full of clients getting their toes done for their holiday plans.

I might not have romantic plans for Valentine's Day this year, unless you count the CSI marathon I have planned with my sister Jordan and my neighbors dog, Sherlock, but I couldn't pass up Autumn, Keely and Zoey's invite to get our pedicures before their dinner dates tomorrow.

I wiggle my toes in the warm, bubbling water of the pedicure bath, letting out a sigh of bliss. This is exactly what I needed after the last few weeks of insistent texts and emails from my boss wanting the Townsend story, and trying not to get caught talking to Reeve about Keely's situation with her dad.

As far as I know, Keely still hasn't told Phil or Sam about her dad, and if my boss ever finds out that I knew about that story and buried it, I'll be looking for a new job. Even after putting my own ass on the line at work, I can't believe that Bex accused me of being the cause of Reeve's performance issues out on the ice.

I thought after our non-interview success a couple of weeks ago that Bex and I would find ourselves in a better place. But his scowl in my direction has barely softened.

Which leads me to believe that the person who deserves performance issues is Coach Bex.

Unfortunately the level of concentration that Bex exudes as a coach, has me almost sure that he's as intense in the bedroom as he is on the ice.

I wrinkle my nose and shake away the thought of Bex having sex. It's the last thing I should be thinking about.

To my left, Keely sits with her eyes closed, her usually cheerful face sporting an uncommon frown. On the other side of Keely is Zoey, who is trying to win a limited edition signed hockey stick on an online auction website for Brent's Valentine's Day present.

On my right, Autumn, the Hawkeyes in-house PR guru and Briggs Conley's fiance, scrolls through a work email that just came up. Though it's technically a work day, Autumn and I both make our own schedules, and as long as Keely doesn't have a therapy session with a player for PT, she's usually free, too. For a weekday, the salon bustles with activity around us, the air filled with the scent of nail polish and chatter from the many conversations all happening around us.

"You okay there, Keely?" I ask, nudging her gently with my elbow.

Keely's eyes flutter open, and she gives me a weak smile. "Yeah, I'm fine. It's just that I can't stop thinking about the text I got from my dad yesterday. I still haven't responded back."

Zoey's head snaps up from her phone. "Your dad? As in..."

Zoey's is the newest of the Hawkeyes WAGs, now dating Brent Tomlin, Tessa's older brother, but our girls group is the blood oath kind so she's been brought up to speed, swearing to take all secrets to her grave.

Autumn leans forward past me to make eye contact with Keely. "You mean the one who just got out of prison last year for racketeering?"

"Yeah," Keely nods, her voice barely above a whisper.

I reach out and squeeze Keely's hand. "You don't owe him a response if you don't want to." She nods, staring down at her toes in the water. "What did he say?"

Keely shrugs and lets out a defeated sigh. "Nothing much. Just that he wants to meet up, catch up on lost time. But I don't know if I'm ready for that. And with everything going so well with Reeve and the team... I'm just worried, you know? I don't want to bring unwanted attention to the team or Reeve over this."

I understand her concern about the news outlets getting a hold of this story. Having a father with a criminal record for paying off players to throw a game isn't exactly something you want broadcast when you're dating one of the star players of an NHL team. And if Charles knew I was holding this story back, he'd probably fire me or at least demote me to Fact Checker.

If she weren't dating Reeve who plays for a professional team, this story wouldn't matter to any reporter anyway, but since it does, it's the kind of click bait that *The Seattle Sunrise* would salivate over.

"Hey," I say, trying to sound reassuring. "The ties to your father aren't easy to find unless someone already knows where to look. And even if it does come out, it's the kind of news story that would barely make the front pages. The press would be onto something new by Monday."

Autumn bends forward in her chair on the other side of me, making eye contact with Keely and nods in agreement. "Absolutely. And with my years in PR, trust me, we could spin this story into a positive faster than you can say *redemption arc*."

Keely's shoulders relax a bit. "You think so?"

"Of course," I say, giving her hand another squeeze. "You became a physical therapist to give back to the sports community, right? That's a beautiful story of overcoming adversity and choosing a different path. People eat that stuff up. And I think a lot of people can relate to wanting to excommunicate a family member."

A small smile tugs at Keely's lips. "Thanks, guys. I don't know what I'd do without you."

"Speaking of your situation," I say, lowering my voice, "Reeve stopped me in the hallway to ask me if I had heard from you yet. I swear the poor guy still thinks you might bolt to protect him if a story gets out about your dad." It's really sweet to see how much Reeve loves Keely. "Bex caught us in the hallway."

Keely's eyes widen. "Oh no, did Reeve tell him about my dad?"

I shake my head quickly. "No, no. Bex was just being Bex. He didn't hear our conversation but I think he's so worried that it's getting to him out on the ice a little. Just talk to him and let him know what's going on."

Autumn leans in, her eyes sparkling with interest. "Oh? And how exactly was Bex being Bex?"

I roll my eyes, recalling our confrontation. "Oh, you know, the usual. Accusing me of distracting his players, demanding to know what Reeve and I were talking about. He even suggested I was 'working an angle' or something."

Autumn's eyebrows shoot up. "Sounds on brand with how you two have been coexisting the last several months. Now that you mention it, I've been hearing some whispers around the office about a huge blow-up in Sam's office two weeks ago. You wouldn't happen to know anything about that, would you?"

I groan, sinking lower in my chair. "God, is nothing sacred in that place? Yes, there was a... disagreement in Sam's office. Bex isn't thrilled about me traveling with the team for away games. I sort of thought we got past it over lemonade and British wieners, but I guess we didn't."

"Weiners?" Zoey gasps.

"It sounds more exciting than it was, trust me," I tell them as they gawk at me.

Keely doesn't miss a beat, she's far too used to me by now. "But the travel arrangements have been set since the beginning, right? So he has no say?" she asks, her brow furrowed in confusion.

"Exactly!" my voice coming off a little too loudly. A few heads turn in our direction, and I lower my voice again. "It was all arranged and approved by Phil Carlton himself. But apparently, Coach Grumpy Pants thinks I'm going to be a 'distraction' to the team."

Keely's face softens. "Aw, Bex isn't that bad. He was really supportive when Reeve was in the hospital after that terrible hit."

I can't help but scoff. "Yeah, well, he has a funny way of showing support. You should have heard some of the things he said. He practically accused me of being some tabloid vulture out to ruin his team's chances at the playoffs."

Autumn hides a smirk behind her hand. "And what exactly did you say in response?"

I feel my cheeks heat up, remembering my sharp response. "I corrected him on some choice words I used to describe him in an article last year."

Zoey gasps. "You didn't!"

"Oh, she did," Autumn chuckles. "I remember that article. What was it? Something about a bridge troll?"

I groan again. "Don't remind me. That article is coming back to bite me right on the tuchus."

Autumn bursts into laughter, while Keely looks torn between amusement and sympathy.

"Oh, Ro," Keely sighs, shaking her head. "No wonder he's been extra grumpy lately."

"But that's just it!" I protest. "He's always been grumpy. I'm not the first reporter to point it out, and I doubt I'll be the last. I just don't understand how everyone seems to love him despite his prickly personality."

Our estheticians return with hot wax and Saran wrap for our pedicure spa treatment, and I get a moment to check the text that pinged in my purse earlier when we first arrived.

"How's the temperature of the wax?" my esthetician asks as she places one foot at a time in the wax and then wraps my feet.

"It's perfect. Thank you."

There's no better time for warm wax to squish between your toes than on a rainy April day in Seattle.

As Keely and Autumn confirm the wax temperatures of their own, I pull out my phone and glance at the message my sister just sent me. A picture from social media that she screenshot of my ex, Drew and his newly minted fiancé... by the look of her holding out her hand in the photo and the caption "Forever Mrs. Lansbury."

> Jordan: He should have captioned it "Mrs. What-a-fucking-tool".

She means that about Drew, my ex, and the man who broke up with me after dozens of doctors' visits and one round of IVF confirmed the prognosis—I won't ever carry my own children.

> Rowan: I'm happy for him.

> Jordan: You shouldn't be. He doesn't deserve it.

I remember the moment I stared down at a positive pregnancy test sitting on the bathroom counter of our shared apartment. It's crazy to think that the surprise wasn't one I was instantly excited about. Drew and I had met while I was interning right out of college for ESPN, my dream job, and he was an affiliate journalist.

We bumped into each other one day in the halls of ESPN and he asked me out almost immediately. We moved in together three months later and the pregnancy test came six months after that. We hadn't even been together a year. So when I saw the test, I cringed at the idea of having to tell Drew that we hadn't been as careful as we thought. Now looking back at how it all turned out, I wish I wouldn't have regretted the possibility of being pregnant for even a second.

Two weeks later, I went to see my OBGYN expecting to get an ultrasound to confirm the gestational age and left finding out that not only was the test a false positive and I was never pregnant, but that the ultrasounds of my uterus left my OB wanting more tests. A month later, it only came with worse news. My doctor estimates that my chances of ever getting pregnant are near one percent.

"But miracles happen, Rowan," she told me.

Drew was optimistic at the time, and we decided that less than one percent means there's still a chance. We tried for nine months and then went on to try IVF. My body didn't handle the injections and hormones well and the transfer didn't take. I missed too many days at work because of feeling ill, and when it came time to offer me a full-time journalist position, they went with a different candidate.

Almost a year to the day that I found out that I wouldn't likely ever have kids, Drew moved out, stating that we'd both regret it if he stayed. But what he meant to say is that he'll regret it one day if he stays with a woman who can't give him children.

It doesn't help that Drew and I still work in the same circles. I still have to see the man at least once a month, usually in a press box.

We're cordial, and now, after so many years, I don't even flinch when I see him at an event we're both invited to.

After licking my wounds on Jordan's couch for four months, I applied for an open position with *The Seattle Sunrise*. They were impressed with my internship at ESPN and my time as the editor-in-chief for my college paper, which turned from paper to digital during the time I was in charge. It was a large undertaking but one of my greatest accomplishments. *The Seattle Sunrise* hired me on the spot, and I've been working my way up ever since.

I decided the day I got off my sister's couch that if I'm doomed to never find a man who will accept me without a baby, then at least I can climb to the top of my career ambitions.

I stare at the picture again, seeing the smile on her face—seeing the smile on his. My heart tightens in my chest as I feel a rush of old pain surface—the familiar ache that never quite goes away. Not the ache for him, but for what won't ever be for me.

> **Rowan:** He was bound to move on someday.

> **Jordan:** You're letting that asshole off too easy.

Maybe so but I just want to move on too and stop thinking about what I can't have.

I blink back the sting of tears, refusing to let them fall. Autumn and Keely are still laughing, oblivious to the inner turmoil attempting to rise to the surface. I take a deep breath and force a smile as I put my phone back down, my mind swirling.

"As I was saying. Coach Bex is harmless," Keely protests.

This isn't the first person to try to tell me that Coach Bex isn't all that bad. Reeve referred to him as a pissed-off T-rex because of his short arms, though Bex has long muscular arms so the analogy never made sense. Even Adele tried to sing his praises as he decided to take the emergency stairs instead of riding down the elevator with me after the meeting with Sam.

"Harmless? You tell that to the dozen or so players whose noses he's broken in his long career that Bexley Townsend is a docile creature, and I can guess what they'll tell you," I scoff. "The man is as harmless as a trigger-happy skunk with irritable bowel syndrome."

Autumn's smirk grows wider. "Maybe there's more to him than meets the eye. You know, Pepe La Pew was a skunk too."

I lift a confused brow. "What's that supposed to mean?"

She shrugs innocently. "Oh, nothing. Just an observation."

Before I can press her further, our nail estheticians return to remove the wax and start on our pedicures. As she begins working on my toes, I can't help but mull over Autumn's words. More to Bex than meets the eye? Unlikely. The man is as transparent as they come – grumpy, stubborn, and seemingly determined to make my job as difficult as possible.

I shake my head, dismissing the idea that something runs deep in that man. No, Coach Bex is exactly what he appears to be – a thorn in my side and an obstacle to overcome in my quest to prove myself and pave the way for me to make a name for myself.

"So," Keely says, breaking me out of my thoughts, "What's your game plan for dealing with Bex on the away games?"

I sigh, watching the esthetician start to apply a base coat. "Honestly? I'm not sure. I was hoping to keep a low profile, you know? Just observe, take notes, maybe get a few quotes here and there. But now..."

"Now you feel like you have something to prove," Autumn finishes for me.

I nod. "Exactly. I can't let him think he's intimidated me into backing off. But I also don't want to overstep and give him a real reason to complain to Sam or Phil."

Keely reaches over and pats my arm. "You'll figure it out, Ro. You're smart and talented. Just... maybe try to stay on his good side to make it easy for you to get what you need."

I laugh. "Me? Stay on his good side? I think you've got it backward, Keely. He's the one who seems to have it out for me."

"You know, sometimes when two people clash like this, it's because they're more alike than they realize," Zoey says with a raised brow.

I nearly choke on air. "Excuse me? I am nothing like Bexley Townsend."

"Are you sure about that?" Autumn challenges, her eyes twinkling. "You're both passionate about your work, dedicated to your respective fields, and from what I've seen, equally stubborn."

I open my mouth to protest, but no words come out. As much as I hate to admit it, Autumn might have a point. But that doesn't mean I have to like it.

"Even if that's true," I say finally. "It doesn't change the fact that he sees me as the enemy. How am I supposed to do my job if he's constantly trying to shut me out?"

Keely leans in, her voice low so that no one else in the salon can hear us. "You know, Reeve once told me that the key to getting through to Bex is to prove your dedication. Show him that you care about the game and the team as much as he does."

I consider this for a moment. "So, what? I should start reciting hockey stats and showing up to every practice?"

Autumn shakes her head. "He thinks you're a reporter that only cares about the story and not about the game, right? Then show genuine interest and respect for what they do. And he's obviously reading your articles. So, show him that you're not just there for bridge troll headlines but to tell the real story of the team's journey."

As much as I hate to admit it, their advice makes sense. I've been so focused on defending myself against Bex's accusations that I haven't really taken the time to prove him wrong. Maybe a change in approach is exactly what I need.

"Alright," I say, a fresh new outlook settling over me. "I'll give it a shot. But if he still acts like the grumpy honey badger that I know he is deep down inside, all bets are off."

Keely and Autumn laugh, the tension from earlier dissipating.

"That's the spirit," Autumn says, raising her hand for a high-five. "Now, let's focus on more important matters. What color are you thinking for your toes?"

I send one last text off to my sister.

> Rowan: We're still on for Valentine's?

> Jordan: Yep, see you tomorrow night.

As me and the girls dive into a heated debate about the merits of 'Ballet Slippers' versus 'Bikini So Teeny', I can't help but feel grateful for these moments of girl talk. In the whirlwind of hockey drama and journalistic challenges, it's nice to remember that sometimes, the biggest decision you have to make is what shade of pink looks best on your toes.

Chapter Five

Rowan

I settle into my seat near the back of the Hawkeyes jet, trying to ignore the butterflies in my stomach. This is it—my first away game with the team. I've been both dreading and anticipating this moment ever since Sam gave me the green light to travel with the players. As I unzip my carry-on, I can't help but feel like I'm stepping into uncharted territory.

A group text comes through on my phone.

> Tessa: Dress shopping for the gala next week. Who's in?

Several chimes come through as all the girls on the group text start to respond.

> Rowan: I'm free after I get back.

Autumn, Juliet, and Shawnie have put a ton of time into making this gala a success. All the news outlets and professional sports teams in Seattle have all RSVP'd. It's gotten so big that Juliet decided to add a red carpet, though this carpet will be turquoise to match the team colors. With all the news coverage, Briggs and Autumn are hoping that the publicity will bring in online donations as well.

Most of the team is already onboard on the jet, and the aircraft buzzes with pre-flight energy. Players shuffle down the aisle, stowing bags and calling out to each other, most of them starting to take their seats. I keep my head down, focusing on unpacking my essentials: laptop, my notebook, and noise-canceling headphones. Just as I'm about to plug in and tune out the world, a familiar voice catches my attention.

"Hey, Summers! I wasn't sure if you were traveling with us this week."

I look up to see Brent Tomlin, the Hawkeyes left defense, grinning down at me. His easy smile is contagious, and I find myself relaxing a bit.

"I wasn't thinking I would be either until the team made it to the playoffs but Phil and Sam want me front and center, so here I am."

Brent chuckles, settling into the seat across the aisle from me. "Yeah, I heard that Sam made it clear that you were going whether Coach Bex likes it or not," Brent says, in almost a whisper, looking to see if Bex is onboard yet. "Coach Bex has been in rare form since he found out you'd be joining us."

I wince internally at the mention of Bex and our infamous meeting in Sam's office. I didn't peg Cammy as the gossiping type, but who else would have told the entire franchise about it? The story is catching on like wildfire. "Is that so? And here I thought his default setting was 'perpetually annoyed'."

"Oh, it is," Brent assures me with a wink. "But you've somehow managed to unlock a whole new level of grumpiness. It's actually kind of impressive."

Before I can respond, I look up to see the man himself, Coach Bexley Townsend, stepping onto the plane. His presence commands attention, though most of the players are all chit chatting with one another or have their headphones already on and are waiting for take-off. Still, I notice.

For a moment, our eyes meet. The intensity of his gaze catches me off guard, and I feel a strange flutter in my chest. It's not quite fear, not quite anticipation, but something... else. Something I can't quite name.

As quickly as the moment comes, it passes. Bex's eyes narrow slightly, and he turns away, making his way towards the front of the plane. I watch as he stows his backpack in an overhead compartment and settles into a seat as far from me as possible.

"See what I mean?" Brent says, pulling my attention back to him. "I think you might be the first person to get under his skin like this since... well, ever."

I force a laugh, trying to shake off the lingering effects of that brief eye contact. "Lucky me. I always wanted to be someone's personal irritant."

"Like his own brand of poison oak," Brent says.

"Hey..." I protest.

Brent laughs. "Oops, sorry. I didn't mean it that way. And just to be clear, the rest of the guys like you just fine."

"Thanks," I say, pulling my phone out to check to see if my sister texted me back about watering my plants while I'm gone.

As more players file onto the plane, a few familiar faces catch my eye. Reeve Aisa gives me a friendly nod as he passes by, while Lake Powers offers a casual fist bump. It's a stark contrast to the cold shoulder I'm getting from their coach.

"I think it's cool having you along. Adds a little excitement to the usual away game routine," Powers says, sitting one row in front of Brent.

I'm about to thank him when the plane's intercom crackles to life. The captain's voice fills the cabin, running through the standard pre-flight announcements. As he speaks, I notice Bex turn in his seat, his eyes scanning the plane until they land on me. His brow furrows, and for a moment, I think he might actually get up and come over.

But then the moment passes, and he turns back around, his shoulders set in a rigid line.

"Looks like someone's keeping tabs on you," Lake comments, following my gaze.

I shrug, trying to appear nonchalant. "He's probably just making sure I'm not corrupting his players or something."

Brent laughs. "Trust me, we were plenty corrupt before you came along. But seriously, don't let him get to you. Bex is... well, Bex. He takes some getting used to, but he's a good coach. Just give him time. But enough about him, how was your Valentine's Day? Zoey said you girls got pedicures?"

My eyes flicker over to Bex for no real reason, but he's not looking in our direction. "It was good. I spent it with Jordan. We watched a movie. Nothing big. How about you?"

Brent met my sister Jordan once when she accompanied me to Zoey's first hosting of a Hawkeyes girls night party at their house in the same gated community as Isla and Kaenan's place. Brent had Zoey moved into his place within the first week they returned from San Diego after Christmas.

Penelope and Slade just bought a place there too. It seems it's the neighborhood where all the Hawkeyes men go to settle down. It's kind of sweet, really.

"I bought Zoey her first set of ice skates and took her to the outdoor rink. She's starting to get the hang of it. I try to get her out on the ice as much as I can."

Zoey told me all about their story. It's the kind that makes you believe that if two people are meant to be together, they'll find each other again. When the time is right.

"What about you, Coach?" Lake asks, reaching over and slapping Bex's arm in the aisle seat in front of him.

Bex doesn't turn around as he responds. "I haven't celebrated Valentine's Day since they made me in primary school. I don't trust naked babies wielding weapons."

That can't be true. He used to be married. Or maybe that's another reason for why he's divorced.

"Good point," Lake says. "Flying around without a helmet and broadhead arrow… that has to be an OSHA violation."

Brent leans forward, gripping Lake's headrest in front of him. "What? No lucky girl getting the full Townsend love experience? What a waste of all that charm," Brent snickers and then winks at me.

Bex shoots a look over his shoulder at me. Our eyes lock and then he turns back around.

What was that about?

As the plane begins to taxi, we all settle into our seats. I mull over Brent's words. Give him time? How much time does he need? It's not like I'm asking to be his best friend. I just want to do my job without feeling like I'm walking on eggshells.

The jet engines roar to life, and I feel the familiar lurch as we take off. As we climb into the air, I can't shake the feeling that this trip is going to be more challenging than I anticipated. It's not just about writing a story anymore. It's about proving myself—to Bex, to the team, and maybe even to myself. The closer we get to the playoffs, the more pressure there is to get this story right.

The vibration of the jet engines soothes me as I lose myself in the smooth voice of Julian Mercer, my favorite contemporary painter. His podcast, "Strokes of Inspiration," has been my go-to lately for both relaxation and creative stimulation. As Julian describes his process for finding inspiration in everyday life, I jot down notes for my upcoming interview with Assistant Coach Ezra Thompson in my notebook. Something about writing down ideas with a pen and paper instead of typing it up in a laptop helps me to work through my thoughts. Maybe it's the physicality of it.

"The key is to observe without judgment," Julian's voice crackles through my headphones. "Every moment, every interaction, holds the potential for the artist to express a feeling, a thought, a question, and most importantly, a story. With every brush stroke, you are the conductor, the author, and the creator of every masterpiece."

I smile to myself, thinking about how his advice applies just as well to journalism as it does to painting. My pen flies across the empty lined pages, ink staining the crisp white paper of my notepad that sits on the folding table attached to the seat back in front of me as I brainstorm questions. Then I'll transfer everything to my laptop.

Just like Julian says, I have a story to tell, which makes me the conductor, the author, and the creator.

My keypad is my easel, my computer screen is my canvas, and unfortunately, at the moment, this team's rise to Stanley Cup victory is the story I'm hoping I get to tell.

I already planned to interview Kaenan Altman this week. Even my questions for him are all laid out and ready on a doc sheet on my computer. But one of the things that artists don't always discuss is that sometimes when inspiration hits, you don't always have a choice to avoid your muse. It consumes your thoughts, even if you wish they wouldn't.

Against my better judgment, I can't stop thinking about the coach sitting three rows ahead of me and on the opposite side of the aircraft. So I'll give in, temporarily, and write the most sensible questions that I think he might actually answer without telling me that they're inconsequential and of no importance to his leadership as an NHL coach.

So I'll stick to the boring stuff.

"How do you balance pushing the team's limits without burning them out?"

"What's your approach to tailoring training methods to individual players' strengths?"

"In your opinion, what's the most underrated aspect of coaching that fans don't see?"

And because I know that my boss will berate me if I don't try to delve a little deeper into Coach Bex as a human, though I'm mostly certain that he's a robot without feelings, I toss in one question that I one-thousand percent know will earn me, at the very least, a deep scowl.

"With all of your achievements and success on the ice, do you feel that hockey still allows time in your life for love?"

I'm so engrossed in jotting down my questions and practically hearing his voice answer the questions how I imagine he will, that I barely notice Reeve sliding into the empty seat beside me. It's only when he gently taps my arm that I look up to see him there.

"Oh, hey, Reeve," I say, pulling off my headphones and closing my laptop before he sees the last question I have on my list, labeled "Questions for the Grump". He'd probably laugh his ass off if he saw the last question I wrote for Bex to answer. "What's up?"

He nods, leaning in closer to speak in hushed tones. "I just wanted to thank you for talking to Keely during your pedicures.

She felt a lot better knowing you and Autumn have her back. It means a lot to both of us."

I feel a warm glow of satisfaction. Moments like these remind me why I love my job. Not just for the thrill of the story, but for the human connections I get to make along the way.

"Of course," I whisper back, matching his low volume. "That's what friends are for. I'm just glad I could help."

Reeve's shoulders relax a bit, but I can still see a hint of tension around his eyes. I hesitate for a moment before asking, "Have you talked to Keely recently? Did she ever respond to her dad, or has he texted anything else?"

Reeve's brow furrows and he opens his mouth to respond, but before he can get a word out, a deep, familiar voice cuts through our conversation.

"Ahem."

I look up to find Coach Bex looming over us, his imposing figure blocking out the overhead light. His face is set in its usual stern expression.

"Summers," he says, his voice low and controlled. "A word. In the back by the stewardess cart."

It's not a request; it's a command. I feel a flash of annoyance that he thinks he can order me around like one of his players. He doesn't wait to hear my reaction or my agreement to meet him. Instead, he continues to the back of the plane, confident that I'll follow.

"We'll catch up later, okay?"

Reeve nods, and within seconds, he's already up and heading back to his seat a few aisles ahead of me. I slide out of my own seat and into the aisle with irritated heat biting at my cheeks but

I try to remain cool and calm. The last thing I want to do is lose my cool at thirty-five thousand feet above ground with nowhere to stomp off to when Coach undoubtedly says something rude during this conversation.

When I reach the small area in the back of the aircraft near the stewardess cart, Bex is standing there waiting.

"After you," he says, and I hate the way his British accent makes the command sound so prim, proper and genteel when it's anything but.

Two curtains separate the little kitchen space back here with snacks and refreshments from the main cabin.

I'm not sure if I'm relieved or disappointed when I realize that there is no stewardess to be found who will witness whatever argument is about to be had between me and the tower of a man taking steps behind me. She must be in the cockpit taking the pilot and co-pilot a cup of coffee.

As soon as I get deep into the small space, trying to keep as much distance between us, I turn around, the airplane's side wall at my back. Bex is right there in front of me, his broad shoulders nearly filling the narrow space.

Up close, I catch a whiff of his cologne—something woodsy and masculine that makes my head spin for a moment before I regain my composure.

"You don't have the right to order me around you know? I'm not a player on your team," I say, crossing my arms over my chest. "If you're worried about me corrupting your players with my journalistic wiles, I can assure you—"

His eyebrows knit together, his eyes focusing directly on me, cutting me off. "You can assure me of what Summers? That whatever dirt you have on Reeve isn't screwing up his game? Go on then... lie to me some more."

I want to tell him to jump out of this aircraft without a parachute but I bite my tongue.

I know that Keely isn't ready to tell Coach Bex and Sam about her father and her fears that if the information came out that it might cause issues with sponsors, so even though I'd like to not be the punching bag for Bex's anger right now, I'll protect Keely for as long as she needs. This isn't my story to tell.

As Bex looms over me, his imposing figure virtually caging me against the wall of the airplane, I can feel the heat radiating off his body. His eyes, usually cold and distant, now burn with an intensity that makes my breath catch in my throat.

"I don't have any dirt on Reeve," I insist, trying to keep my voice steady. "And I resent the implication that I would use anything against him or the team."

Bex leans in closer, his voice dropping to a low growl. "Then why the hushed conversations? The secretive glances? Don't think I haven't noticed, Summers. You're holding something against him aren't you? Something that has him distracted."

I can feel my heart racing, a mix of anger and something else I don't want to name. Something that has my nipples hardening beneath the padding of my bra. "Has it ever occurred to you that maybe, just maybe, people might confide in me because I actually listen? Unlike some people I could mention."

His jaw clenches, a muscle ticking in his cheek. "Are you suggesting I don't listen to my players?"

"I'm suggesting that maybe if you weren't so hell-bent on making everyone think that you only care about hockey and winning a championship, you might actually learn something about your players besides their stats," I snap back.

"You're right, I don't care about anything besides hockey," he says, his eyes searching mine, curious if I believe him.

I don't.

"I wouldn't be so sure about that," I say.

Autumn, Keely, and most everyone in the Hawkeyes franchise seem to see something that I don't, but I'm not planning on digging under Bex's gruff exterior to find the supposed heart of gold underneath. Without the option of building a family someday, this career is all I have and getting too close to the source could jeopardize it all.

"What's it going to take for you to believe me?" he asks, his voice low and steady.

We're so close now I can see the flecks of gold in his darkening hazel eyes, the slight stubble on his jaw as if he forgot to shave this morning. His full lips are dangerously close—too close.

"An interview. A real one," I tell him firmly, though I know Sam or Phil will force him into it eventually if they have to. Still, I'd rather he come willingly.

"Not a chance," he says, the challenge clear in his eyes.

I won't back down. Straightening my spine, matching his gaze. "What are you so scared of?"

His brow twitches at the question, but he doesn't flinch. His intimidation tactic might work on the ice, but it won't work on me.

And then, he catches me. I see it in the slight shift of his expression, the moment he notices my gaze lingering on his mouth. Ever so subtly, his tongue peeks out to wet his lower lip, and the air between us shifts, thickening.

"Who's Jordan?" he asks, a flicker of vulnerability I've never seen in his eyes before, but he covers it quickly.

Suddenly, the plane hits turbulence, lurching violently, causing me to lose my balance and fall sideways against the Stewardess's snack counter and then I lose my balance, stumbling forward. Before I can hit the floor, Bex's strong arm wraps around my waist, yanking me back up and steadying me back on my feet. I find myself pressed against his chest, my hands instinctively gripping his shoulders as if he's my lifeline.

I hate the way I'm clinging to him as if he's the safest place on this aircraft, but in this moment, he feels like it

"Are you okay?" he asks, searching my body for signs of injury. "Are you hurt at all?"

"No, I'm okay," I tell him, surprised by how his first instinct is to check on me, to make sure I'm alright—even after our heated conversation.

Who is this guy, and where is Bex? Is this a glimpse into the softer side that everyone else seems to know is there but me?

Time seems to stand still as we lock eyes. His eyes soften from irritation to something akin to curiosity as he searches my face. The tension between us shifts, morphing into something electric, maybe even dangerous.

Bex's eyes drop to my mouth. "You should stop me, Summers. I'm about to kiss you."

Before I can process what's happening, Bex bends his head down and seals his lips with mine. I take a sharp inhale the second the heat of his mouth warms mine.

His kiss is nothing like I imagine. His lips are soft and tender yet blaming hot—demanding yet giving—aggressive but also gentle. How can he be so many things?

There's something too. Something deeper that I can't quite pin down. A need in him that I never thought I'd never thought he'd let me see. He takes control, pressing tight against my lips again, as if the first kiss was merely him testing the waters.

He pulls me tighter and I let out an approving hum, my hands sliding up the back of his neck and into his hair. It's been so long since anyone's kissed me like Bex, or maybe no one ever has, and it feels too good to stop. That's all this is. Just a need to feel this heat from someone.

I should break away, but I can't bring myself to do it. I should break loose of his embrace but somethings telling me not to.

Bex maneuvers us, pressing me back against the side of the plane. His body cages me in, one hand still at my waist, the other braced against the wall beside my head. I can feel every hard plane of his body against mine, and it sends a shiver down my spine.

"Bexley..." I whisper into our kiss.

He releases his grip around my waist and caresses down the low of my back until he palms my ass cheek, pulling me tight against his growing erection, and groans the moment my body presses against him.

I gasp into our kiss and pull him tighter to me.

"What the hell are you doing to me, Rowan?" he says, taking my mouth again.

Rowan... he called me Rowan. He never calls me by my first name.

The sound of my name off his lips causes my heart to thump even harder.

His tongue slides against my lower lip and I open to take him, his tongue testing and tasting.

Just as I'm losing myself in the kiss, a gasp breaks through our heated moment. "Oh! I'm so sorry, I didn't realize—"

I break away from him, both of us gasping for air, I stare at him in shocked disbelief, my kiss-swollen lips parted. His pupils are dilated with the kind of arousal that I've never seen in his eyes before, let alone focused on me. I peer over his shoulder to find the source of the woman's voice. The stewardess shields her eyes but continues her job. I wonder if she's seen worse since joining the mile-high club is a thing.

Finally, Bex glances over his shoulder to see her too, but he doesn't take a single step back from me, as if he plans to keep me here longer.

I break away from him, the stewardess shields her eyes but continues her job. There's nothing to see but I'm sure she's seen plenty on her flights.

Finally, Bex glances over his shoulder to see her too, but he doesn't take a single step back from me, as if he plans to keep me here longer.

While he's distracted, I duck under his arm, his hand around my waist, releasing me without putting up a fight. He knows as instantly as I do that the kiss was a mistake. So why am I the only one fleeing the scene while he doesn't move an inch from where he had me up against the wall?

I push past the stewardess, who's trying to pretend that she didn't see me in the coach's arms, his body pinned against mine—our mouths locked together. My cheeks burn with embarrassment as I hurry back to my seat, leaving Bex behind.

He's probably standing there, still trying to process how a fight between us turned into... *whatever that*.

As I sink into my chair, pulling my noise-canceling headphones apart and snapping them against my ears as my mind does somersaults over what just happened. My heart is racing at full speed while the rest of my body is thrumming with a need for a man I can't stand.

I hear the pilot come over the inflight speakers as the seat belt sign turns on, letting us know that there is some light turbulence up ahead and that our flight might be a little bumpier than anticipated.

I hear Bex finally walk out from behind the curtain.

His feet stop near the back of my aisle chair.

He bends close to my ear, pulls the one of the headphones back gently and speaks only loud enough for me to hear over the jets.

"Buckle up, Summers, this is about to be a bumpy ride."

Chapter Six

Bex

I stride through the hotel lobby after checking in, my plastic rectangular room key in one hand and my small rolling suitcase trailing behind me in my other hand, with a duffel bag slung over my shoulder. The posh interior of the five-star hotel barely registers as my mind churns with thoughts of the flight—and more specifically, of Rowan Summers.

What the hell was I thinking kissing her like that?

The moment replays in my head for the thousandth time since we landed. The way she felt in my arms was soft but unyielding. The little gasp as I pulled her against me, keeping her from falling. The way she pressed into me, matching my intensity with her own.

I shouldn't have wanted her—but damn it, I did. I can't remember the last time I've wanted any woman that bad. Not in a long time.

I can't even remember if I wanted to kiss Lily on our first date as much as I wanted to kiss Rowan.

Seeing her lose her footing and almost hit the ground, sent a surge of concern through me. Instinct took over, and I pulled her close to steady and protect her. Years spent on the ice have given me solid footing and balance, allowing me to keep us both upright.

I shake my head, trying to dislodge the memory of the look in her eyes when I asked if she was okay. She looked at me like I had grown two heads. And then, like an idiot, I leaned in and kissed her.

It would have been a mistake. A moment of weakness brought on by turbulence, close quarters, and her sharp tongue. Nothing more.

And it won't happen again.

Rowan is a reporter, and if there's one thing I've learned in my years in this business, it's that reporters can't be trusted. I should know; it was a news outlet not unlike *The Seattle Sunrise* that sold gossip that I had been unfaithful to Lily, and that she ended our marriage because of it. My agent threatened to sue for slander but they retracted the story later—much good that did. The damage was done.

Reporters will sell their own granny for a juicy story, and I'll be damned if I give Rowan Summers ammunition to use against me or my team.

I reach the lifts in the hotel, jabbing the 'up' button with perhaps more force than necessary. As I wait, I replay our interactions since she joined the Hawkeyes' inner circle, trying to gauge her motives. So far, besides the less-than-flattering article she wrote about me before the Hawkeyes agreed to give *The Seattle Sunrise* full access to the team, her articles have all been lighthearted, yet informative pieces meant to give fans an inside look at each player and who they are on and off the field.

The lift doors slide open with a soft 'ding', and I step forward, only to stop short. There, looking equally surprised, stands the very woman occupying my thoughts.

Rowan Summers, her golden hair slightly mussed from travel, a small suitcase at her side. Our eyes meet, and for a moment, neither of us moves.

"I was just coming up from the basement floor. They have a gym and spa down there," she says.

I give a curt nod and step into the lift.

She's been avoiding me since the *incident* on the plane. Taking her time to exit the aircraft, hanging back as far from me as possible and hopping on a different bus to the hotel. I should be avoiding her and dodging her invasive questions, not the other way around. But now, here we are, face to face with nowhere to hide.

I could have saved us both from having to ride up together by telling her that I'll take the next one, but Rowan Summers won't have me running, even if the idea of being enclosed in a small elevator with her closely resembles the situation we were in mere hours ago.

The silence stretches for a few seconds and then Rowan clears her throat.

"All checked in?" she asks, her voice slightly higher than usual.

"Yup," I say simply.

I bend forward to hit level seven while level five is already illuminated.

Good, we're not on the same floor.

The team usually stays on the same level of the hotel together, Penelope always books, but since Rowan was a last-minute add-on, I suppose there weren't any rooms left for her. That's one less thing to worry about. Knowing that she won't be sleeping next door to any players.

"So," Rowan starts, clearly trying to break the awkward silence. "Big game tomorrow. Feeling confident?"

I arch an eyebrow at her. "Fishing for quotes already, Summers?"

She rolls her eyes, a flash of the fire I've come to expect from her. I kind of fire she uses to draw me in. "Believe it or not, Coach, sometimes small talk is just small talk. Until the head coach kisses you in the back of an aircraft."

I feel a twinge of guilt, even though nothing happened since we were interrupted by the stewardess. "About the incident on the plane, I think we'd both do well to forget it. I made a poor judgement—it shouldn't have happened. But I'll give you a quote... if you drop it." I say, glancing over at her. When she lifts a brow at me without a verbal response, I continue by answering her question. "The lads have been training hard. I believe we're in good form for tomorrow's match."

Rowan nods, a small smile playing at the corners of her mouth. "That's good to hear. The team seems really focused."

"They are," I agree, then can't help adding, "When they're not being distracted, that is."

Rowan shakes her head.

"Look, I know you don't trust me," she says softly. "But I'm not your enemy, Bex. I'm just trying to do my job, same as you."

"Just stay off of level seven, and we'll be fine."

Her eyes narrow slightly. "And what exactly is that supposed to mean?"

The elevator dings as we get to her level. Thank Christ.

I look up at the red number five lit up above the lift door. "Look at that, fresh out of time. Just as well. You and I don't fight well in closed spaces. Best we don't tempt fate again," I say, reaching out a hand to keep the door open as she exits. The last thing either of us needs is to be stuck in this lift together any longer than necessary.

She stomps out of the elevator with that air of confidence that amplifies all the ways that I'm attracted to her.

I pull my hand away to let the lift door close, but just before the doors begin to move, Rowan glances over her shoulder at me. "Don't forget Bexley, you're the one who kissed me. Not the other way around."

The use of my first name catches me off guard; it's the second time she's used it—both today, and the sound of my name off her pink glossy lips against my mouth, sending an unexpected thrill through me, just like it did on that aircraft.

"Goodnight, Coach," she calls over her shoulder, not glancing back.

She starts walking down the hall and I can't stop from watching her hips and ass sway right to left, before the doors close completely.

For a moment, I'm tempted to hit the 'open' button on the elevator doors to stop them from closing. The need to close the distance between us and feel her sweet lips on mine and her soft body pressed against me again has me tightening my fist, bending my plastic room key in half.

"Fuck," I curse out loud.

I'll have to go back downstairs and get a new one.

I hit the button to send me back down to the lobby to get a new key, giving me time to consider one undeniable truth:

I can't stop thinking about Rowan Summers.

And that, more than anything, scares the hell out of me.

It's the next day at the game when I realize that we've just ended our second period and I haven't seen Rowan in the crowd around us.

She'd been on the bus with us, chatting with some of the players at the back of the bus. I'd caught snippets of her conversation with Briggs, something about his pre-game rituals. She seemed so at ease, laughing and joking, while I'd sat at the front, pretending to be engrossed in last-minute strategy notes.

But now, as the team files out of the locker room and back onto the ice for our last period, there's no sign of her. It's not like she needs my permission to go anywhere, but a nagging worry tugs at the back of my mind. This isn't our home turf. The away crowd can get rowdy, especially when there's alcohol involved. And Rowan, with her golden hair and quick wit, stands out in a crowd.

I scan the seats again, my eyes drawn to the seat five rows back where she usually sits during home games. It's strange how accustomed I've grown to her presence there, like a persistent shadow always in my peripheral vision. Now, the seat is occupied by a man twice Rowan's size wearing the opposing side's jersey and giving me the stink eye.

"Coach!" Ezra's voice cuts through my thoughts. "We're ready to get back on the ice."

I turn to my assistant coach, forcing myself to focus. "Right then. Let's go, shall we?"

As my team heads down the players tunnel and out onto the ice for our final period, I push all thoughts of Rowan to the back of my mind. We only have a one-point lead and the third period is turning into a nail-biter. I can't afford any distractions, not with so much on the line. We're in a crucial part of the season, each game a steppingstone towards the playoffs. My team needs me at my best.

The referee's whistle blows, and the game begins. Almost immediately, I'm swept up in the familiar rhythm of play. My eyes track the puck as it zips across the ice, my mind already three moves ahead, analyzing patterns and planning strategies.

"Conley, watch your left!" I shout, before Briggs narrowly avoids a brutal check. He recovers quickly, snagging the puck and racing towards the opposite goal.

I bark out a protest to the referee, who waves me off. Frustration bubbles up inside me, but I take a deep breath, regaining my composure. Losing my cool won't help the team and the last thing I need is Rowan writing something about me flying off the handle at a ref.

Before I know it, the buzzer signals the end of the game and we win 3-1, making another goal in the final seconds of the period.

In the locker room, the team all clammers with excitement, their energy high after another win. This is why I love hockey – the thrill of the game, the camaraderie of the team. This is the world I understand, not the art magazine that my dad built from the ground up before me or my brothers were born.

My mind drifts back to Rowan as Ezra takes the lead on congratulating the team and giving kudos to a few impressive plays that he and the rest of the coaching staff saw out there tonight.

Rowan's probably in the press box, furiously scribbling notes or chatting up other journalists. She's more than capable of taking care of herself, so why can't I shake this nagging feeling of concern?

I pull out my phone and look through the text messages that Cammy sent me about hotel and travel information, as well as Rowan's number.

I type in Rowan's number and send off a text.

She might be capable of taking care of herself, but as long as she's traveling with my team, it's my responsibility to make sure that everyone gets back home safe, and that includes getting back to the hotel.

> **Unknown number:** We're going to head down to the media room soon. – Bex

> **Rowan:** I'm already down here. See you in a bit.

My shoulders relax when her text comes through.

She must be okay if she's texting me. That's a good sign.

Whatever this is with Rowan, it needs to end. It's becoming too complicated, and even if I could get past her career choice, collecting dirt on my players, and writing reviews about me as a coach, it would never work.

In the end, I'll do what I always do.

I'll choose hockey, and she'll end up broken-hearted.

Chapter Seven

Rowan

The Hawkeyes just finished up game three tonight, a 4-2 win over North Carolina, and tomorrow morning we get on a plane and head home.

I take a sip of my water, trying to focus on the conversation around me instead of the fact that it seems as if Bex has done everything in his power to avoid me the last few days out on the road. We haven't spoken about the moment in the back of the aircraft on our first flight out here, and I'm content to pretend it never happened, but the tension between us still feels raw whenever our eyes meet and it's hard to ignore.

Sitting next to Coach Ezra on my right, I listen in as he tells a funny story to a small group of players all sitting at one end of a large table at the restaurant after the game, when I noticed a commotion near the restaurant's entrance. A family of five has just walked in. The father steps forward to reserve a table while the mother tries to corral three energetic boys, wearing North Carolina jerseys, all sporting well fitting youth sizes except the youngest who's sporting a bright blue cast on his right arm and sporting a jersey that looks like his father should be wearing it.

It hangs down almost to his ankles and his mom bends down to roll up the arms for what I imagine she's done a dozen times already if they came to the game tonight.

As the hostess leads them to their table, the boys' excited chatter grows louder. Suddenly, the youngest lets out a high-pitched squeal. "Mom! Dad! Look! It's Townsend!"

The parents try to shush their son, looking embarrassed, but it's too late. The entire restaurant has turned to watch, including our table. I watch, waiting for Bex to react, unsure if the pint sized opposing team fan is about to fire some insults for crushing their team tonight.

But to my surprise, Bex waves at the little boy. The father tells his family to take a seat in the booth in the corner and then he makes a beeline for our table, stacked full of Hawkeyes players. "I'm so sorry to interrupt your dinner, Coach Townsend," he says, his voice low. "It's just... my son Corey, is a big fan," he gestures to the boy with the cast, "He broke his arm trying to make a save on his junior hockey team. It would mean the world to him if you'd sign his cast."

As Cory shifts in the booth talking to his mom with big hand gestures, I see the name on the back of the old North Carolina jersey.

Townsend #14

It's not a surprise to see Townsend Hawkeyes jerseys at home games. In fact, it's common to see a dozen or so in the crowd. Sometimes a hundred or more when the stadium is packed. But this is the first time I've seen a Townsend jersey for a team he used to play for back in his earlier years.

I hold my breath, waiting for Bex to answer. I have no idea what to expect. I hardly see Bex leave the stadium early enough after a game for fans to still be around to ask for an autograph, and he gets in too early for anyone to be waiting for him to show up to the stadium.

He nods, pushing back his chair. "Sure mate," he says, his voice gentler than I've ever heard it. "I'd be happy to."

As Bex stands and makes his way over to the family's table with the father, I can't help but stare. This is a side of him I've never seen before – a side I didn't even know existed.

I hear Bex's voice as he addresses the three wide eyed boys. "I've got a niece about your age back in England."

The boys' faces light up as Bex approaches Cory, their eyes wide with awe. Cory, the boy with the cast, looks like he might faint from excitement. Bex kneels down beside him, bringing himself to eye level with the child.

"So, you're the one making the saves on your team?" Bex asks, his accent somehow softer, less intimidating. Cory nods vigorously, sliding over to give Bex room to sit down on the booth, four deep—him and the boys with wide cheesy grins and their parents smiling as they watch on from the other side. "Let's see that cast. I think it needs a proper signature, don't you?"

As Bex signs the cast, the other two boys crowd around, each thrusting various items at him—a napkin, a North Carolina cap, even a ketchup-stained menu. To my continued amazement, Bex doesn't rush or show any signs of impatience. He takes his time with each boy, asking their names, listening to their excited chatter about their favorite players and the junior hockey teams they each play on as he signs anything and everything that they ask him to.

I watch, transfixed, as Bex transforms before my eyes. The hard lines of his face soften, his eyes crinkle at the corners as he smiles—real smiles—at the boys' enthusiasm. He laughs at their jokes, nods seriously at their earnest questions about hockey strategy, and even demonstrates a few stick-handling moves using a breadstick as an impromptu hockey stick.

Time seems to stretch as Bex interacts with the family, and the waiter starts to hand us our checks since we've all finished our meals.

The rest of the team went back to their conversations, but I haven't moved an inch, watching carefully from my seat a few tables away, dumbfounded by the way Bex is with these kids.

What started as a simple autograph request has turned into a full-fledged meet-and-greet session. The parents look on, clearly touched by Bex's kindness and patience with their children.

Finally, after what must be at least fifteen minutes—far longer than would typically be considered polite for a celebrity encounter in a restaurant—Bex stands up. He ruffles Cory's hair gently. "Keep practicing those saves, yeah? And listen to you mum and dad," he says with a wink.

The boys chorus their thanks, practically vibrating with excitement. The parents, too, express their gratitude before he leaves.

As Bex turns to head back to our table, I quickly avert my gaze, not wanting him to catch me staring. But I can't help sneaking glances as he makes his way back, noting how the tension seems to have melted from his shoulders, how his step seems lighter.

Just as Bex is about to sit down, a waitress approaches with a water pitcher. "Can I refill your glass, sir?" she asks.

"Yes, thanks," Bex replies, then pauses. He reaches into his pocket and pulls out his wallet, extracting a credit card. Leaning in close to the waitress, he speaks in a low voice, but I'm close enough to catch his words. "Take care of the family's bill with this. But don't tell them until after we've left."

The waitress's eyes widen, but she nods in understanding. "Of course, sir. I'll take care of it."

As if sensing my gaze, Bex's eyes find mine across the table. I watch as the realization dawns on him that I've witnessed this entire exchange. The smile dies slowly on his lips, replaced by his usual guarded expression. It's like watching a shutter close, blocking out the light.

For a moment, we just stare at each other. I want to say something—to acknowledge what I've seen, to tell him how touched I am by his kindness. But the words stick in my throat. How do I let him know that I've seen a glimpse of the man behind the gruff exterior without making him feel exposed?

Before I can figure it out, Bex breaks eye contact, turning to engage in conversation with another assistant coach beside him. The moment is gone, leaving me with a whirlwind of conflicting emotions.

As the dinner continues, I find myself stealing glances at Bex, trying to reconcile the man I thought I knew with the one I just witnessed. The gentle way he spoke to those boys, the genuine interest he showed in their excitement, the quiet generosity of paying for their meal. None of it fits with the image of the grumpy, unapproachable coach I've been battling with for months.

As a journalist, I pride myself on my ability to see beyond the surface, to dig for the real story. But have I failed to do that with Bex? Are Keely and Autumn right that there is more to him?

I participate in the conversations around me as our bills start coming back and everyone finishes off the last of whatever they were drinking. It's time for us to head back to the hotel for our early morning flight back home tomorrow.

As we all stand to leave, gathering our coats and saying our goodbyes, I find myself lingering. I want to say something to Bex, to acknowledge what I saw, but I'm not sure how. As I debate with myself, I see him heading for the exit.

Making a split-second decision, I hurry to catch up with him. "Coach Bex," I call out, just as he reaches the door.

He turns, his expression guarded. "Yes, Summers?"

I take a deep breath. "I just... I wanted to say that what you did for that family was really nice. Those kids will remember this night for the rest of their lives."

Bex stares at me for a long moment, his face unreadable. Then, to my surprise, the corner of his mouth twitches up in a small, almost shy smile. "Yeah, well," he says. "Some people believe that I don't let my fans know me at all," he says, giving me sideways glance." But I never turn down an autograph for kids. I'm not a monster like you portray me to be."

"I've never thought that you're a monster," I say, following him out to the sidewalk of the building, our hotel is only a few short blocks away. We all walked here so we might as well walk back. There's no need to hail a cab.

He tucks his hands in his pockets and stares up at the dark night sky, not making any effort to continue our conversation, so I continue.

"Paying for their meal was really sweet. You took an extra step to make that family's night magical."

His eyes whip down to mine, his eyes back to their usual guarded stare. He doesn't like something I said.

"That stays out of the article... in fact, all of tonight does. Got it?" he says.

"Your fans would love to hear about the boy with the cast and how you sat with them while they asked you questions about—"

"No," he says, cutting me off.

I hear the friendly chatter of the rest of the team pushing past the doors of the restaurant, completely unaware of the conversation that just passed between Bex and me.

He watches them head in our direction and then he turns and starts walking away from me.

Soon the sound of the rest of the group envelopes around me as I get gobbled up into the group and start walking with the herd of hockey players and staff.

Fine, if I can't use the moment with the family to show Bex in a different light than what he shows the world, I'll dig deeper into Bexley Townsend.

Something tells me that his stern stare and don't-touch-me attitude are only surface-deep. Now that I've seen that there's more to him, I'll have to find a way to flush it out of the man... whether he likes it or not.

Chapter Eight

Rowan

I'm curled up on my couch, a fluffy blanket draped over my legs with Sherlock, my neighbor Hans' Boston Terrier, snuggled against my side. The opening credits of the latest CSI: Las Vegas episode play on the TV, but my attention is split between the exclusive interview with Bex that I don't have and how the Hawkeyes are doing this season.

My sister, Jordan, who's sprawled on the other end of the couch, a bowl of popcorn balancing precariously on her stomach, lets out a relaxed sigh.

"So," Jordan says, tossing a piece of popcorn into the air toward me. I miss the toss, and the popcorn hits me on the corner of my mouth, bouncing off and landing right in front of Sherlock, who gobbles it up before I can steal it back, "How was the trip with the hockey team and the outrageously Sexy Mr. Bexley Townsend?" she asks, wiggling her eyebrows and using that ridiculous title she's given him

Jordan is four years younger than me and put off college in lieu of working her way up as manager of a large hotel in the city. She has her own apartment that she pays for without the help of a roommate. At twenty-four, she's doing so well and I'm proud of her and all that she's accomplished.

I've filled my sister in on all things "Bex" and his growing grudge against me. When I first told her about Bex, she whipped out her phone and internet stalked him immediately. I remember the look on her face the second his old team picture popped up on his Wikipedia page.

"Christ on a cracker... Please tell me this man is single."

"He's twenty years too old for you, Jordan."

"Perfect, I have daddy issues, and so do you," she smirked. *"Want to share him? I call dibs on the bottom half."*

I don't know about daddy issues but our parents divorced when we were little. I don't think Jordan even remembers our parents being married. Our dad got remarried and moved away after he got a big newscasting position in New York. I try really hard not to think about how I ended up choosing a similar career path as him.

Jordan and I didn't hear from him much after he moved, though for some reason he now talks more to our mom than he's ever tried to reach out to us.

I still get texts ever so often.

> Dad: Hey, squirt. Mom said you got into Northwestern. Good job!

> Dad: Congratulations! Mom said you got an internship with ESPN. That's huge.

> Dad: Hey Ro, mom said you got a big promotion at work. You're traveling with the Hawkeyes? I'm proud of you.

But never a phone call or an attempt to reach out and ask how I was doing. Everything went through our mom.

Mom says that dad feels too guilty to reach out himself but that sounds like a bunch of excuses to me.

Jordan tosses up another fluffy piece of popcorn into the air and catches it in her mouth.

I clear my throat, debating whether or not to tell her about what happened on the trip, but I can't keep this from her. I tell Jordan everything. She and I don't have secrets. "It was... eventful, I guess you could say."

Jordan's eyebrows shoot up. "Ooh, do tell. How did it go traveling with Coach Bex? I know he's the Grinch and his heart is three times too small... but his cock must be huge, right?"

"Jordan!" I say, whipping a wide-eyed look in her direction.

"What? The mean ones always have the biggest cocks. It's nature's cruel injustice," she says with a straight face.

"Oh my God Jordan, we are not talking about the size of the man who hates my guts."

Not that I would know his *measurements* anyway since I've never seen it.

Jordan doesn't seem the least bit fazed by the shock written on my face about her choice of conversation topic.

"I guess you're right. Besides, Drew was average sized right? And that guy is the biggest tool of them all," she looks over at me. "Or rather an average-sized tool," she winks.

"Jordan—"

She cuts me off before I can demand she drops this line of questioning. "Here, I'll go get a ruler and you could show me where Drew falls *short*."

She makes a move to pull the bowl of popcorn off her lap but I whip out my leg that I had tucked underneath me and plop it on her thigh. "Don't you dare move a muscle. This is sister bonding time since I haven't seen you in days. We're not talking about anyone's dick size, okay? Can we just watch our show and talk about *anything* else?"

"Okay, fine," she says, snuggling back into her spot, and then grabs a handful of popcorn and throws it at me.

"Real mature," I mutter

I scoop as many pieces as I can before Sherlock gets too many but he's already eaten several pieces. It's the light butter version but he still shouldn't have too much. If he gets sick from eating the popcorn, Hans won't ever let me puppy-sit again. I'm on a thin line with that man.

"You at least owe me a breakdown of your trip. Tell me everything."

I snort, reaching over to steal a handful of popcorn. "Okay, something did happen."

Jordan sits up straighter, nearly dumping the popcorn bowl, as she reaches for the remote to mute the TV. "Spill. Now."

I take a deep breath, preparing myself for my sister to lose her shit. "We kissed."

The popcorn Jordan was about to eat falls from her hand, scattering across the blanket. "I'm sorry, what? You and The Outrageously Sexy Mr. Bexley Townsend kissed? And you didn't think to tell me about this until sooner?"

"When would you have preferred I told you?"

"The *minute* it happened, duh!"

Of course she would have.

"While in mid-air? You're not supposed to make phone calls while on an aircraft. It could do something to the plane."

She waves her hand in dismissal. "Psht, that's a myth. And even if it weren't a myth, you should have risked it," she says, her eyebrows down turning in annoyance with me.

She actually expected me to run to my phone the moment after it happened.

To be honest, it took a while to process the whole thing, and I'm still not sure that I understand what happened.

"Well, I'm telling you now."

"I need to know everything. "How? When? Where? Why?"

I groan, burying my face in my hands. "It was in the back of the plane. We were arguing, as usual, and then there was some turbulence, and suddenly..."

"Suddenly, you were playing tonsil hockey with the coach?" Jordan finishes, a mischievous glint in her eye.

I feel my cheeks heat up. "It wasn't like that. It was... intense. Unexpected."

"Please tell me he took off his shirt."

I just shake my head at her and chuckle. It can't be helped when she's like this.

"Was it good at least?" she prompts, leaning forward. "I mean... duh, it had to be good but what happened after?

I hesitate, remembering the feel of Bex's strong arms around me, the passion in his kiss, the way he pulled me against him protectively. "Yeah, it was good. Really good, actually; then the stewardess walked in, and I panicked."

Jordan whoops, punching the air. "I knew it! I knew there was some serious sexual tension brewing between you two! I can't believe you were hiding this from me."

"I wasn't hiding it... I'm telling you now. And besides it was one kiss and nothing else happened. And anyway, I've been a little too busy trying not to get fired."

"What do you mean fired? You're one of the best sports reporters that *The Seattle Sunrise* has."

I groan at the thought of what I have to do to keep being the best sports reporter there in order to get the promotion. "Charles wants an exclusive with Bex and there's no way that Bex is going to sit down with me. He already thinks I'd be willing to sell out my own grandmother for enough new subscribers to the newspaper."

Jordan's expression softens. "That's because he doesn't know you the way I do. Plus, if he knew Grandma Charlene, he wouldn't put it past you. She's a cranky old witch." Jordan is teasing. Our grandma isn't all that bad, she just spends most of our visit still cursing out my father, as if that helps mend anything for Jordan or me.

"Yeah well, go down to the Hawkeyes stadium and put in a good word for me because he won't believe it if in comes from me," I sigh, absently stroking Sherlock's fur.

"With pleasure," she winks.

I roll my eyes. "Don't even start, you'll only make it worse trying to come onto him. He'll just think that I'm prostituting out my sister for a promotion, which is exactly the sort of thing he thinks I'd do," I shake my head. "I just don't know what to do at this point. My job depends on it." I let out a defeated sigh.

"You know what you have to do. You have to go down there and face him on his terms. Don't take no for an answer and find some common ground with him."

I hate that she's right. I really wish there was another way to get him to open up.

"Face him on his terms," I repeat, mulling it over.

"Yeah. You've been studying him like the amazing reporter you are, right? His schedule, his habits, his coaching technique. So... what is he likely doing right now?"

I don't have to wonder. I can almost guess with certainty. "He's probably alone out on the ice shooting pucks into the net. It's like his way to decompress." I tell her, thinking of all the times I've seen him out on the ice.

"Ok. We can work with that. Do you have a set of skates?"

"No, I don't. And I don't think I've ice skated since we were kids. And I wasn't very good even back then when gravity was a little nicer to me." I never took well to ice skating, skiing, or even gymnastics.

I do pretty good on a pair of stilettos but that's where my balancing ability starts and ends.

She shoots me a look like I'm being picky. She's right, if I want this exclusive, Coach Bex is going to make me work for it—figures.

"I don't have skates... but I know someone who does."

I pick up my phone and text Penelope asking if she has a set of ice skates I can borrow. I already know that we're the same size, and then I set my phone back down.

Penelope is going to be happy when she finds out what I need them for. If I didn't know better, I'd say Jordan and my sister planned this.

"He can't be all that bad. It seems like his team respects him and the fans love him."

I nod. "I can't deny that he's an incredible coach. The way he connects with the players, the strategies he comes up with... it's impressive. And when he lets his guard down, even for a moment, there's something about him that's just... magnetic. You should have seen him with these little boys at the restaurant." My lips pull into a wide grin at the memory of Bex crammed into the booth next to the boys.

Something about seeing him dote on those kids has me imagining him as an amazing father to some lucky kid. Or maybe that's just me projecting since I can't have kids of my own. I often see people in two different categories: good with kids or bad with kids. A habit I should break since children aren't in my future.

Jordan nods. "Sounds like someone's got a crush on the Grinch.

I grab a handful of popcorn and toss it at her. "I do not have a crush, and that kiss was a mistake. It probably happened because the air is thinner up there. My brain was being depleted of oxygen."

Jordan ducks, laughing as she throws more popcorn at me. "Right. And that's why you're blushing like a schoolgirl after her first game of seven minutes in heaven."

I stick my tongue out at her, trying to catch a piece of popcorn in my mouth. It bounces off my nose and hits Sherlock between the eyes. He's too busy trying to eat it before I can scoop it all up.

"Okay, fine," I admit. "Maybe I'm a little attracted to him. But it doesn't matter. We're way too different, and I don't need that kind of drama. If I'm going to date someone, it needs to be the right person."

Jordan's smile fades a bit. "You mean someone who's okay with adoption."

I sigh. "Or someone who's fine with not having kids at all. I can't go through what happened with Drew again. I don't want to feel like I'm not enough."

"You've been through a lot, I get it. But Drew's a fool. The right man will accept you for who you are. Don't give up hope."

"I'm not giving up. I just want to focus on my work for now. No more talk about babies or boyfriends for a while."

Jordan reaches over, squeezing my hand. "I know, Ro. I'm not rushing you. I just want to make sure you're not shutting out someone who could be important."

Part of her speech might be right, but thinking of that "important" someone being Bex has heat rising up my neck.

I shake the thought of the grumpy coach for now, and besides him, the dating scene feels like a complete mess. It's easier to just focus on what I can control.

"Let's just watch our show," I say with a sigh.

Jordan grins and throws one last piece of popcorn at me. "Deal. Now, let's see if they catch this killer before I lose my mind."

I laugh and settle back into the couch, pulling Sherlock closer as Jordan hits play on the TV remote. "Ten bucks says the killer is the neighbor."

"You're on," she says.

For now, the stress of work, life, and whatever tomorrow will bring out on the rink with Bex, will have to wait. I have ten bucks to win.

Chapter Nine

Bex

The sound of my skates scraping against the ice fills the quiet rink as I take another shot. The puck slams into the back of the net with a satisfying thud.

Practice ended over an hour ago but after the team all left I couldn't sit still in my office.

The weight of everything.

The team, the season, my family wanting me to finish out my contract next season and come home... and the unsettled conversation constantly going around in my head about her. It all feels especially heavy today, like a puck lodged in my chest that I can't shake off.

Rowan Summers.

It's maddening how she's managed to get under my skin. Every time I think I've got her figured out, she goes and does something else that sets me off. My head's a mess, and I've been avoiding her, focusing on the one thing that's always made sense to me—hockey.

Another slap shot, another echo through the empty rink. It's not enough.

"Looks like you're trying to murder that puck," Sam's voice calls out from the bench.

I glance over, seeing him leaning casually against the boards. He's wearing his usual black Hawkeyes windbreaker, and a pair of trousers.

"Need to work out some frustration," I grunt, sending another puck flying toward the goal.

Sam watches for a moment, his eyes narrowing slightly before he speaks. "She's got you all twisted up, doesn't she?"

I pause, resting the stick against my knees, breathing hard. "It's not just her. It's the team. The season. Everything's on the line."

Sam steps onto the ice, his movements steady and deliberate, each stride gripping the slick surface with the confidence of years spent navigating it. "I get it. But you're not just angry at her, Bex. You're angry at yourself, too."

I raise an eyebrow at him. "What're you on about?"

He sighs, rubbing the back of his neck. "I see it in you. The way you look like you're carrying the weight of the world on your shoulders. Hockey is everything to you, just like it was to me. And we both know that it costs us more than we care to admit."

His words hang in the cold air between us, and I know exactly what he's referring to. Sam's ex-wife left him when she felt that hockey was the real love of his life, not her. They couldn't make it work, and though Sam doesn't say much about her, I know he's never moved on.

"It wasn't the same for me and Lily," I say, shooting another puck into the net, the sound more hollow this time. "I cared about her, but I didn't love her like she deserved. I broke her heart because I couldn't love her more than the game."

Sam nods, his eyes distant. "And that's where we're different. I still love my ex-wife, always will. But that didn't make a damn difference when it came down to choosing between her and the game. Hockey... it consumes you. But I know I made the wrong decision. I should have picked her. I should have given Penelope the childhood she deserved."

"But Penelope turned out brilliant. She seems happy. You managed it alright," I say.

"Maybe, but hockey never made me whole. When Caroline refused to move to Seattle, I should have made a better choice and kept my family together."

I grip my stick tighter, the tension in my chest not letting up. "Do you regret it?"

"Every day," Sam admits, his voice quieter now. "And if I could do it over, I don't know what I would do. Being on this side of things, it's easy to say that I might have made the wrong choice, now that my skating days are over, but had I done it before I accomplished everything I wanted to in the sport...

I might have resented letting my window close on my career. That's the thing, Bex. The game—it's always going to demand more from you than anyone else ever will. The question is, how much are you willing to give and when is it time to move on?"

I look down at the ice, the question echoing in my mind. How much more can I give before there's nothing left?

"How much are you willing to give it?" I ask.

"I've given the sport more than its fair share. Now it's time to give Caroline back the time I took from us."

Did he just say what I thought he did?

"You're getting back together with your ex-wife?"

A lopsided grin pulls at the corner of his mouth. "It's a little too early to tell, but I'm going to spend the off-season back home trying to convince her to take me back." He chuckles. "I promised Phil that I'd give him one more year to make sure that Penelope is ready to take my place. She's going to need a strong head coach by her side, which is why I'm curious how many more years you're willing to give this franchise."

Before I can answer, Sam's gaze shifts, and he gestures toward the players' tunnel. "Looks like you've got company."

I follow his line of sight and see Rowan standing there in a pair of skates and a smart black dress that stops at her calves, designed for the office and not for a skating rink. At the very least, she's wearing some puffy jacket that looks like Penelope's. The skates look like Penelope's too. I wouldn't be surprised if Rowan skating out here was the new Assistant GM's idea.

She wobbles slightly as she tries to step onto the ice. She looks completely out of place but determined.

Sam smirks and claps me on the back. "Be nice. She's here for a reason, and if she's got questions, you might as well practice answering them. There will be press at the gala in a couple of days anyway. And think about what I said. Maybe you've given the game enough years of yourself."

I sigh as Sam heads back toward the bench. I skate slowly toward Rowan, watching as she hesitates before taking a tentative step onto the ice. She wobbles as she skates onto the ice. She's trying to hide her nerves but I can see it in the slight shake of her ankles and her stiff posture, her eyes locked on her skates and the ice below her. My guess is she's never ice skated before.

I skate up to her with ease, my hockey stick still in my hand. "What are you doing out here? You're a reporter covering a hockey team, but you don't know how to skate?"

She glares up at me, peering through her long dark eyelashes. "I'm a sports journalist— I cover more than just hockey, and as shocking as this might be to you, knowing how to ice skate was not part of the job requirement."

"Maybe it should be," I mutter under my breath.

"We all start somewhere, Coach Bex. I doubt you came out of the womb dressed in full hockey gear."

My mum would laugh at that. In fact, I think there's a lot about Rowan that my mum would like. They have a similar fiery personality.

"Actually, I did." I shoot back.

She rolls her eyes and makes a tsking sound with her tongue. "Figures."

She wobbles again and attempts to bend her knees and straighten out her arms on either side of herself in an attempt to gain better balance.

My hands flinch forward as if prepared to reach out and grab her before she falls like I did on our flight, but she stabilizes on her own. Just as well. The last thing I need is an excuse to touch her again.

"You're wearing a dress out on my ice. Don't you own anything warmer?"

She blinks at me twice as if my question doesn't make logical sense. "I'm at work. It's hard enough to be taken seriously as a female in my field. I need to dress as professional as possible, and this is what I've always worn to press interviews. Besides, I'm not here on a social visit. And why do you care what I wear? Penelope wears less than this when she iceskates and I doubt you've ever commented on it."

She makes a point. I've never once commented on Penelope's figure skating apparel before. But Penelope doesn't wear a lot because she needs the freedom to move around. Rowan can barely skate out here at all.

"I don't care what you wear. You just look cold, that's all." I say, glancing up into the stands to see if we have an audience of one... Penelope Roberts. But when I glance around, it only confirms that Rowan and I are alone together.

"Since when do you care what temperature I am," she asks, a glint in her eye.

"I don't," I say quickly, not wanting to admit that I unwillingly notice her temperature every time I glance back during practice, witnessing the tip of her nose turning red and her knees bouncing to keep warm. "Now why are you out here anyway? Practice is over, and if any of the players are still here, they're in the gym lifting weights. If you want interviews, you should have gotten here earlier."

"I came to see you," she says.

"You came to see me? Why?" I ask, narrowing my eyes slightly, suspicion creeping into my voice.

She glances around the rink as if to make sure that we're still alone.

"We're going to be working together for a couple more months, and rumors are already swirling around the franchise about how much we don't get along. I thought we could come to an understanding."

She's not going away, that I realize.

I reach out my hand for her to take. If we have to talk, at the very least, I should get to hit a few pucks. She is, after all, encroaching on my time.

Her eyes flick up to mine, a mix of uncertainty and distrust. Does she really think that I'd let her fall on her ass after what happened on the plane?

"Where are you planning on taking me?" she asks.

"Just over there," I say, pointing to where a bucket of pucks is sitting. "You're interrupting my shooting practice. The least you can do is let me hit some pucks while you try to convince me why gossip around the franchise matters. It's never been a secret that we don't get along."

This is as close to cooperation as she's going to get and she knows it. After a moment, she reaches out, gripping my hand with her black gloves.

The feeling of her warm cotton hand fitting right inside of mine like it belongs there is unnerving.

We skate together, slowly, toward the spot where I've been shooting pucks. She stumbles a bit, and I hold her steady, trying not to think about how natural it feels to help her like this. To have her out here on the ice with me. To have her invade the space I usually go to clear her out of my head.

"Where did the skates come from?" I ask, though I'm sure I know the answer.

I'd like to know who to personally thank for this intrusion.

Rowan glances down at the skates I'm referring to as she glides slowly next to me.

"Penelope had an old pair, and we wear the same size. Lucky don't you think?"

"Lucky... right," I say, knowing that there's no "luck" involved when Penelope decided to stick her nose in it. What is she up to?

She clears her throat as we stop. I let go of her hand once I'm sure she's stable on her own. "I wanted to talk to you about this job. About why this is so important to me."

I stay silent, pulling another puck from the tipped-over bucket with the end of my hockey stick, and then wind up and hit it. The puck makes a loud thud noise as before, the sound ricocheting off the walls of the rink. In the corner of my eye, Rowan jumps at the loud crack. It's a lot louder out here than it is behind the plexiglass.

I slide another puck into position and wait for her to continue.

"I know we're never going to be friends, and that's fine. I don't expect us to get along, but this job means everything to me. It's my career, my way of proving myself and it's the only thing I have for myself."

The only thing she has for herself?

I want to ask her exactly what that means, but she continues, and the less I know about Rowan, the better.

"And after the Hawkeyes win the Stanley Cup. You'll see much less of me. But until then, I don't want to be enemies anymore."

I let her words sink in, the honesty in them disarming me. For the first time, I see the one attribute that Rowan and I both share. We're both dedicated to our careers. I'm just still not sure what lengths she'll go to keep hers.

"You're asking for a truce?"

I stare down at her, the ice reflecting off her big blue eyes, causing them to shimmer.

There's something disarming about her, something that makes it hard to keep my walls up... but I can't let myself fall for her, not when my team is on the line.

"Yes, a truce. For the sake of the team and the championship, so that both of us can do our jobs."

I think for a second. I don't know if she's trying to pull one over my head, so she'll have to earn a truce.

I hand her my hockey stick. "If you can sink this puck into that net, you've got yourself a truce."

I skate around to her back to help guide her into position.

"Sink the puck?" Rowan looks over her shoulder at me, eyebrows raised in disbelief. "And if I miss?"

"If you miss, no truce," I say, reaching around from behind her to adjust her grip on the stick. Her scent lingers in the air between us, subtle but distracting, and the way her body fits between my arms feels dangerously natural.

"But like I told you before," I murmur, my voice low. "We're not enemies. I just don't trust you. Not yet."

Her eyes meet mine, something unreadable in them, but I force myself to look away, focusing on the puck. She draws a deep breath and lines up the shot, clearly out of her comfort zone. My hands grip her hips, positioning her body into place, feeling her heat through the thin material of her dress.

For a split second, I almost want her to make the shot–to force us to play nice–to address what is or isn't happening. But then I know better. It's a bad idea that will likely end badly.

Rowan winds back and hits the puck. The puck flies off to the right, missing the goal by a long shot.

Her shoulders slump, disappointment etched on her face, the brightness in her big blue eyes dimming just slightly. I should feel satisfied that the bet worked out in my favor, but there's a part of me that wonders what would happen if we agreed to a truce.

"Well, I guess that settles it," she mutters, handing the stick back to me. "No truce."

I grip the stick but don't pull away. Her effort was decent, and for someone who's clearly out of her element, she tried, I'll give her that. "You gave it a fair shot," I say, my voice softer than I intended.

Rowan shrugs. "Guess I'll just have to work on my slap shot. Maybe I'll beat you next time."

She says it with a touch of humor. I pause, watching her for a moment longer.

"You can try again," I say, gesturing toward the ice. "But be sure you're ready next time. I won't go easy on you."

Rowan's eyes sparkle with the challenge, her confidence returning. "Oh, I wouldn't expect anything less, Coach."

I pull the stick back, sliding another puck into position for myself. As I line up my next shot, I glance over at her, standing there on the ice, wobbling but determined. She may have missed the shot, but she's far from defeated. There's something resilient in her, and despite everything, I'm starting to see that.

I take the shot, the puck sailing cleanly into the net with a loud thud. Rowan doesn't flinch this time, and that makes me grin. She's learning.

As I skate over to her and extend my hand to help her back to the player's tunnel.

Do I trust her enough for a truce?

No, not yet. I can't afford that. Not with everything at stake.

I still don't have an answer for the hallway whisperings and concerned looks shared between Reeve and Rowan.

"Thanks for helping me back. I need to get going. I'm meeting Tessa and Brynn for dress shopping for the gala."

I nod, releasing her hand as she steps off the ice. For now, the truce may be off, but something tells me this isn't the last time we'll be standing here, facing off on my turf.

Chapter Ten

Rowan

The bell above the boutique door jingles as I enter the gorgeous French inspired boutique dress shop located outside of the city. This is where Tessa, Brynn and Cammy told me to meet them to try on gowns for the gala.

Tessa is already leaning against the mirror, rubbing her pregnant belly, focused on her screen. She's probably checking the Hawkeyes' social media account as she usually does throughout the day to respond to fans and questions on posts about game schedules and where to buy tickets online. She glances up and grins as soon as she spots me.

"Finally, you're here! We were about to send a search party for you. Brynn's in the back trying on half the store," she greets, her voice her usual teasing tone, her hand still absentmindedly tracing circles over her belly.

The sight stirs something in me I wasn't expecting—a pang that settles somewhere between my chest and my gut. It's not jealousy—more wistful, and quiet yearning that sneaks up on me.

I force a smile back at her, not wanting her to see it in my eyes and feel sorry for me, but my mind wanders for a fleeting second. Isla just had her baby a little while back, and now Tessa is due at the end of the season. The thought catches me off guard, my imagination leaping ahead of me.

What would it feel like to be a part of this group, not just as the reporter they've accepted into their inner circle, but as someone sharing the journey of building a family? To have a little life growing inside me and get to raise that baby surrounded by this tight-knit, loving community of women who seem to rally around each other no matter what?

But then the weight of reality crashes in, reminding me why that thought is so dangerous. Being this close to them—to their lives and their families, is already a conflict of interest. As a reporter, my job is to stay impartial, not to dream about what it would feel like to belong in their world.

I hear Brynn's muffled voice behind one of the changing room doors, breaking me from thoughts. "And Tessa only tried on one dress and bought it instantly so she could keep working. She's no fun. I need someone to try stuff on with or I'm going to start feeling self-conscious for grabbing so many gowns."

"I'm pregnant, it doesn't exactly lend to a closet full of couture. But I got lucky and found something that fits," she says, pointing to a long plastic dress bag hanging by the register.

"The Hawkeyes' social media account has been blowing up from the pictures I've been posting of Juliet and Shawnie's decorations for the gala that just started going up around the stadium. Fans are hitting up the comment section asking for last-minute tickets to the gala or to find out if players will be available for autographs at some point that night. And besides, I already know what looks good on me; I'm an easy shopper... so sue me." Tessa teases, saying the last part loud enough to make sure Brynn can hear it.

"I would if I could," Brynn mutters.

I laugh, stepping fully into the boutique, hoping that girl talk will chase away my disappointment at my failed attempt at a truce with Bex. "Sorry, traffic was a nightmare, but I'm here, and I'm ready to shop," I say, pulling off my jacket and laying it down on the kind of chair I would imagine Marie Antoinette probably had in her salon. "Where's Cammy?"

"She just texted. She's running late from a study session but she's on her way," Tessa says, looking down at her phone as she types something up and hits send. "But wait, what's this about traffic? I thought you lived only a few minutes away from here."

Unlike most everyone on the team who either live downtown Seattle or live in the wealthy gated community nearby, I live in a studio apartment further out of town. Being a journalist pays the bills, but not the kind of bills that allow city living without the need for a roommate to share the expenses. It's fine with me. The city can feel suffocating at times anyway, and since I work out of the office most days, I only have to commute to work when there's a game I need to be in the press box for or a staff meeting at *The Seattle Sunrise*.

"Yes, I do live close by, but I came from the stadium," I tell her.

Tessa shoots me an inquisitive look, but before she can dive into her question, a tall woman with a name tag and shiny jet-black hair pulled up in a tight bun makes her way toward me, sporting a smile that says she plans on making a commission today.

"Hi, you must be Rowan."

"Yeah, that's me. Sorry I'm late," I tell her.

She gives my body a once over as if scanning me for my measurements.

"That's not a problem at all," she assures me. "Based on the event and your friend's description of you, I pulled a few things to start us off, but of course, if you don't like any of them, you're welcome to look around or tell me what you have in mind."

I move my gaze over toward the changing rooms to find that one of the doors has a handful of dresses hanging on a metal rack. She wasn't kidding when she said that she already pulled items for me.

There must be over twenty dresses bulging off the rack.

There's a slinky gold dress that catches my eye as I follow the saleswoman. When we get closer, I notice a pink satin one with a full skirt, a black and white striped one with a lot of tulle, and an emerald, green dress that looks like it belongs on the red carpet. It would look killer with Keely's auburn hair. I wish more of the girls were here tonight, but most of them had conflicting schedules, so we all had to divide and conquer to get gowns for the event. Still, I'm glad that Tessa, Brynn and soon Cammy are here to do this with.

"No, I trust you. I'm sure whatever you picked out will be a great place to start."

The saleswoman nods and then opens the changing room that she has waiting for me.

"Now that I've seen your body structure in person, I'll pick my top favorites for you if you're open to my suggestions. You can tell me which ones you like and which ones you don't like, and then I can narrow it down to the perfect dress."

Tessa finds a chair in front of the waiting room and sits as if she's waiting for Brynn and me to start modeling the dresses for her.

"That sounds great, thank you," I tell her.

I walk into the dressing room and then the saleswoman returns with four dresses. She hangs them up for me and then leaves, telling me that she's going to go check on another client at the end of the dressing room but to let her know if I need help in or out of a dress.

I close the door and begin to undress.

"How's it going in there?" Tessa asks Brynn.

"Good, I think. I found a couple I like so far, but I need your opinion. This is the first major event Seven and I are going to as a couple. I just want to make sure that I make him look good."

I hear Tessa make a tsking sound. "You're kidding, right? First of all, you're so gorgeous you could make a dumpster look classy as shit. Second, Seven practically worships you, so stop putting this pressure on yourself. Instead, consider your choice of footwear carefully. I have a feeling that there will be an impromptu walk to Wally's Burgers after the gala ends at one in the morning."

I chuckle at the mental image of a group of Hawkeyes players and their girlfriends, all dressed in formal wear, walking six long blocks to Wally's Burgers.

"Don't forget to model the dresses for me," Tessa says. "And speaking of arm candy, are you bringing a plus one to the gala, Rowan?"

"A plus one?" I ask, trying to sound as if the idea had never occurred to me. Although it actually hadn't happened because this is more of a work event for me than one for pleasure, with all the stunning art pieces that Autumn says are coming in for auction, I'm really looking forward to seeing them in person. "No, I'm not bringing anyone, but if I were to, it would probably be my sister Jordan."

I scan all four dresses and pick a red full-length dress with a plunging neckline to try on first.

"You sure you wouldn't just want to go with someone who is already going to be there?"

I can hear the teasing tone in Tessa's voice, like she's trying to lead me to the answer that she wants to hear.

"Like who?" I ask, playing into her game.

"Word around the Hawkeyes stadium is that things between you two are getting steamy. Something about you two disappearing for an extended period of time on the flight out and then emerging later, both appearing a little more disheveled than when you went in."

For the love of God, does anyone keep their mouth shut around here?

And then a thought comes to me that hadn't before. Is Bex bringing a plus one?

And do I care if he does?

I shake the idea away. Of course, I don't care. He'd be a miserable date for some poor girl.

"Wait, what? This is the first time I'm hearing of this. What happened on the aircraft?" Brynn asks, the sound of taffeta rustling around like she's either taking off a dress or putting a new one on.

"Nothing," I say, pulling the dress up my body and then trying to zip it up as far on my own as I can.

I turn toward the mirror and take in how I look in the first dress I'm trying on so far. I like it, but it's not giving me the vibe I want. Maybe it's childish, but I know that Drew and his fiancé are invited and though I still don't hold a candle for our relationship since it ended three years ago, the last thing I want him to think is that I'm not doing well and that dumping me was the right move on his part.

"That's not what I heard. I heard that at every game, Bex was always looking for you—asking players, if they had seen you—eye fucking you every chance he got—dragging his feet to get on the bus until he physically saw you onboard."

Did he really do all of that?

Tessa doesn't travel with the team so she must have heard this from Lake.

"Rowan! Are you seriously holding out on us?" I hear Brynn say, and then her door opens.

I open my door too and walk out in the first dress.

Tessa looks at the dress I'm wearing and gives an unsure twist to her lips. "I'm not sure about that one," she says.

"Yeah, me either," I say, and I glance down the hall of changing rooms to see that the saleswoman is staring at me in the dress and seems deep in thought—making her own opinion of the dress on me as well, only she keeps it to herself.

Then Tessa and I both glance over at Brynn and shake our heads. It's not form fitting enough and she already mentioned in our group text earlier this week that she wants a Jessica Rabbit look to make Seven drop to his knees.

I think the man already does.

Brynn and I both turn back and head into our dressing rooms to pull off our dresses and try another one.

"I don't know where you're getting your information from but—"

"From Lake. He said he saw it all with his own eyes, so don't bother denying that something happened," Tessa says.

Damn it. I can't exactly call out her fiancé as a liar.

"Wait, something happened between you and Bex on the plane?" Brynn asks.

The sound of hangers clinking together in her room tells me that she is moving on to another dress.

I consider my options in the safety of my changing room without the prying eyes of Tessa Tomlin. The way I see it, I only have two choices: either I lie to my friends even though there was an eyewitness to the moment between Bex and me, or I come clean about the kiss he and I shared on an aircraft and seek out advice. Though the last advice from Keely, Autumn, and then

Jordan was to meet him on his turf to get some perspective and let him see that I'm trying. Some good that did me. But Tessa is a human lie detector, so there's no point in lying.

I grab another dress off its hanger and step inside, pulling the soft, silky gown up over my hips.

This dress is a sleek mermaid flare in black satin, and it's glorious but almost too refined and sophisticated. I want to be noticed, not blend in with the scenery. It's not the one but Tessa will probably still expect to see it.

I open my door

Tessa takes notice of the dress, giving it a once over, but shakes her head.

"Pretty but not quite right."

"I agree."

I turn back and head for the changing room, unzipping the second dress and sliding it off my body.

"So? What happened?" she asks. "Don't think you're getting out of this conversation, Ro."

"Okay, fine, we kissed," I admit, hanging the black dress back on the hanger. "But it was an accident, and we quickly agreed never to discuss it again."

Brynn gasps on the other side of the changing room. "You kissed!?" she yells loud enough for everyone in the shop to hear.

"I knew it! Spill. Now." Tessa giggles in triumph.

"It was nothing. He thinks that I have some dirt on Reeve or Keely, and he pulled me aside to threaten me off his team. I slipped during turbulence, and he caught me. He kissed me—it was barely a peck." A little lie won't hurt. They got the story they wanted anyway.

"He knows about Keely's dad?" Brynn asks.

"No, he doesn't know anything. But now that Keely's dad is trying to re-enter her life, Reeve keeps pulling me aside to ask if I can reassure Keely that it's all going to be okay. Bex keeps finding us together, and he thinks that I've got something on Reeve."

"So, he thinks you're going to run a nasty story on Reeve?" Tessa clarifies.

Ever since Keely and Reeve decided to be together, I've convinced Keely to let more of the girls know what's going on with her so she doesn't feel so alone, and just as I suspected, no one judged her for the sins of her father. She still hasn't been ready to tell Sam or Bex... or pretty much anyone else on the team, but I'm proud of her for starting to trust more. And all of the girls in our group are fiercely protective of her. Autumn, Tessa, and I even have a contingency plan ready in case the news ever breaks out, and we need to help bury the story, though I truly think that Keely's ex-boyfriend and the athletic director from her old team blew this whole thing out of proportion.

But colleges are weird about protecting their recruiting ability since it means money for their program, and her ex... well, that guy just seems like a selfish tool. I covered the Boeing Classic two years ago that's part of the PGA tour, and her ex threw his driving iron and kicked over his golf clubs when he made a shot that landed in the pond nearby. I'd say he's a bit of a drama queen.

"Yep. Basically, if you ask Bex, I'm the story-hungry enemy who has no soul." I say, rifling through a few more dresses that the saleswoman flung over the door for me to try on.

"Can you find another way to talk to him? Get him to see that you're not a threat to his team, while still keeping Keely's secret?" Tessa asks.

"I tried. I went to see him after practice. I thought we could clear the air, maybe find some common ground so we're not constantly at each other's throats. But then it didn't work. He told me we're not enemies, but that he doesn't trust me. Then he handed me his hockey stick and told me if I could make a shot, he'd call a truce—I missed," I say.

I pull on a third dress, this time a delicate blue beaded gown. A darker hue than the Hawkeyes' turquoise team color. The second it's on, I know. This is the one. The way the beads shimmer in the light, the plunging neckline that flatters without being too much, the way it hugs my curves—everything about it is perfect.

I've worn beautiful dresses to events and galas before... but this dress—this is something else.

Tessa raises her voice in confusion. "He challenged you to a *hockey* duel?"

"Yeah," I confirm.

"The man needs to find a better way to end a feud because that's just ridiculous. What if that's how he makes all of his life decisions?" Brynn asks.

Maybe she's right, but right now, I don't care about anything else except for this dress. It has me in a trance the way it accentuates every curve on my body. The beads glitter in the lighting like a blue waterfall and I'm almost tempted to ask if I can wear it out.

I check the price tags.

It's way more than I wanted to spend—double actually, but I have a feeling that this dress will be worth every penny, plus some.

"Ro? You still in there?" Tessa asks when I don't say anything.

I open the door instead, slowly making my way out to find Tessa and Brynn there; Brynn is in another dress.

Both of their jaws drop, shocked into silence.

Brynn's mouth falls open. "Holy hell. You look incredible."

Before I can respond, the bell over the door jingles again, and Cammy walks in, eyes immediately locking onto me. She grins.

"Rowan, he's going to die when he sees you in that dress," she says.

I raise an eyebrow. "Drew?"

Cammy snorts. "Who gives a flying rat's ass about Drew Lansbury?"

"Then who is going to die seeing me in this dress?" I ask.

Cammy looks at Tessa and then Brynn who are all grinning back at her.

"Bexley Townsend. And it won't be a quick death either... that dress is going to torture him slowly," she chuckles. "And I can't wait to watch."

Chapter Eleven

Bex

The ballroom of the convention center downtown is filled with the sound of laughter, conversation, and the clinking of glasses from the open bar. I tug at the collar of my perfectly tailored jacket, the fabric feeling tighter than it should. Galas like this have never been my scene—too much small talk, too many forced smiles, and an overwhelming amount of posturing. If I had my way, I'd be back on the ice where things are simple, straightforward, and free of all this pretense.

But tonight is essential. Briggs and Autumn asked for support—even sent a limo to The Commons to pick me up tonight, though it was unnecessary, I could have taken a cab. They sent a limo for Sam and one for Phil and his wife as well.

Considering how much they're doing for these kids and the families that they sponsor, the least I can do is show up, smile, and help earn some money for Kids With Cancer— a charity that I believe in and have donated a sizable yet deserving amount over the last two years since Briggs started it.

I'd just as soon write them a fat check and then be out of here tonight, but it's not a total loss of an evening. There are always a few alumni players who show up for Hawkeyes events. And Tucker Evans, the coach for the Seattle NFL team, texted me asking if I'd be here tonight. He and his wife Lexi should be around here somewhere.

I scan the room, not entirely sure of who I'm looking for as my eyes skip over faces, silk-covered tables with flower arrangements, ice sculptures, and expensive gowns until they land on *her*. The woman that it seems I'm always looking for in a crowded room and packed stadium. She's standing by one of the art pieces up for auction in the left corner of the event center. She looks stunning—self-assured—graceful even. Like she always does.

But she's more than all of that— she's utterly captivating. Witty, intelligent, with a career focus that I can respect, even if I don't appreciate that writing about my team is her ticket up the corporate ladder.

Men rubber neck to check out the gorgeous blonde in the blue dress as they walk by her. I can't blame them for admiring her, even if the sight of it has my bow tie feeling tighter around my throat than it did when I walked in.

The blue dress she's wearing clings to her as if it was tailor fitted, the intricate beading shimmering under the soft lights and her blonde hair up in some kind of knot that I wouldn't know the first thing about how to take down, not that I'll ever get the opportunity to learn. The dress is completely backless, stopping just above her ass and showing off those two sexy dimples that I imagine running my fingers over after sneaking her off to some dark broom closet around here. Only, Rowan's too smart to let me guide her anywhere, and I know well enough to keep my hands to myself.

Or at least I did before I walked in and saw her dressed like that.

A long slit runs down the seam of her dress that shows off the back of her legs each time she shifts from one leg to the other, studying a painting, with one arm folded over her rib cage and the other one holding a program in her hand of the items up for auction. The same program I was handed when I walked in.

A man in a tux with his hair slicked back, about forty years older than her, takes a spot at her side before I can get there. He grins at her in a way he has no right to, but I keep at my pace, not speeding up. Maybe I'm interested in how she'll handle him or maybe I don't want to draw attention from other guests of the target I've zeroed in on.

A waiter steps into my path, balancing a tray of champagne flutes as I nearly brush past him. I stop in my tracks, my gaze fixed on her, ensuring she stays exactly where she is. She doesn't seem to have a drink in hand, at least not that I can see.

I set the program I'm holding onto the waiter's tray and grab one of the champagne flutes with a curt "Thanks." Sliding a hundred-dollar bill from the money clip I brought tonight, I tuck it into his hand. "Do me a favor," I say, keeping my eyes trained on her. "Grab me a beer—something half decent—and keep 'em coming."

It's an open bar, but the tip should incentivize the waiter to bring me a few beers at least, saving me from having to stand in the long bar line and make small talk with people I don't know. Besides, something tells me that I'll be looking at *art* all night.

I continue toward my target, watching as Rowan entertains the man's presence next to her, pointing at the painting and discussing something about the piece based on the way he nods, staring at the artwork. I've spent enough time around art and in galleries, growing up with parents who lived, breathed, and worked in the art world, that I know the pieces displayed here are collector items

Juliet's sister-in-law, Harper, is an art curator, and she pulled together an impressive showing for this event.

Rowan continues to talk to the man as I draw closer.

"The thing about impasto technique," she says, motioning toward the painting in front of them, "is that it's all about texture. Do you see how the artist laid the paint on thick? It's almost sculptural. Like you could reach out and touch the ridges, that's what gives it such depth—almost as if the painting is a window that you can reach out and touch and not just a canvas hanging on a wall." She traces the air in front of the painting, to help explain her point. "Van Gogh was famous for using this style. His work was filled with movement and emotion, and you can see how this artist was clearly inspired by him."

Just as soon as I think I have Rowan figured out, she does something to throw me off kilter. I had no idea that she knew that much about art. And the way her face lights up as she discusses it with the man not worth her breath has me wanting to be the one she's explaining painting techniques and brushstrokes to. To have those happy, eager eyes on mine instead.

I could listen to her talk about Van Gogh all day even though I don't care about art—not the way my family or Rowan care about it, anyway.

I hear the man struggle to add to the conversation, it's obvious that he's not standing there for the painting. However, I could be persuaded tonight to agree that Rowan in that dress looks like a priceless piece of art. Only, I don't want her hanging on my wall... I want her in my bed. And that's the reason why I should turn around right now and find someone else to talk to, but I'm too invested now.

The man standing next to her is completely out of his depth but nods appreciatively, his eyes narrowing as if trying to make a show of critiquing the painting. "Ah, yes, Van Gogh," he says, but he doesn't have a damn clue. "Quite... quite impressive."

I bite back a grin. He probably couldn't pick Van Gogh out of a lineup of dogs playing poker.

I finally reach her side and stand next to her, close enough to catch a whiff of her usual perfume and to make sure that the moment the man standing next to her sees me, he'll back off, noticing that I'm staking my claim. Though my only intention is to protect her, not to claim her for myself—that would be a mistake that we'd both pay for later when Rowan realizes that she'll only ever be number two to hockey, just like every woman before her. That is, if I could get past the fact that she's a reporter, always looking for a story. But he doesn't need to know that.

I'd do the same thing for Keely, Penelope—any of the Hawkeyes girls, if I thought they needed me to run interference on unwanted attention and I guess Rowan is a part of that now.

She hasn't noticed me yet, and her attention is still on the painting.

"It's one of the more abstract pieces in the collection," she says, her voice thoughtful, her eyes scanning the brushstrokes. "But if you look closely, you can see the story in it. The artist uses these sweeping strokes to create motion, almost like a gust of wind, but if you focus on the smaller details, you'll notice little touches of red, symbolizing... I think, hope."

Her words catch me off guard. I didn't expect her to know so much about art.

"You know your stuff," I say, behind her.

Rowan whips around when she hears my voice, her eyes wide and her lips parted. She didn't see me coming, which was my intention.

"Coach Bex..." she says almost in a whisper.

The man's eyes widen a little.

"Coach Townsend," the man says, coming around the other side of Rowan to offer up his hand. "It's an honor to meet you. I was hoping you'd be here tonight."

I shake his hand, the champagne glass I brought for Rowan in the other hand. I squeeze his hand a little tighter than I should, making a nonverbal point that I don't like him around Rowan.

He makes a muffled sound of discomfort.

"Sorry," I say, releasing his hand. "Hockey grip—occupational hazard."

"Right, of course," he says, pulling his hand from mine, attempting to discreetly shake off the pain.

I offer the champagne glass to Rowan, and she takes it, eying me cautiously.

I bend close to her ear, keeping it between us. "I didn't poison it. I promise."

A glint sparkles in her eye and the corner of her lip turns up a little. "Good to know," she says and then takes a small sip, an appreciative hum as soon as the sparkling liquid hits her lips.

I use the politest scowl I can muster and stare back at the man. Finally, he catches on that I'm not the one intruding... he's now no longer welcome to stand by Rowan.

"Oh, are you two...?" he asks, his pointer finger wagging between us to ask if we're together.

I say, "Yes," quickly before Rowan can say no.

She shoots a death glare up at me, but he doesn't notice because his eyes are fixed on me.

"Will you excuse me... I think I see..." he doesn't finish his excuse before he leaves as quickly as he can.

Rowan's lips pinch together, her eyebrows stitching together. "You didn't have to be rude. And you lied–we're not together."

"I didn't like the way he was looking at you," I say, satisfied that the man made my job easy.

I didn't have to physically remove him from Rowan's side. I would have done it if he had forced my hand, but I'd rather not make a scene. This charity is important for the kids who need our help, and I don't want to make Briggs, Autumn, or the Hawkeyes franchise, who are co-hosting this event, look bad.

"And how was he looking at me?" she asks and then takes another sip.

"Like you were up for auction," I say, sliding one hand into my dress pant pocket.

She gives me a narrowed look.

"Wouldn't you love that? Someone swooping by, picking me up and whisking me out of your life? Problem solved, right?"

"Only if you'd like to see a bidding war."

She scoffs. "What bidding war?"

"The one where I empty my entire bank account to keep that creep from taking you home."

She stares at me for a second as if to gauge my sincerity about spending all of my money to win her in an auction.

I would have done it if I had to, but Rowan has too much spirit to let anyone own her. That much, I know. She sees something in my eyes, swallows hard, and cuts our connection to focus back on the painting.

"Don't do that," she says.

"Don't do what?" I ask, leaning in closer.

"Don't pretend to be a knight in shining armor who suddenly has an interest in where I am, who I'm with, or where I end up tonight. The Bex I know only cares about my proximity to his beloved team. Let's not kid ourselves, you'd never pay a dime for me. And by the way, he wasn't a creep, he was very polite. We were having a lovely conversation about art before you showed up and interrupted by the way."

"He's at least thirty years older than you. He's a creep."

She shifts her weight from one side to the other, jutting out her hip in a casual yet confident stance.

"Oh really. You're eighteen years older; what does that make you?" She challenges me.

I take a step closer, watching as she holds her breath at my nearness.

"What do you want me to be?" I ask.

A waiter stops in front of us, breaking Rowan's eye contact with mine. She clears her throat and stares up at the waiter with a forced smile.

"Your beer, sir," the waiter says, handing me the ice-cold long neck. "Can I get you another miss?" he asks of her champagne glass.

Rowan's champagne glass is nearly empty, so she takes the last sip of it and then places her empty glass on his tray.

"Actually, can I get one of those?" She points to my beer.

He nods and then leaves us.

She turns back to the canvas, not returning to my question.

Just as well.

There's a moment of silence between us before I break it. "You know more than I would have guessed about art," I say, turning to study the piece as well, standing side by side with her.

A small smile plays on her lips. "Is that a compliment, Coach Bex? I don't think you've ever paid me one before. Did it feel weird rolling off your tongue?" she teases.

"A little," I admit, taking a pull off my beer.

She shoots me a playful scowl in return for my honesty and then eyes my beer longingly.

I hand her the bottle.

I've never shared a beer with anyone like this before but maybe I feel a little like a wanker for shutting her down when she came by to ask for a truce. However, I'm not completely ready to let my guard down. This is as close to "I'm sorry for being a horse's ass" as she's ever going to get.

She takes a sip and then answers. "I've always loved art," she says softly. "It tells a story without needing words. When I first dreamed of becoming a journalist, I thought I'd end up writing about travel or art. But then..."

She pauses as if considering how much to say. I take a sip of my beer. It tastes like some of her lipstick left on the rim of the bottle—I don't mind it. "Then my dad happened. He's a big-time sportscaster. I applied for an open columnist position with Northwestern's campus newspaper, but when the editor-in-chief found out who my father was, she put me in the sports section of the paper. I didn't get much of a say, but it ended up working out," she says and then takes another sip of my beer before handing it back. "I don't know if it was growing up as a kid watching my dad on TV to feel close to him, but sports journalism comes naturally to me. Not that I'd ever admit that to my dad. He might feel vindicated that leaving me as a small child to chase his dreams was good for me or something."

Shit, I didn't know her father left her when she was little. That must have been hard. Now Rowan's resilience makes sense in this new light.

I watch her as she speaks, taking in the way her eyes light up when she talks about art, and her voice tightens just a bit when she mentions her father. I feel a strange pull, like I'm seeing a side of Rowan I haven't before. A side I... don't dislike.

I take a pull off my beer, taking the faint flavor of her lipstick and the champagne she drank earlier. The taste of her shouldn't have me wanting to guzzle down this entire beer just to get another taste, but it does. I hand it to her again and she chuckles.

"You're sharing?"

"I think you need it more than I do."

More like, *"I need to pace myself or I'll get drunk off the taste of you."*

She takes a long pull and I memorize the way she tilts her head back as she drinks. The way her red lips look around the lip of the beer bottle, the way her throat swallows.

I clear my throat and glance away. She hands me back my beer after she finishes her sip.

"Have you ever thought about going back to that? Writing about art or travel, that is?" I ask, curious.

Art journalism is completely different from what she's doing now.

One thing is for sure, we wouldn't be at odds if she were writing about a hole-in-the-wall art gallery in Italy as my younger brother Archie does for the magazine. He travels around the world, writing about art in all the unique places he travels to.

I think about how different things between Rowan and I might have been if we had met while she was a journalist for my family's magazine instead of as the woman who wrote a less-than-flattering article about me... and might have more unflattering articles to write about my players.

She shrugs. "Sometimes. But the world of sports keeps me busy. And I can't deny I love the thrill of it—the rush of the games, the stories behind the players. Traveling with the team has shown me a totally different side. You're all so close when you're on the road—like family."

I nod. I'm glad she's seeing what I see, why giving up this game—this family, is so hard to walk away from. I'm lucky to have a supportive family outside of hockey, but not all of these guys do, and maybe I want to stick around for them.

The waiter comes back by and hands her the beer she ordered. I drop another hundred on his tray that she doesn't see, and I nod at him as if to say, "Keep them coming for her, too." He smiles and then heads off to give away the rest of the champagne glasses on his tray.

I might be a little disappointed that we won't be sharing my beer anymore, but I don't let it show.

"Not all teams are that way. I've been a part of some teams that can't stand each other. It can be a toxic working environment as a player and as a coach."

"Sure, I can see how egos, testosterone, and vying for the same positions could lead to a hostile working environment. Journalism can be just as ruthless," she says, raising an eyebrow. "What about you? Do you know much about art?"

I shake my head. "Enough to get by, but I should know more, considering my family owns *The Painted Easel*."

Rowan gasps, her eyes going wide. "Wait—your family owns *The Painted Easel*? The Painted Easel… as in the magazine? As in the magazine printed in Liverpool, which is one of the biggest art magazines in the world?"

I can see the minute it clicks for her when she remembers where I'm from. There's not a lot of information about my connection with my family's magazine, mostly because I never tell anyone, and I haven't done an interview since my rookie year.

I nod, suppressing a grin at her surprise, and obvious pleasure in the idea of it. "Yeah, it's popular."

She looks genuinely stunned. "Popular? I subscribe to that magazine. I get one every month in the mail. How did I not know that your family owns it?"

"Because it's not something I talk about much. My older brother Leo runs it, and my younger brother Archie is a photographer and journalist for the magazine. They've been trying to convince me to move back home and get involved, but... I'm not really an art connoisseur. Not much of a writer or photographer either."

I pause for a moment, considering how much to tell her. "I still own a place back in Liverpool. One day, when I retire, I'll move back— become a professional uncle to my brother, Leo's, kids. Maybe Archie's if he ever settles down."

Rowan's eyes brighten toward me as if I'm telling her the most interesting thing she's ever heard.

"No plans for a wife and kids of your own?" she asks, her tone light, but there's something deeper in the question.

I shake my head, glancing down at my beer as I swirl the liquid in my glass. "No. Not anymore. I chose a career in hockey instead."

I just now realize that in the span of minutes, I've told her more information about me and my family than I have to any reporter over the last twenty-five years in the NHL.

Before I can tell her that everything I said is off the record, someone clears their throat behind us. I turn to see a man and a woman standing there. Rowan stiffens beside me, and I immediately pick up on her discomfort.

Then it dawns on me who it is. This is the first time I've seen him outside of the press box.

Drew Lansbury.

Rowan's ex and the ass who wrote that article about me recently.

I place my free hand gently against the back of her arm to let her know that I'm here in solidarity, letting her know that I won't leave her side unless she asks me. I know she and I don't always see eye to eye, but no one should make her feel this uncomfortable; she doesn't even stiffen like this with me when we're at each other's throats.

Rowan forces a polite smile. "Drew, hi."

"Hi, Rowan," he greets with a smile, and then his eyes drift over to me. "Coach Bex," He reaches out to shake my hand and I decide not to crush his phalanges like the last guy since Drew is a reporter who could use it against me. He's also not currently making eyes at Rowan so I have no reason to hurt the guy except for the article he wrote about me. "Nice to finally meet you outside of the press box. You're not an easy man to find out in the wild. This is my fiancée, Claire."

I nod at the brunette that he has his hand wrapped around, keeping my expression neutral. I'm not particularly interested in small talk with the man who's made a career out of taking cheap shots at my coaching record and the coaching careers of my friends. But it seems Drew can't resist stirring the pot for a guy who never made it past little league tryouts. He has no idea what it takes to compete at this level, he just hides behind his laptop, that is if he even bothers to show up in the press box at all.

He's made a career of "phoning-in" his commentary, and it has me wondering what a driven beautiful woman like Rowan was ever doing with a lazy tosser like Drew Lansbury.

Then I start to notice the small ways that Rowan is fidgeting at my side.

Not that Drew or Claire seem to notice.

Maybe I'm starting to get used to Rowan's body language.

"So, Coach," he starts, voice dripping with a smug edge, "It's been, what, six years? Playoffs twice, but no Stanley Cup yet. Must be... frustrating for the fans. And for you, I imagine. You really think *The Seattle Sunrise* should even bother following the Hawkeyes around this year?"

I feel Rowan tense beside me, her fingers curling around the stem of her beer bottle. Before I can fire back with a retort, she speaks up, her voice calm but carrying an undeniable edge.

"It's interesting you bring that up, Drew," she says, setting a calm and cool gaze on him. "Because when you look at the numbers, Bex has one of the best win records as a coach in the league. Not only that, but he's built a team that's shown consistent improvement, despite all the injuries and setbacks they've faced. If you'd spent any amount of time watching the games in person instead of watching the highlight reel, you'd see that Coach Bex is one of the fiercest coaches in the NHL."

Drew blinks, visibly taken aback, but Rowan isn't finished.

"And as for the players," she continues, her voice unwavering, "They respect him because he's more than just a coach. He's someone who's dedicated to every practice, every game, and who's built a team culture that's as strong as any in the league. You might not see that in a stat sheet, but anyone who's actually paying attention knows it."

I stare down at her, taken off guard. What she just said contradicts everything that she claimed in the article she wrote about me last season. She just defended me against someone on her side of the press box when she didn't need to. Journalists usually try to play nice, at least to each other's faces. This was a bold move and she did it for me–there's no other explanation.

Except, I'd like to know why.

Drew opens his mouth, but words seem to fail him. After an awkward pause, the waiter passes by with another beer for me and a tray of champagne flutes, Claire places a protective hand over her stomach and declines with a soft smile. "No champagne for me. Not with the baby on the way."

The words hang in the air, and I feel Rowan go board stiff next to me. I glance down at her, noticing the tension in her jaw and the way her hand tightens around her beer bottle.

"Excuse me, will you?" she asks suddenly, her voice tight. She doesn't even manage a forced smile.

She turns and walks away before anyone can stop her, leaving me standing there with Drew and Claire. I watch her go, concern telling me that I should follow after her.

She sets her beer bottle down on a table in the middle of the ballroom as she flees, picking up her pace.

Drew says something, but I'm not listening anymore. I'm already planning my escape from this conversation. After a few more polite nods, I excuse myself, muttering something about needing to find Tucker Evans and his wife before the night is over.

I weave through the crowd, searching for Rowan, but she's nowhere to be found. I ask a few of the Hawkeyes girls if they've seen her, but no one has. My concern deepens as I scan the room, wondering where she could have gone.

Finally, after what feels like forever, I find her in a dark hallway near the back of the ballroom. She's leaning against the wall, her back to me, her shoulders shaking slightly. She's crying.

"Rowan, Jesus," I say softly as I approach. Did something happen to her after she took off? Did someone hurt her? I scan her body for any visible signs of trauma, but I don't see any. "Are you alright? What happened to you? Do you need me to grab Tessa or Keely?"

She quickly wipes at her eyes, trying to pull herself together, but the pain in her voice is unmistakable. "I just... I need to go home, Bex."

Her words take me off guard; I wasn't expecting this. I don't know what's going on with her, but I do know that I can take care of what she needs right now—what she's asking for. I can get her home.

"Okay, come here," I say, gently offering my hand for her to take. The minute she does, I slide my fingers through hers and carefully pull her with me. "I'll get you out of here."

I don't mind leaving early. In fact, if I hadn't been so worried that something had happened to her, I'd have welcomed the excuse to leave early. I wrote my donation check already and signed as much memorabilia for the silent auction as Autumn could hand me in my office earlier this week. They don't need me anymore. And Tucker and I will see each other another time.

I pull out my phone to call for the limo Juliet and Shawnie ordered to pick me up.

She doesn't protest, just nods, and squeezes my hand tighter as I lead her behind me toward the entrance, checking over my shoulder every few minutes to make sure she's okay. But she keeps her head ducked down to hide her tears from anyone who might see them and try to ask questions.

I don't know what happened between her and Drew, or why seeing him with his fiancée affected her so much. But right now, I don't care. All I care about is getting her somewhere safe, away from this place, where she doesn't have to keep pretending everything is fine.

The limo pulls up to the front in the pouring rain. I don't know where her jacket is but I'm not going to make her wait while I retrieve it from the coat-check. I'll send a text to Autumn to ask her to grab it at the end of the night and get it back to Rowan.

I pull off my tux jacket, pulling it over the top of her head to shield her hair from the rain and wrap the rest of the material around her body.

Fuck, I don't even remember the last time I cared to keep a woman's hair from getting wet. It's been so long since I've had to worry about something like that. None of the women I've been with since Lily have ended up long-term. A date here and there—sometimes ended at her place, sometimes not. But I've never thought about their hair getting wet in the rain as a problem. Not until now.

"Your jacket." she protests. "But you'll get wet?" Her glassy eyes stare up at me, my jacket draped around her face.

If I hadn't just found her in tears, I'd laugh at how damn cute she looks drowning in the coat of my tux.

"We live in Seattle, Rowan. If I was worried about the rain, I would have moved a long time ago," I smirk, wrapping an arm around her, getting ready to make a run for the limo but wanting to make sure I have a good grip on her, so she doesn't fall.

She looks back up at me. "That's the second time you've called me Rowan."

I don't look back down at her. I use the movement of the driver running out to open the door for us as my excuse to ignore her observation.

We make a run for it. Rowan's high heels make it difficult for her to match me step-for-step, so I turn back and scoop her into my arms, one arm braced behind her back and the other behind her knees.

"Bex!" she squeals. I take off running with her gripping tight around my neck.

As soon as we reach the limo, I tell the driver that I'll close the door so he can get back in the driver's side and out of the rain. I make sure Rowan gets inside first, then I settle into the seat next to her, closing the door behind me.

"Thank you," she whispers, her voice barely audible.

"You don't have to thank me."

"Where to, sir?" he asks, his eyes reflecting back at us through the rearview mirror and the open window between the limo and the driver's side.

I look to her for instruction. "Where do you want to go? He'll take us anywhere you want."

"Home, please," she tells me. I nod, and then she gives the driver her address.

I know the area she gave him. It's outside of town, which means we'll have more time if she wants to tell me what happened. I want to push her for answers. If Drew did something, or anyone else, to make her react the way she did in that dark hallway, I need to know before the gala ends so that I can break someone's nose or, worse, hurt him. But I won't pressure her to talk to me if she doesn't want to.

We ride in silence, the city lights flashing by outside the windows. And as we drive, I can't help but feel like something between us has shifted—something I can't quite put into words yet.

I can't stop this need to protect her. From the turbulent flight, to the rich asshole twice her age trying to pick her up, to whatever happened back at the gala that made her want to get out of there so quickly.

But I know one thing for sure.

I'm not ready for us to get to her apartment just yet.

However, there's one more thing I should be protecting her from, and my ex-wife can vouch for it—me.

Chapter Twelve

Rowan

Bex shuts the door, sealing us inside the dimly lit limo and out of the wet Seattle evening. The sound is like a final exhale, shielding us from the chaos of the gala and the torrential rain that's now pelting the roof. My heart is still racing, my chest tight, and my breath uneven from the rush of emotions that's been threatening to spill over since Drew's announcement. I can't stop trembling—whether from the chill of the drenched bottom of my dress or the heartbreaking moment that Bex witnessed.

Oh God... Bex witnessed it all.

I want to pull Bex's jacket back over my head and hide. I can't believe I ran away like that, and I can't believe that Bex ran after me.

He sits beside me, silent but watchful. His hands rest on his knees, clenched, as if he's willing himself to stay calm for my sake. The quiet inside the limo feels starkly different from the usual back-and-forth banter that Bex and I find ourselves in when we're anywhere near each other. The city lights blur outside as the car melds into traffic, and for some unknown reason, I feel like I need to unload what just happened in there with my ex.

"I'm so sorry, Bex," I blurt out, my voice shaky, barely holding back the tears threatening to spill. "I shouldn't have run like that. It's just... Drew, he..."

My voice breaks, and I struggle to find the words. The humiliation of Drew and his fiancée announcing their pregnancy, of seeing their happy faces while my heart felt like it was being ripped apart, rushes back all at once. Didn't Drew consider that the news would shatter me?

Not the news that he's moved on, or that he's engaged, or even that he's expecting a baby. No... the thing that guts me is that he proved tonight that leaving me gave him a brighter future with a wife and kids—all the things he wanted.

What's to say the next man won't do the same?

"Did he do something to hurt you? Should we go back so I can beat the living—"

I cover my hand over his hand to stop him. "No! No. It's nothing like that. I mean, he hurt me, but not like you think." I clamp my eyes shut for a second and then glance back up at him at my side. "I thought I could handle it—I thought I was getting stronger and had come to terms with what I couldn't have. But seeing him so happy with his decision to end us, and then hearing her mention the baby..." The words tumble out. I don't even know if I'm making sense, but Bex listens intently, though he doesn't look happy.

"He's your ex," he says, somehow already knowing.

"Yes, and she's his new fiancée."

He nods.

"If you wanted him back, you probably shouldn't have come to my defense. It didn't win you any points," he says. "Is that why you needed to get out of there? He broke your heart."

I meet his eyes, needing him to understand. "I said those things about you because he was wrong. And leaving was... well, it's hard to explain. It's not that I want him back." I pause, swallowing hard. "It's just that he's getting the family we wanted. The family I thought I'd have someday, and now all that I'm left with is..."

I trail off, the words hovering between us.

"Me?" Bex raises an eyebrow, a hand pressed to his chest in mock offense. "Ouch, Summers."

Despite myself, I laugh softly, shaking my head. "Your feelings aren't hurt," I say, giving him a sideways glance.

What's wrong with this man?

If I come to him with my tail between my legs, basically humiliating myself at what a horrible ice skater I am, and ask for a truce, he challenges me to a hockey duel. But if I insult him, he grins.

He shrugs. "Fair enough. But why not just find someone else to put a ring on your finger and give you a house full of kids? You're gorgeous—clever—fiery. Find someone better suited and start the family you want. Drew's a lazy sod anyway. He'd only hold you back from what you're really capable of."

My jaw practically hits the limo's floor.

Bex is on a roll with the compliments.

"What?" he asks, watching me as I blink back at him.

"Did you just call me gorgeous and clever?" I ask.

He licks his lips. "And fiery, don't go forgetting that one. I doubt just anyone can meet you at your level."

And there it is.

What I know to be true.

Finding a man who challenges me, interests me, and is willing to take a woman who can't bear her own kids. As if it weren't already hard enough to find a man-unicorn.

"Yeah..." I say, exhaling slowly, turning my head to gaze out the window.

"I meant that as a compliment, you know," he says. "You'll find someone better than that knobhead."

"He's not a knobhead."

He turns to me in his seat.

"Fine, he's a filthy wanker, and he did you a favor because you deserve more."

"I can't have kids," I say, dropping the bomb right there between us. "So he ended it."

He freezes, not a single blink.

Then he turns back to face forward and rolls up the sleeves of his wet dress shirt. It's the first time I've seen the tattoos on

Bex's forearms. He's always wearing his Hawkeyes Coaching windbreaker at the stadium or his suit during postgame media. He looks ten times more intimidating with ink peeking past his shirt than he usually does. "Driver, please turn around and head back to the gala. There's a prick back there that I need to beat some manners into."

Drew hurt me but it's not worth Bex going to jail on assault charges, even if the offer warms my heart a little.

"No!" I yell back to the driver, gripping Bex's forearm as if he might jump out of the limo and run the rest of the way there if the driver doesn't turn around. Bex glances down at where my hand grips around his arm and then back up at me. "We're fine. No need to go back. And can we get some privacy, if you don't mind?" I call out to ensure that Bex can't make his request to turn around again.

The driver does as I ask even though Bex is technically the passenger that gets to make the calls. The driver probably just doesn't want to be an accessory to murder by taking Bex back to find Drew, and I don't blame him.

"Summers, what he did was fucked up. Someone needs to tell him so. I'm the perfect bloke for the job," he says, leveling me with a stern gaze.

"He has a baby on the way. And besides, you told me that I'm better without him, remember?" I say, releasing him.

"Alright, let me get this straight. You ran off when you heard that his fiancée is pregnant, but you're telling me you don't want him back."

I rub my lips together. He's going to make me tell him, and some part of me wants to—I'm not sure why.

"We tried to have a baby," I say. "After my OBGYN told me that I have less than a one percent chance, we decided to try for a miracle. He was so optimistic. I don't think he even considered that it might not work. He had me believing it too. We even went as far as IVF, but nothing took. After a year of us trying and three years together, Drew told me that he wanted his own kids and that we'd resent each other if he stayed."

I feel Bex's hand reach for mine, intertwining our fingers together. My whole body tingers just from the warmth of his hand in mine. There's something so reassuring about Bex's touch.

I work up the courage to look at him. Hoping not to find the sad puppy eyes that I get so often. Just as I hoped, Bex is sturdy, solid, unyielding to silly emotions like pity or empathy... good. Still, there's a softness in his eyes towards me. Something that makes me want to turn into him and be wrapped up against his chest–to be held in the safety of his hold, under his protection like I was tonight, though I didn't ask for it.

"He was wrong," he says softly, his thumb grazing over my knuckles. "You're worth so much more than that."

I don't know what comes over me but before I can second guess myself, I push up out of my seat and wrap my hands around his neck, his damp hair under my fingers as I press my mouth against his.

Bex doesn't hesitate. He reaches for me, his strong arms pulling me into his chest. I don't resist—I can't. His warmth seeps into me, his solid presence anchoring me as he deepens the kiss, biting at my bottom lip and then soothing it with his tongue. He murmurs soft words against my mouth.

"Beautiful"

"Brilliant"

"Sexy as fuck"

"He's wrong Rowan, so fucking wrong."

Bex's hands slide under his jacket coat still engulfing me His fingers brush against my bare skin, tender and reassuring, sending a ripple of warmth through me. The heat radiating from his body, the hard, defined muscles beneath his damp clothes, grounding me in the moment

I feel his hands slide down to my hips, and then pull me over his thighs to straddle his lap. My dress stops me from widening my legs, it's too form-fitting, and with the heavy beading, it has no stretch to it. Bex tries to pull my dress further up my hips but it doesn't work, it's too tight. I can see the bulge through his tuxedo pants below me, waiting for me to grind down on and I'm getting as anxious as him.

"Hurry," I tell him, sliding his jacket off my arms and discarding it onto the limo floor behind me.

He tries again but the dress doesn't budge.

Finally, I feel his hands reach around the back of the dress, his fingers curling into the slit at the back and I gasp the second Bex rips the dress from the bottom of the slit all the way to the top zipper, beads pinging and ricocheting off every surface inside the limo.

"Oh my God" I say, my eyes widening.

I can't believe he just tore my dress off my body.

"You begged, Rowan. Now you know what the sound of you begging does to me."

The notion that I have any effect on him sends a thrill through me.

"That dress was expensive." But my objection is only half hearted.

Seeing him rip my dress in half to get to me has me wetter than I've ever been in my entire life.

"Then send me the bill," he says, offering a devilish grin.

Now, with the dress no longer attached in the back, the thin spaghetti straps slide over my shoulders and down my arms, gaping the dress open for him, and without a bra, my breasts are on full display. He groans at the sight of me, pulling what's left of the dress out of our way and pulls my hips down against his lap.

I let out a moan the minute my soaked panties land on top of his thick bulge, his eyes darken with arousal, as they stare into mine.

"Last chance to change your mind," he warns, his voice strained with desire. "Tell me to stop, Rowan. Because if I don't stop now, I won't be able to."

I shake my head, my breath coming in shallow. "Don't stop. I want this. I want *you*."

With a groan, Bex cups my breasts, his fingers brushing against my hardening nipples before his mouth follows. I whimper at the feeling of his mouth on me, my head falling back as he sucks hard on my sensitive nub, flicking it with his tongue, the sensation shooting straight to the ache between my legs.

I moan out loud as he grinds himself against me through our damp clothes. Sparks shoot up my spine, desire warming low in my belly.

I'm aware that we're still in a moving car, but the world outside no longer exists. There's only Bex and the way he's making me feel—wanted–special–protected.

I know this can't last. Sex won't make him trust that I don't have some secret story I plan to drop. But just for tonight, we can have this.

He reaches down between us, his middle finger running over my drenched silk panties.

"You're torturing me with these," he says, "So wet—so soft—goddamn perfect."

I whimper as he slides my panties over, coating his fingers in my heat.

"More— I need more," I beg, his mouth exploring my breasts.

"I showed you what the sound of you begging does to me. Be careful what you beg for Rowan because I have every intention of delivering on everything you want from me tonight," he says, his voice low.

His fingers grip the top of my waistband and rips my thong, tossing the thin material somewhere in the limo.

"Bex!" I protest, though I've never experienced anything as sexy as Bex ripping my clothes off my body.

"Bill me for that too," he says with a smirk, pulling me down in a rough but passionate kiss.

"I want you inside of me. I need you now."

"Tell me that you're sure, because you've been through a lot tonight. I just want to make you feel good. That's all I'm after."

Somehow, I know that without him telling me.

I nod. "I'm sure. This is what I want to remember tonight, not the gala. Being with you," I say.

He knows we both need this. The growing tension between us has been leading to this moment. Soon enough, I manage to free him from his belt, tuxedo pants, and boxer briefs. I reach for his erection, loving the feel of his arousal in my hand. It feels hot and heavy as it pulsates for me—this man makes me almost dizzy with need. I stroke him gently at first, loving the way he jerks in response, and then his hips take over, rocking into my hand.

"Bloody hell, Rowan..." he growls, his head falling back against the limo headrest and he watches me through hooded eyelids.

I can't wait another second. We'll be at my apartment soon enough and I don't know what will happen after. Right here–right now–this is all I'm promised.

I position myself over him, the tip of his cock notching at my entrance.

Skin to skin—this is what I need to forget tonight.

He grips my hips, guiding me down onto him in one smooth motion. We both groan at the feeling of him entering me, the fullness of him inside me making my toes curl.

"Fuck, your so damn tight." He stalls for a moment—his eyes fluttering closed—his teeth grinding. The sight of Bexley Townsend trying not to come undone under me causes more wetness to pool at my entrance, coating his cock.

Then he begins to move, rolling his hips in slow motion, finding the spot that I need him and stroking it with expert precision. I meet each of his thrusts with a roll of my own, my nails digging into his shoulders as I ride him. I might be on top, but Bex is the one in control.

Reality breaks through the heated moment when something comes over him; he grips my hips to slow our motion but still keeps our rhythm moving in and out. "Rowan... shit, I'm not wearing a condom."

A flash of concern washes over his face, but I shake my head, grinding down on him harder, coaxing him to keep going. "I can't get pregnant, remember? And I'm clean."

I can't believe we got this far without discussing it, but then again, I never expected Bex to feel so safe—so open. I didn't expect him to come find me tonight and to comfort me the way he has. I lost my head with an unexpected desperation to be with him—I guess we both did.

"I'm clean too. But I never *usually* go without. I want you to know that," he says, his thrusts increasing again as if he couldn't stop himself from fucking me bare even if he wanted to, hitting the spot inside of me that has my belly on fire—tingles spreading through my body.

"Rowan... Christ, I can't stop fucking you like this. I don't think I could pull out of you even if I wanted to. You feel so fucking good."

"Then don't. Take me just like this," I tell him. "I'm so close."

Bex increases his tempo, thrusting into me hard and deep until he bottoms out inside of me. He grips my ass, pulling me unbelievably tight to him. I've never had someone so deep inside of me. Our bodies melding together as we both take what we want from each other—our grunts getting louder and the thick smell of sex filling the back of the limo.

Our mouths find each other once again—but he takes my mouth so differently than he takes my body. It's needy and desperate but smooth and passionate. Our bodies chase after each other's orgasms, but our mouths are taking more time to explore—to tease.

There's so much more to Bex than he lets me see. And now I'm more curious than ever to unlock it.

His hand slides between our bodies and finds my clit, I shatter apart, crying out his name as my orgasm rips through me, my body pulsating over his cock, gripping him so tight that he growls as he comes, spilling into me, emptying every drop as deep as he can.

We stare at each other for a moment, and the reality of what we just did in the back of this limo sets in.

As the car approaches my apartment, Bex wraps me back up in his jacket, and he smooths my hair back from my face, before pulling on his suit pants and button up shirt. He gives a soft smile, but there's also an unspoken understanding that this won't happen again.

We're still at odds, even if he came to my rescue... and then I came to his. We still have to work together, and Bex doesn't trust me. Not to mention that Bex mentioned early tonight that he plans to retire in Liverpool with no wife and no kids.

When push really comes to shove, I think I also held out hope that I'd meet a man who would want to adopt at some point. And Bex doesn't even want a wife, let alone adopt children. And then, of course, there's our age difference. Maybe the eighteen years between us have us both planning for different futures.

There's just too much between us.

Tonight, will just be tonight—nothing more.

I won't even be the least surprised if Bex is still trying to convince Sam not to let me go on any more away games.

"You okay?" he asks softly, pressing a gentle kiss to my forehead.

I nod, a slow smile curving my lips. "Better than okay. That was... something else entirely."

Bex grins, but it's tinged with something bittersweet. He pulls his jacket around me tighter. "I owe you a new dress, but if it's any consolation, I'd say you look better in my jacket anyway."

My belly flips with the thought of him enjoying the sight of me in the coat of his tux.

"Is that right? You like me in your jacket?" I ask, intending to keep the mood light.

"Look... Rowan..." he starts.

Oh God... He'd better not be starting the *"it's not you, it's me"* speech.

"You don't have to say anything—really. We're fine." I tell him, leaning up off my seat to head for the limo exit but he reaches, gripping around my wrist gently— the concern in his eyes triggering the whole reason I ran away from Drew.

I actually thought he and I might make it out of this situation as two normal adults, with no awkward conversation afterward.

But he continues.

"I'm too old for you. You deserve someone who's not..." He pauses, searching for the right words. "Not broken down. Someone who can give you the life you deserve. Art. Travel. A family."

"I can't have kids, remember? You don't know me as well as you think you do," I say pulling my wrist back slowly—he releases me.

I should just let it go—nod and exit, but that's just not how he and I are when we're together.

We both have a point to make, and neither of us like to relent.

I should say, "*Thanks for the mind-blowing sex; see you on the opposite side of the sideboards,*" but I can't make the words come out.

"There are other ways to make a family, and you will someday. Besides, you wouldn't want me," And there he goes. It's back to Summers, no more Rowan. "I'm a bloody wreck half the time. My knees are shot. I've had more surgeries than I can count, I'm married to this job, and I wouldn't make anyone a good boyfriend, let alone a husband. You need someone you can start a life with."

"Sounds like you're putting yourself out to pasture," I say.

"I had the chance to have all of that. The wife, the kids... the family. I chose hockey instead and hurt someone who didn't deserve it. If given the chance, I'll do the same thing to the next person who gets too close," he says, a look of regret in his eyes. "You deserve better than me or Drew and I hope you find it one day."

I don't know why I care that he's closing a door that I never considered would be open.

My heart clenches, but I nod. "Thank you."

He opens the door, stepping out first in his slacks and dress shirt with the buttons not perfectly aligned.

He offers me his hand and I grab what's left of my thong before I climb out in only his tux and my matching beaded clutch, with my heels in my hand.

"The beads?" I ask.

Glancing back over my shoulder, it looks like a bead shop blew up in there.

"I'll tell him to charge me for that and I'll give him a big tip to keep quiet. I don't need a news article out there spreading a rumor about how I massacred a dress in the back of a limo, it wouldn't be good for my antisocial grumpy honey badger image."

He's kidding but it's also a reminder that we're still at odds. He thinks my loyalty is to *The Seattle Sunrise* and not to the Hawkeyes like he is.

"Right. That could be bad for your brand," I say, forcing a grin.

"I don't know what I should do here. Should I walk you up?" he asks, staring up at the four-story apartment building that I live in.

"Don't pretend that I'm the first girl you've had a one night stand in the back of a limo with," I say, rolling my eyes.

He stands there, his hands in his pockets and stares down at me for a moment. "I'm not a saint, that's a fair assumption, but that," he says tossing a thumb over his shoulder, "Was a first for me. What about for you?"

I try to stop the heat from warming my cheeks at the thought of owning one of Bexley Townsend's first.

"A lady doesn't give up all her secrets Coach Bex."

He sucks in his lower lip and nods. "Are you sure you don't want me to walk you up?"

"No, that's okay. I've been walking myself home for long enough at this point, and I'm really good at it. Besides, I'm sure Hans will be front and center, ready to read me the riot act for coming home past dark," I say, looking up to Hans' dark window.

The lights are already off in his apartment, which means I may get a pass tonight if I'm really quiet.

"Hans?" he asks, his eyebrows stitching together as if he'd like more information about the man waiting for me to come home.

"He's my grouchy eighty-year-old neighbor," I tell him. "Actually, now that I think about it, I bet you two would get along. Maybe you two can exchange pager numbers."

"How old do you think I am?" he asks, faking insult.

"Too old for me, if I recall."

Then I turn and head up the stairs of my apartment building and down the long walkway.

By the time I input my front door code and push through the unlocked door, I look over my shoulder to find Bex right where I left him, his hands in his pockets, watching me until I enter my apartment building.

As soon as I make it up to my studio apartment, I quickly race to the window and peer down to find Bex in the same place. His eyes turn up to meet mine as if he was waiting to see me safely home. Bex lifts his hand to say goodbye and then turns to climb back into the limo.

The limo pulls off the curb, and with it, my Cinderella night with the anti-prince charming.

Chapter Thirteen

Rowan

I sit down with a sigh at Serendipity's, the café busy with people coming in to get their caffeine and sugar fix, and I'm no exception.

An email comes through from Charles. I already know what he wants.

Rowan, I need an update on the Bex story, ASAP! Or do you need me to take you off this story and put someone else who can do it?

Best regards,
Charles Albright

His email threatens to ruin my appetite for lunch with the girls. If Charles take me off this story, kissing the promotion goodbye will be the least of my worries. I'll be looking at a demotion, or even worse, looking for a new job. And with Charles being a big fish in the media pond around here, it could hurt my chances at getting another job in sports journalism—or any reporting job, for that matter.

It's the perfect place to unwind with the girls, a little pocket of warmth where laughter and friendship thrive. It's been two weeks since that gala night with Bex, a whirlwind of a night that's left me with enough moments to replay in my mind. But after a few lingering glances from my spot on the stadium seating behind him for the last couple of weeks, there hasn't been a single word uttered about the night in the limo. Even during last week's out of town games, Bex has been polite but distant in a different way than usual.

As I settle in with my coffee, Keely, Autumn, Cammy and Penelope slide into the booth, all smiles and chatter. Autumn's the first to notice my distracted expression, her brows knitting together. "What's up with you, Ro? You look like you're a thousand miles away."

I force a smile, not wanting to dampen the mood. "Just thinking," I reply, taking a sip of my latte. "It's been a busy couple of weeks."

Keely nods, shaking out a hand. "Tell me about it. The guys are all coming in more regularly for therapy. My hands are killing me."

Penelope nods in understanding, her eyes sympathetic. "Speaking of injured players, how are things going with you and Reeve?" she asks gently.

Keely bites her lip, hesitating for a moment before she speaks. "Better since I opened up to him about my dad contacting me. He's been so worried that I'm going to break things off because I'm worried about his career," she admits, her voice soft. "He wants me to come clean with Sam and Phil and find a way to put this behind us. And he wants to do it this week."

A hush falls over our table as we take in her words. I reach across, my hand finding hers, giving it a supportive squeeze. "That's a big step, Keely," I say gently. "And a brave one."

Autumn sitting next to her, reaches over, taking her other hand. "We're here for you and we'll go with you to talk to Sam if you want. I think you're going to feel relieved to get this out in the open and move on."

Keely looks up at Autumn and then to me, her eyes grateful, but there's a flicker of uncertainty. "I just... I don't want it to blow up in his face. He's worked so hard, and this feels like it could undo everything."

Autumn leans forward, her expression fierce. "Whatever happens, we'll be there. I met someone at the gala that I think can help. I'll make a call, okay? I promise I'll be discreet about it."

The word 'gala' sends a flutter through me, thinking of Bex and the limo again.

Keely's shoulders relax, a small smile tugging at her lips. "Thank you. That means the world to me. Really. Can we talk about something fun now? The "dad went to prison thing" is a total buzz kill."

We all smile and nod.

"I think we should talk about how Rowan hasn't gone through her Hawkeyes girls initiation yet," Autumn says. "What's the hold up?"

"I'm not dating a player on the team. It's part of the requirement. But it's fine, I already feel like part of the group."

"You mean you're not dating a player yet," Penelope smiles and winks at Cammy.

I glance between them both. "Hey! What was that? Hidden winks and such. If this has to do with me I think I should be notified of the scheming."

Penelope takes a sip of her and then sets it down. "You and Coach Bex seemed awfully cozy at the gala two weeks ago and Cammy spotted you two leaving together, which you failed to mention at our last girls brunch."

"Cammy! Girl code," I demand.

Cammy covers her mouth and giggles. "I'm sorry. Penelope should have been a CIA lie detector operative. She got it out of me. And don't blame me, anyone in the gala could have seen you two leaving together. You two were holding hands as he guided you out of the party, and the man looked like he was about to burn down the whole world for you. It was hot as hell. Please tell me you broke off a piece of that."

I watch as all three of my friends turn and stare straight at me. I broke the one cardinal rule in our group.

Rule #1 - Thou shalt always tell the group when you're having hot sex.

Damn it!

"Oh.My.GOD!" Autumn starts. "You slept with Coach Bex?"

Penelope's grin widens and a few older ladies from a table over start to lean closer to our table.

"Shush it!" I say, waving them to be quieter. "The whole city block doesn't need to hear you. And we didn't *sleep* together. It was once in the back of the limo."

Autumn shakes her head and stirs in a sugar packet into her tea. "Well at least I can tell Juliet why we got charged an extra large cleaning fee. She's been hounding them about dropping the charge for two weeks. What the hell did you guys do back there anyway? They said it took hours to clean up."

I cock a brow at her, Bex said he was going to pay off the limo driver so no one would know. "Hours to clean up? That seems dramatic. It was a beaded dress, not a jello fight."

Keely laughs. "He ripped your dress in the act! You're in so much trouble. Just wait until Tessa and Isla find out what juicy secret you've been keeping, you naughty girl."

"It didn't mean anything and it was only one time. We haven't spoken about it since and we never will." I tell them.

Cammy rolls her eyes. "If you think it's over, then you don't see the way Bex looks at you when you're not watching. Or how he can't stop glancing over during practice at the seat you usually sit in when you aren't there."

Penelope nods, "I agree. You'll be an honorary Hawkeyes WAG by the end of the season, mark my words. Whatever's going on between you two, that was just a warmup."

Oh God, I hope she's wrong. I don't think I can handle any more if that was Bex's "warm up".

I roll my eyes, trying to play it off, but I know there's truth to her words. "Alright, alright. So, maybe there's... something there. But whatever it is, it's complicated."

Keely squeezes my hand. "Complicated or not, we're here for you. Whether it's just a fling or something more, you deserve happiness, Ro."

I smile, feeling a bit of the tension ease as the girls dive back into their usual banter, swapping stories, and making plans for who's apartment they'll watch all of the out-of-town games at, and who's bringing what snacks. But in the back of my mind, I can't shake the image of Bex in that limo—the warmth of his hands, the steady, unflinching look in his eyes as he took care of me.

Tomorrow, I'll go down to his office and clear the air. If there's something between us, I need to know.

Chapter Fourteen

Rowan

Walking through the small waiting area of Sam's office, I notice that Cammy isn't at her desk. She's probably out to lunch, but she's not the reason for my visit.

I don't have a scheduled appointment with Sam, but with Charles on my case, and a hunch on a lead that might distract my boss away from Bex, I walk up to Sam's closed office door and rap my knuckles against the solid wood door.

I hear the sound of Sam pushing out of his rolling office chair and then the sound of his heavy footsteps coming closer to the door.

The moment the door opens, I'm greeted with a warm smile. "Rowan. What brings you to my office? Come in," he offers, leaving the door open for me to walk through.

I take a deep breath, clutching my notebook a little tighter than necessary, and then close the door behind me. What I have to ask is private in nature. I don't know if anyone else in the franchise has caught on to some of the hints I've noticed and with gossip the way it is around here, I wouldn't want to be responsible for the spread of a rumor if it turns out not to be true.

"I was hoping to get a few minutes of your time. I need to interview you about your future plans."

It's a weak cover, but Sam's too laid-back to call me out on it. His expression doesn't change; if anything, his smile deepens as he waves me over to the chair opposite his desk. "My future plans? Is there something I should know about, or is this your way of subtly asking if I'm about to announce my retirement?"

I laugh, though it's more out of nerves than amusement. "You know, just doing my job. People have been speculating for a while now. You've had a long successful career and with the Hawkeyes practically creating the Assistant GM position for Penelope, people are beginning to ask questions."

Sam leans back in his chair, stretching his arms above his head. "People are always speculating. That's what they do best, right?"

"True," I admit, glancing down at my notepad and pen in my hand. "But if anyone could set the record straight, it's you."

Sam doesn't immediately respond. He looks past me, out the window where the city's skyline stretches against the horizon, his face softening. "I've been with the Hawkeyes for a long time— longer than I anticipated. First as a player and now as the GM. I've had a long career in the sport but I can't do this forever. It's time for new blood and with it, a new GM," He pauses, meeting my eyes again.

"Penelope," I say, knowing the answer.

He nods. "The grind wears on you after a while and it makes you start thinking about what comes next."

There isn't a sadness in his voice like what I thought I'd expect to find. He seems almost hopeful for this next chapter. And I think I might know why. It's not because he's looking forward to what *might* be waiting on the other side of retirement—it's because he already knows *who* is waiting.

"I don't want to push you into anything," I say carefully. "If you're not ready to make an official statement—"

Sam interrupts with a grin. "Relax, Rowan. I know you're just doing your job. If anyone's going to report on it, I'd rather it happen with someone I trust. And I'd like it to come out on my own terms—after we win the Stanley Cup. Next year will be my last season but Penelope will be stepping into a large role, and I think it's time that the fans hear it from me," His tone is easy, reassuring. "I don't want to distract from the playoffs. Do I have your word that you won't release the article until I give you the 'okay'? And I want a chance to read it over before you send it out into the world, as has been our agreement thus far."

A rush of gratitude fills me. "Of course. You'll have final approval before anything goes live."

He nods, seemingly satisfied with that. "Good. Now how's traveling with the team? Is Bex treating you okay out there on the road? You can tell me if I need to have a word with him."

His question pulls me back to the present, and for a moment, I forget about the article, about the potential headline. All I can think about is Bex. The memory of our night together flickers to life in my mind, and I feel a heat rising in my chest.

"No, he's been as welcoming as Bex knows how to be, I think," I say, though my voice sounds distant to my own ears. "I think we've reached an understanding," I lie, though I'll call it wishful thinking.

Sam tilts his head, eyeing me as if he knows I'm fibbing. "You'll let me know if he steps out of turn?"

I freeze, my breath catching in my throat. How does he know?

"Of course, thank you Sam."

He nods. "Bex and I aren't all that different if you'd believe it." he says.

What did he just say? "Actually, I have a really hard time believing that. You both seem completely different. You seem even keeled, while Bex seems..." I fight to find a word that doesn't insult Bex right in front of Sam.

"Passionate?" Sam says, but that's not exactly the word I would use to describe Bex.

"Yeah, something like that," I say, thinking more along the lines of "hot-head".

But then again, there was something calming about Bex at the gala and then again in the back of the limo. Something that put me at ease in a way no one else has ever done before. And Bex is the last man on earth I thought would be capable of doing that for me.

"I'm several years older than Bex and my passion for the game has morphed more into a respect. I suppose I see it differently from the owner's box than I did from the ice," he says. "Perspective, I think. Something that Bex needs more of. He's too close to it sometimes. He needs a reason to look up from center ice once in a while."

"Something to remind him that there's more to life than the game... or maybe, *someone*."

Wait a second.

Is he referring to me?

"Sam," I say, already shaking my head. "If you're insinuating that Bex has any interest in me, I can assure you that nothing could be further from the truth."

Sam just smiles. "Just do me a favor. Whatever happens between you two, just remember that Bex is a complicated guy. He's not what he seems from the outside at first glance. But you already know that don't you?"

I nod, my heart heavy with the truth of it. "Yeah, I think I might have an idea."

Sam studies me for a moment longer before offering a small, understanding smile. "You'll figure it out, Rowan. One way or another, you will."

I manage a weak smile in return, but the uncertainty lingers. I don't know if I will figure it out, or if there's even a way to untangle the mess I've gotten myself into. But as I leave Sam's office and head back into the heart of the arena, I know one thing for sure—the story may be big, but it's not the only thing on my mind.

Bex is still there, in the back of my thoughts, a constant presence that I can't seem to shake.

Chapter Fifteen

Bex

I'm in my office, pouring over game footage from our last match, when I hear a familiar voice drifting through my open door. It's Rowan, and she sounds... agitated.

"No, just give me more time," she says, her voice low and urgent. "I have a feeling this could be a big story. I can get it, I promise."

My head snaps up, every muscle in my body tensing. A big story? About what? Or more importantly, about whom?

I rise from my chair, moving closer to the door. Something in her tone sets off alarm bells in my head.

"Yes, I understand the deadline, but..." Rowan continues. I can hear the frustration in her voice, and if I had to deal with Charles Albright, the Chief Editor of *The Seattle Sunrise*, I'd probably take a long swim into Puget Sound and never return to shore. If lawyers have ambulance chasers, then journalists have Charles Albright. The man doesn't care about facts, he only cares about appeasing his stockholders. "Look, I just need a little more time to piece it all together. This could be huge for the paper, and a great headline."

My head snaps up, the tension in her tone sending a ripple of unease through me. The words themselves set every nerve on edge.

A big story. Huge for the paper.

The pieces fall into place with alarming clarity. The conversations I've caught her having with Reeve in the hallway. The extra time she's been spending around the stadium. The way she's been watching everything lately, as though she's piecing together a puzzle.

The realization hits me hard—she's digging. And I know exactly whose dirt she's trying to uncover.

I push back from my desk, rising to my feet as the frustration and anger build inside me. It doesn't matter what her intentions are; if she drags one of my players into her story, it won't just affect the team—it could ruin a career.

The sound of her footsteps nears, followed by a soft knock at the door.

"Coach Bex?" she says, her voice hesitant. "Do you have a moment?"

Was the gala a set up just so I'd be too distracted to see that she's still digging up dirt?

Did she think she could lower my defenses the minute she told me about Drew and then proceeded to straddle me in the limo.

Here I was, the last two weeks, concerned that I might have taken advantage of her when she was vulnerable.

This is my chance to find out what dirt she has on one of my players and convince her not to run the story.

I'll pay whatever she wants.

There's not a dollar amount I won't pay her to protect my team.

Hell, I'll give her the penthouse that the Hawkeyes lease for me for as long as my contract lasts if that's what it takes.

"Come in, " I say, trying to keep my voice neutral.

The door creaks open, and there she is. The woman I haven't been able to stop thinking about since the gala, standing in the doorway with her hair cascading in soft waves around her face. Her floral dress clings in all the right places, making her seem more like someone who walked out of a daydream than a bloodthirsty reporter chasing her next scoop.

"Am I interrupting?" she asks, her eyes scanning the room as though checking for witnesses.

"No," I reply tightly, gesturing for her to step inside. "What can I do for you?"

She closes the door behind her with a soft click, and I can't help but think how ominous it feels, sealing the two of us in here together. The smell of her perfume wafting into my office, filling my space with something so addictive it should be illegal.

"I thought we should talk about... the gala," she starts, her voice softer now.

The gala? That's what she wants to talk about?

I stride around my desk, heading straight for her. My sudden movement makes her freeze, her eyes going wide as I close the distance between us. She takes a step back, but I keep advancing, until her back meets the wall.

"Is that what you really care about Summers? The gala?" I say, my voice low and steady as I lean in closer. "Because I heard you on the phone. You're planning a big exposé, aren't you? Something 'huge for the paper.' Care to share who the target is this time?"

Her eyes widen, she knows now that I heard her outside of my office.

"Bex, it's not what it sounded like—"

"I don't like being lied to, it's insulting," I say, my voice low and steady.

For the last two weeks, I've been avoiding Rowan because the night of the gala changed things between us. I've been keeping my distance, knowing that Rowan being with me will only end up causing her more pain when I ultimately end up letting her down like I did my ex-wife.

I know better to think that I can give Rowan the kind of life she deserves, but now hearing her outside of my office, I know I made the right call keeping her as far from me and my team as possible.

"I've seen you whispering with Reeve in the hallways, his distraction out on the ice—You're planning to air out his personal business for all the world to see, aren't you?" I ask.

Understanding dawns in her eyes, quickly followed by indignation. "What? No! That's not what—"

"What will it take, Summers?" I press on, leaning in closer. "What will it take to make this story disappear? Money? My penthouse?"

Her mouth opens to answer, but instead, her gaze drops to my lips, and for a moment, everything shifts. The air between us grows heavy, charged with something far more dangerous than anger. Need–lust–connection, all things I can't seem to shake when it comes to her.

And I'm pulled into her again, just like I was in the limo.

She's here for career advancement, to tell a story that could decimate one of my players, setting fire to the season me and my players have been working everyday toward, all I can think about is the taste of her lips.

A flash of understanding hits me like a bolt of lightning. The tension between us, the constant push and pull, it's all been leading to this moment. Without conscious thought, I find myself sinking to my knees in front of her.

"Drop the story," I murmur, my hands sliding up the side of her thighs, lifting her dress with it. "And I'll make sure you don't regret it."

Her lips part in protest, but I don't give her a chance to respond. My mouth finds her bare thigh, my lips pressing against her, pulling a gasp from her, as her hands flatten against the wall behind her, unsure of what to hold onto.

For a moment, the world seems to stand still. I can hear my heart pounding in my ears, feel the heat radiating from Rowan's body. This is madness, a voice in the back of my mind warning me to choose a different course but I silence it, too caught up in the moment.

"Bex, we need to talk—" she starts, but her words dissolve into a moan as my mouth finds her skin.

"Tell me to stop if you don't want this," I offer, giving her an option out, but she only licks her lips in response giving me my answer.

I'm not thinking anymore, just feeling. The heat of her, the way her body trembles as I press my lips to her cotton panties still in place but dampening quickly before me. Her hands clutch at my shoulders, her fingers digging into the fabric of my shirt as though she's trying to ground herself.

I hook my thumbs into the side of her thong, pulling them down over her hips with practiced precision, sliding it down her legs with agonizing slowness. I look up, her eyes catching with mine. She doesn't tell me to stop, instead her eyes are hooded, the same need in her eyes mirroring mine, her chest rapidly rising and falling, matching my rhythm.

I dive back in, my tongue flicks against the perfect cleft at the apex of her thighs, causing her entire body to jolt. The sound she makes—a soft, breathless whimper—is enough to undo me completely. My hands grip her hips, holding her steady as I work her with my tongue, exploring every inch of her, drawing out sounds I never thought she'd make for me.

Her legs tremble, and I shift, hooking one of them over my shoulder to give myself better access. She's lost now, her head tipped back against the wall, her breaths coming in quick, shallow gasps, as I press deeper, my tongue lapping up every drop, swirling through her clit. Her fingers slide through my hair, pulling me closer as she moans, pulling me closer, begging for more.

She tugs my hair closer as she moans my name. "Bex... oh god..."

I feel her start to unravel, her body tightening, trembling, as she teeters on the edge. And then, with one final flick of my tongue, she falls apart. Her cry of release echoes through the room, her body shuddering, her legs giving out but I hold her up as wave after wave of pleasure crashes over her.

I stay with her, drawing out every last bit of her climax, until she finally goes still, her body slumping against the wall. Slowly, I lower her leg off of my shoulder and rise to my feet, keeping a hold on her as my own need for release throbs painfully in my trousers. But this wasn't about me. This was about her, about protecting my team, about keeping whatever secret she has about Reeve safe from the prying eyes of the media. Or... at least that's what I tell myself, because her conversation outside of my office confirms that even if I was capable of putting someone before hockey, Rowan has her sights on making a splash to make her slimy boss happy.

I made my point, and hopefully, she'll see reason.

Rowan lifts her head, her eyes meeting mine. There's a vulnerability in her gaze that wasn't there before, a connection that goes beyond the physical. But I can't let myself get caught up in it. I can't let myself care for her the way I know I want to. I've been down that road before and it never ends well.

"Bex," she whispers, her voice barely audible. "We still need to talk about this, the gala, the limo, and what you think I know about Reeve."

I shake my head. "My tongue said a lot just now. Mostly, that I was right not to trust you. I knew this whole time you had a big story. We both got something out of what just happened," I say, adjusting the painful erection that I'll have to sort out later in the private shower of my office. "I think we can both agree that this will be the last time."

She steps forward, reaching out to touch me but pulls her hand back as if realizing that there's no point. "You're not listening. The story isn't about Reeve. It's about Sam and he already approved it."

I'm not sure how to process what she just said. "Sam knows there's a story about him coming out?" I ask.

She nods but there's no light in her eyes for me anymore. I should have listened—I should have heard her out.

"Row—" I say, reaching out for her but she takes a step out of my reach.

Then a loud knock pounds against the door.

"Bex, are you available?"

We both freeze, the reality of what we've just done inside the Hawkeyes stadium crashes down around us. I quickly adjust my clothes, trying to regain some semblance of professionalism, while Rowan scrambles, searching for her panties.

Rowan's eyes are wide with panic, but she manages to find her underwear and quickly steps into them.

"Just a moment, Sam," I call out, my voice steady.

I turn to Rowan, finding her pulling her panties into place and quickly smoothing out her dress with trembling hands.

I fight the urge to pull her against me to stop her from shaking and to reassure her that we'll talk about this later. That I made a rash judgment that I'll rectify if she just lets me me.

Suddenly, I see her standing before me so differently than when she first walked in. She never dresses like she's dressed right now for game day or media. Where a steely gray pant suit should be, is a floral spring dress. Where I should find a slicked back ponytail or bun, I find her hair down with soft blonde curves round her face. She didn't come here on a work errand, this was personal. She wanted to talk about the gala–about us. This no longer feels like a back-alley trade deal I made with a cunning journalist who has in her possession a hard-hitting story.

Her lips tighten, her eyes staying fixed on the door as she walks toward the exit of my office. The look in her eyes – a mix of hurt, and something else I can't quite name – hits me like a physical blow.

I thought I was protecting my team—protecting Reeve. And yet, something tells me I'm going to regret the way I handled this.

"Rowan," I say again softly to stop her, but she takes the last steps, reaches for the door, and twists the handle, pulling the door open.

"Oh. I didn't realize you were in a meeting," Sam says, his eyes on Rowan first as she walks past him.

"It's officially over and I was just leaving, he's all yours," she tells him with a forced smile and then slips past him, her words echoing in my head with double meaning.

I watch as she retreats down the hall, unsure of what the hell I just did or how I'm going to fix it.

"What was that about?" he asks.

"It's complicated," I tell him.

"Well, might I suggest a hat? Unless you want everyone to know that Rowan had something to do with that," he smirks, gesturing to my hair.

And then I realize that I didn't slick back my hair after Rowan had her hands in it.

Fuck.

"It's not what it looks like," I lie.

He chuckles to himself and shakes his head. "For your sake, Townsend, I hope it's exactly what it looks like. She's exactly what you need. What you both need. Though, take it back to your penthouse next time, alright?"

Chapter Sixteen

Bex

I catch Cammy's eye at the reception desk as I head for Sam's closed office door. She glances up, nods, and says, "Go right in. He's waiting for you." There's a hint of something in her tone, something that puts me on alert.

Sam texted me ten minutes ago to meet him here. It's not often he summons me without a heads-up. If Sam has something on his mind, he usually heads straight to my office or finds me on the ice or in the gym. But here I am, being called up to his office with zero explanation, and I don't like the mystery of it.

As I reach for the handle, I hear muffled voices on the other side of the door. One voice cuts through the others—familiar, soft, but slightly strained. It's Rowan.

A cold twinge grips my chest. Is this about what happened in my office last week? Does she regret it, or has she said something to Sam? I take a steadying breath, hoping to shake off the unease in my gut. Whatever it is, I'm about to find out.

I twist the handle and step in, taking in the scene. The room's more crowded than I expected. Keely and Reeve are standing off to the side, both looking tense. Keely's expression flickers with guilt as she glances at me, then quickly looks away.

"Bex," Sam's voice breaks the silence. "Come on in. Close the door behind you,"

I shut the door and scan the room, feeling the weight of every eye on me. In the corner, Phil's leaning against the wall, hands shoved deep into his pockets. He nods at me, tight-lipped, his expression unreadable. And then I see them—Autumn and Rowan, standing together by the window, speaking softly as they exchange glances, barely noticing me walk in. My pulse spikes, though I keep my face blank.

"What's going on here?" I ask.

Keely clears her throat, shifting her weight from one foot to the other. "This... is actually about me," she says, looking as sheepish as I've ever seen her.

Keely takes a breath, eyes flicking to Reeve and then to Sam before she finally speaks. "I was just... confessing, I guess. Telling Sam and Phil about my father's history and the fears I have about how it might affect the team."

"Your father?" I echo, struggling to make sense of this. "What does he have to do with the Hawkeyes?"

Keely glances over at Reeve, who gives her a slight nod of encouragement. She visibly steadies herself, then looks back at me, her expression tightening with something between fear and determination.

"He used to work for the mob." Her confession has my chest tightening at the thought that Keely might be in some kind of trouble. "He went to prison for organizing the throwing of the World Cup fifteen years ago. Rowan's been keeping her ear to the ground in case there's anyone in the media that might be stirring up a story about my connection to my father, but so far, she hasn't heard anything."

There's a beat of silence, and I piece it together, though her explanation only brings on more questions. Suddenly, Reeve's concerns over Keely since Thanksgiving, and the whispering in the hallways with Rowan are all starting to make sense. "So you're worried about his reputation sticking to you," I conclude, my tone gentler.

Keely nods, her shoulders slumping in relief. "But more than concern for myself, I am concerned about the Hawkeyes' reputation and Reeve's sponsorships dropping him."

"You know I don't care about that. They can drop me if they want. It won't change us being together." Reeve tells her reassuringly, pulling her hand into hers.

She nods. "I just don't want anything from my past to cast a shadow on this team—or on Reeve."

"Nothing is going to happen to the team or to Reeve. Even if a reporter got their hands on this, it might last a week or two at most. Then they'll move on to something else," Rowan says.

"The media might move on, but what about the investors for the Hawkeyes? Will they forget so easily?" Keely asks.

"Rowan's right. If anyone wrote an article about the Hawkeyes PT having a father that was involved in an incident a decade and a half ago, it would have to be a slow week. We'll support you if the story comes out. Though I wish you would have given us a heads up a lot sooner so that we could have prepared our backers about any possible angle the press might take on this."

I glance around the room, taking in the faces of everyone here, realizing that this is more than just Keely's confession. They're all here to figure out how to shield her—and by extension, the team—from any potential fallout. And while this is Keely's story, it's clear that everyone in this room is affected by it in one way or another.

I meet Sam's gaze, silently asking what he expects from me in this conversation.

"We're trying to come up with a strategy," Sam explains. "Something that will put distance between Keely's family past and her role with the team, while also getting ahead of any potential stories that might try to dig this up."

Autumn raises a hand. "I have a connection with Woman-Fit magazine. They are one of the biggest magazine brands for athletes out there right now. The Editor loves Briggs' charity and she donates a huge amount each year. I briefly spoke to her about how we hired a female head PT for our men's hockey team and she was thrilled at the idea of doing a monthly edition of women in sport related careers."

Phil rubs his chin. "Interesting. What's your angle on this?" he asks.

Autumn looks to Rowan who takes the lead. "We might not be able to hold this story back for long. Keely and Reeve have been getting a lot of publicity lately over Reeve saving her and Keely nursing him back to health. It's a feel good story, but with it, people are snooping around."

Sam crosses his arms over his chest. "You think that someone is going to find this story?"

"Eventually," Rowan says. "But this magazine is an opportunity to control when, how, where and with all the facts told from Keely's point of view."

I stare over at her and she finally meets my eyes after Sam and Phil nod in agreement.

"You knew about this? For how long?" I ask.

She swallows and then looks around the room as if she feels guilty too for keeping it from everyone.

Keely steps forward toward me. "It wasn't Rowan's fault. I asked her to keep my secret. If it weren't for her, Reeve and I wouldn't be dating. But I should have told everyone sooner. Reeve has been worried they've been trying to come up with a solution."

My eyes search out Rowan again. That's what the hallways whispers have been about and why Reeve has been distracted. "This would have at least brought it some click-bait readers. Charles isn't happy about this, I'm sure."

"He doesn't know," she says, her eyes narrowed on me.

She kept this from her boss? A story like this?

"You kept a story from your boss to protect the team and Keely?" I ask.

"Can we do this another time? This is about helping Keely, not about *The Seattle Sunrise*. I have other loyalties than just my chosen profession," she says, already turning her eyes back on Autumn as if to cut me out.

I deserved that.

I thought for sure that she had something on Reeve and now I know that I was wrong.

Phil clears his voice. "I think Autumn and Rowan have a good plan. Let's excuse this and keep me apprised of any sponsorship squabbles. Nothing a few executive box tickets to the game won't remedy."

"Thank you, sir," Reeve says, Keely, Autumn and Rowan quickly agreeing.

"You're all excused, Phil and I have a few things to discuss. Have a good day everyone," Sam says. "Autumn and Rowan—keep me in the loop about the magazine spread."

They both nod, and we all make our way toward the exit. I hang back, keeping my eyes on Rowan as she lingers at the rear of the group, exiting last.

"Can we talk?" I ask, leaning closer to her ear as she passes by me, my voice low enough that only she can hear.

She glances over her shoulder, her eyes sharp, then takes a quick scan to ensure we're far enough away from Sam and Phil before speaking.

"I thought you said your tongue did enough talking yesterday," she says, her tone laced with both challenge and irritation, a hint of a smirk tugging at her lips.

I deserve that.

But I'm not about to let her brush me off, not after everything that just came to light.

I gently hook my hand around the inside of her elbow before she takes another step away from me. She shoots me a look over her shoulder, but she stops and I release her.

I got her attention, now it's up to her if she wants to stay and discuss the misunderstanding we had earlier.

"I'm sorry about yesterday. About what I said when you came to see me... and how I acted. What did you really come to talk to me about yesterday?"

"The gala, as I said when I knocked on the door," she says, crossing her arms over her chest and peers past me.

I turn to see Cammy sitting at her desk behind me with a smirk on her face.

"Can we discuss this somewhere more private?" I ask.

"We've tried privacy Coach Bex. It seems that privacy is the last thing you and I need any more of. If that's all you had to discuss, I need to get back to work," she says, already turning away.

That's not all. It's not even close to what I need to say to her, but Sam's office isn't the time or the place for this conversation.

My mind is still reeling with what I just learned in Sam's office.

Reeve and Keely, along with all the Hawkeyes WAGs have been keeping a huge secret from the franchises for all these months, and Rowan not telling her boss about this story could have gotten her fired.

I'm beginning to see that Rowan isn't who I thought she was.

Chapter Seventeen

Bex

There's a knock at the front door of my apartment as I debate whether or not I'm going to head down the Oakley's later tonight. Tonight is Shawnie's birthday, and all the women are headed out to the club for girls night and the men are all headed to Oakley's for beer, pizza and pool.

It's the night before we have to leave for our out-of-town games, which means the bar should be mostly us.

There aren't a lot of people who have access to the penthouse level of The Commons. It's probably Reeve coming up to make sure I'm coming out tonight. The elevator requires a code to get up this far and the only three people who have a code to give out are Ryker Haynes, Lake Powers, and myself.

I open my front door to find Ryker standing outside of my door. He must have gotten in last night from Canada. He's still not allowed to live in the states for another year and a half but he's allowed to travel here like any normal Canadian citizen, with a passport. And he does, often, as the Head Coach for the Vancouver Vikings NHL hockey team.

He and Juliet drove down from Vancouver last night, a quick two-and-a-half-hour trip to Seattle, for Shawnie's birthday party tonight.

He's dressed in gym attire, standing outside of my door as he stretches his arm across his body. He's either preparing for a run, or just returned from one.

"I'm going for a run. Shawnie and Juliet are getting ready for tonight and the apartment looks like the aftermath of a storewide clearance sale. I needed to get out of there."

It's been a while since I've ever been forced out of my own place. Come to think of it, I'm not sure that ever happened with Lily. I wasn't around enough during the few years we were together to experience anything like that.

If I was in town, I was at the stadium practicing or in the gym strengthening. And if she had friends come in from out of town, hell if I would have noticed.

"Give me a minute," I say and turn for my bedroom.

Ryker catches the door and waits for me inside.

In less than two minutes, we're out the door, headed out of the apartment building, our footsteps pounding the pavement as we pick up a steady pace. It's the middle of March and the spring weather is starting to show around Seattle.

We settle into an easy rhythm that feels familiar from back when he was still a player on my team. But now as the Head Coach of the Vikings, he and I are peers, and with it, a new found level of respect.

I've always admired Haynes as a player, as a leader and as the captain of the Hawkeyes before he was forced to leave the country for a couple of years for faking a marriage to a woman he now shares a life with in Canada.

In the end, it all worked out for him. He and Juliet renewed their vows in Canada last summer with the entire Hawkeyes and Vikings teams in attendance, and a guest list that would rival some celebrities' weddings. Now he's set out to do something he's always wanted to do— bring his late father's team back for a playoff victory. With his leadership, I think they've got a shot. But since we play them next week, I don't intend to offer that up.

We cross the street and head toward the park a few blocks away, the sunset starting to color the sky in reds and oranges, the tall skyscapes standing tall around us and the sounds of traffic on the busy streets around us.

"Juliet's brother, Jerron… how's he doing?" I ask, keeping my tone casual as we stride side by side.

Ryker glances over, and a surprised grin stretches across his face. "You remember his name?"

"Why does that surprise you?" I huff, a bit annoyed as we match each other's strides. It's not like I don't care about my players' lives just because I keep things professional. Even if I wasn't the most sensitive coach, I knew that Juliet's need to provide for Jerron was the reason she agreed to marry Ryker so he could get his green card.

"Didn't peg you for being sentimental," he replies, trying to keep his breathing steady through the pace we're keeping.

"Does everyone reckon I'm an asshole?" I ask, with a bite to it, thinking about how Rowan's been dodging me every chance she gets for the last two weeks since the meeting about Keely's father.

Once Autumn's connection at the women's sports magazine heard about the story, they were quick to move on it. The issue went out a few days ago and though questions have come up during interviews with Reeve at our last home game, Autumn and Tessa coached him on his responses to move the conversation forward.

Tessa's been managing the conversation on the Hawkeyes social media pages, and as far as I've heard, the publicity only caused a spike in ticket sales and more buzz around the team. Phil and Sam saw the opportunity as a chance to touch base with sponsors and renew contracts.

"Touched a sore spot, did I?" he laughs, his tone turning slightly mocking as we cross a green crosswalk, scanning around for cars. No point in taking chances, this team's been through enough injuries as it is.

"Piss off," I tell him. "I don't have sore spots."

He just shakes his head, letting that one pass. We turn onto the path leading through the park, trees rising around us as we cut into the softer light under the branches. I let the quiet sink in for a beat, but it's clear he's still thinking about something, his brow creased in concentration.

"Wait..." He finally says, giving me a side-eye. "This doesn't have anything to do with that reporter who's got the exclusive, does it? What's her name, Rowan, right? I read her piece on you last season. She nailed you right on the head, didn't she?"

I shoot him a glare, but he just chuckles, clearly enjoying this.

He wouldn't have put that together on his own, which means, I probably have Penelope gossiping with Juliet to thank for this. Rowan likes to share a good story, but now I know she can keep a secret better than anyone I've ever met too, and she doesn't give up much about herself freely.

"Well, fuck you too, traitor," I mutter. I'm trying to stay serious, but his laugh is loud enough to echo through the park, and I feel the corners of my mouth twitch in spite of myself.

"Christ, I'm kidding!" He grins, struggling to catch his breath. "She was way off base; she doesn't know you like the team does. But it was funny as hell, I'll give her that. 'A feral cat at a garden party'? Where'd she come up with that one?"

The problem is, Rowan knows me a lot better than Ryker thinks. And if I don't get a hold of myself and remember my boundaries, she's going to end up knowing a hell of a lot more about me than anyone else ever has. More than anyone in that locker room, that's for sure.

Still, I shake it off. I didn't bring up Juliet's brother just to get on the subject of Rowan. I wanted to feel Ryker out, see if he'd even consider coming back to Seattle to take over coaching when the time comes, whenever I decide to hang it up. So I change the topic, sidestepping the chance for him to dig deeper.

"It doesn't matter," I say, focusing my gaze on the path ahead. "Like you said, she's off base."

Ryker glances at me, eyebrows raised, but turns his eyes back forward with a quiet, thoughtful "Huh."

"What?" I demand, annoyed. "What was that?"

"Nothing." He shrugs, feigning innocence. "It just seems like she's getting off easy."

I brush off his comment with a shrug. "She's got the team by the balls. I'm playing nice, that's all."

Ryker throws me a sidelong glance, a smirk curling his lips. "Just the team's balls?"

I give him a good hard shove, and he has to dodge out of the way of a bicyclist coming in the opposite direction.

"Fucker," he yells with a laugh.

I keep my pace as he comes back around, meeting back up with me and falling back in sync.

"I've got no idea what you're on about," I mutter.

"Yeah, sure you don't. Bexley Townsend, man of mystery," he teases, breathing heavily as we keep up the pace. "Look, I'm only saying, I've been where you are before. If there's something there, just... don't go blind trying to pretend it's not there. Especially if she's got her claws in your head."

"Trust me, mate, I know what I'm doing," I say, feeling my jaw tighten.

"Alright, if you say so," Ryker replies, though I can see he's not convinced. "Anyway, we've got bigger things to worry about."

We stop at our usual park bench to stretch before we head back for the apartment building and get ready for Oakley's.

I take the opportunity to shift the conversation back to where I wanted it. "Right. Bigger things—as in finding a coach who might be up for taking over the Hawkeyes after next season if I call it quits."

Ryker stop mid lunge, his eyes shifting to meet mine. "Wait...you're serious?" he says "I thought you'd be stuck in that rink until they scraped you off the ice."

"Maybe it's time I take a good look at the future. Consider what else might be out there for me. My family wants me to move home, and my mum isn't getting any younger. My dad isn't around to take care of her as she gets older, Leo has a family of his own, and Archie might stay a nomad forever."

Ryker doesn't answer right away. We're both silent as we turn down a narrow, winding path through the park, surrounded by tall trees and the faint rustling of leaves in the breeze. I wonder if he's going to press me on what's waiting for me outside the rink. I've been keeping it close to the chest, mulling over what retirement might look like. Hell, I never thought about it seriously before now. Hockey's been my life, my constant, even when the rest of my world turned upside down. But lately... lately, there's been more than just hockey waiting for me when I walk out of that stadium.

"I think you could handle it," I say finally, glancing at him out of the corner of my eye. "Juliet's brother's well looked after now, yeah? And you're already splitting your time here and Vancouver. It wouldn't be a stretch to make it permanent."

Ryker lets out a long breath, considering. "Jerron's in a great place now. He's thriving and even has a part time job with Juliet's new step-dad at the rock climbing gym. But I made a promise to myself that I'd bring the Vikings to the playoffs for my dad," he says, glancing at me. "Are you really ready to leave it all behind and move back to England?"

I exhale, feeling the weight of the question settle between us. The truth is, I don't know. But with Rowan there, a glimpse of something more than just hockey, something that feels like home... I can picture it. I've tried not to let it settle in, but it's there, tugging at me more than it should.

Her life and her career is here, and my future is in Liverpool. I've had someone move an ocean away for me before. Even if I could get Rowan to not hate me, I can't ask her to give up everything for me.

"Maybe I am," I say quietly.

Ryker nods, as if understanding more than I'm saying out loud. We turn back toward the street, picking up the pace as we head back to the apartment building, but there's a quiet resolve in his expression that tells me he's considering it.

Chapter Eighteen

Rowan

Shawnie's girls' night took an unexpected detour when Ground Zero—the club we'd planned to celebrate at—had a fireplace malfunction earlier in the day.

Luckily, no one was hurt, but some lounge couches and flooring weren't so lucky. With our original plans literally going up in flames, the unanimous decision was to crash the boys' unofficial Hawkeyes pool tournament instead.

The energy shifts as soon as we enter Oakley's, a bar filled mostly with Hawkeyes players, friends, and Oakley's usual patrons. The place pulsates with competition in the air as the large blackboard hung on the left wall of the bar is covered with white chalk outlining the pool tournament bracket currently underway.

When we arrive, Oakley already has a table cleared off and waiting for us to make sure that Shawnie still gets her night. Everyone's having a good time, ordering drinks and teasing Shawnie for a night that seems destined to be memorable.

Zoey leans in toward me as if about to ask a question until something catches her eye behind me. I turn to see what has her smirking. Across the room, Bex stands by the pool table, his usual self—sharp, composed, holding a cue stick in one hand and a beer in the other, seemingly unaffected by the joy all around him as he carries on a conversation with Seven. Just as Oakley heads to the bar, Bex steps in his path to stop him. Bex asks him a question, I don't know what it is, but Bex's eyes shift to Shawnie and then to me as he speaks. Oakley nods and then heads back to the bar.

What did he say?

But Bex returns to his conversation with Seven and doesn't bother to look this way again.

Soon enough, drinks are passed around, and the guys respectfully leave us to our girls' night, moving back to their pool tournament. Bex is close by, though, sipping from a glass of water now, his beer long gone. I tell myself I've noticed him switch from beer to water because I'm observant—a reporter's instinct. But if I'm honest, there's more to it than that. I can't help but keep track of his every little habit, like how he exhales right before he lines up a shot, or how he crosses his arms with his right hand lifting his thumb to graze over his lower lip when he watches his opponent take theirs. It's like I've memorized all these small details without even meaning to.

Without warning, Shawnie waves him over. "Coach Bex! It's your birthday too, isn't it?"

My ears prick up. It's his birthday? How did I miss that? Some reporter I've been lately if I can't even catch something as basic as the head coach's birthday.

"Yesterday," he says simply, shrugging as if it's no big deal.

Penelope frowns, clearly disappointed. "Why didn't you tell us? I would've gotten you a cake!"

He raises a brow at her. "That's exactly why I didn't tell you," he replies, the tiniest trace of amusement slipping through his usual guarded expression.

"Did you make a birthday wish?" Shawnie asks, looking playful but curious, and maybe just starting to feel the birthday drinks.

His gaze shifts to me again, his eyes softening as they settle on my lips before dipping down just slightly, almost like he's caught up in some thought. His tongue darts out, brushing over his bottom lip, and my heart does a somersault. He breaks his stare and turns back to Shawnie, with a shake of his head. "I'm too old for birthday wishes," he says with a touch of humor. "But if you want, you can have mine too, Shawnie."

"Too old, my ass," I say, unable to resist. This man thinks he's too old for me, and now too old for birthday wishes.

Bex shifts his eyes back on me and takes steps in my direction. "Did you have something to say about it?" he asks.

"If you're not going to make a wish, then what's the harm in sharing it?" I ask, and then hide my grin by taking a drink of my martini.

I should be careful not to drink too much in this situation. I didn't bring a car to town, I'll take a rideshare when I'm ready to go home, but I'm already loose with my words when it comes to Bex. Any looser and I might say something I can't take back.

He lifts a brow, clearly intrigued by my challenge. "What's in it for me if I share it?"

I smirk, eyeing the pool table behind him. "I'll tell you what," I say, stepping closer. "If I make your last shot, you have to spill the wish."

A glint of amusement lights his eyes, but he folds his arms, giving me a half-smile. "You think you can make it?"

I shrug nonchalantly. "You think I can't?"

He doesn't waste another second and holds out his cue stick for me, the weight of it solid in my hands as I grip it, setting my stance. The room falls into a curious hush, the energy shifting as everyone waits to see if I can pull it off.

I take a deep breath, lining up the shot with my gaze zeroed in on the last solid ball left on the table—Bex's last shot before the eight ball. The whole bar feels like it's holding its breath as I pull back and send the cue forward in one smooth motion. The solid ball sails cleanly across the table and drops into the corner pocket without hesitation.

Next I have the eight ball, and I do the same. Lining up and taking a deep inhale before making my shot. Within the second the eight ball too drops into the side pocket and disappears from view.

The bar erupts into cheers, everyone clearly impressed, and when I glance back at Bex, his expression is unreadable for a moment. But there's a glimmer in his eyes. I didn't make his wager for a truce on the hockey rink, but now we're on an even playing field, and I won this round.

"Nice shot," he says softly, the hint of a smile tugging at his mouth. "Didn't realize you had that in you."

I hand him back his cue stick with a grin. "At least my dad taught me something useful. Now pony up. What was the wish?"

He leans in, his voice low enough that only I can hear it over the noise. "If you want to hear it, you'll have to wait until the end of the night."

There's a challenge in his tone, the kind that dares me to see where this night could go, and I can't help but feel the thrill of it, the way he's got me wondering about that birthday wish more than I probably should.

I should still be upset about the way he didn't believe me about Reeve and Keely until that meeting in Sam's office, but in fairness, the whispering and Reeve's distraction on the ice isn't exactly Bex's fault. And now with things out in the open about Keely's family history, things will get better.

Keely's gotten some hate on social media, mostly from people who had money on the game or are die hard soccer fans. And honestly, just a couple internet trolls as it is, but it's only been a few days since the story broke, and all in all, she and Reeve are handling it really well.

"Fine, but don't keep me waiting for long. I'm not the patient type," I say, closing my arms.

"No, I don't think anyone who knows you would find that surprising." And then heads over to re-rack the balls for the next two players on the bracket to play and I head back to the table with the girls.

For the last two hours, my mind has been a broken record, replaying the same thought.

What's Bex's birthday wish?

I've tried everything to distract myself—conversation, pool games, even scrolling aimlessly on my phone, but it's no use. Bex Townsend is a mystery I can't stop trying to solve. The anticipation has me bouncing my knee like a caffeine addict, but I'm not about to let him think he's got me this wound up. That wish could be anything, but with Bex, anything feels priceless.

The pool tournament ended ages ago, and the night is winding down. Across the room, Lake heads toward Tessa, his easy smile still intact even though he's clearly ready to call it a night. "Are you ready to go home? That baby needs some sleep," he says, his hand drifting to her pregnant belly.

"Momma needs some sleep too," Tessa agrees, taking his offered hand and carefully sliding off her stool. She pauses to hug Shawnie. "This was such a great night. Happy birthday."

Shawnie smiles wide, gripping Tessa's wrist warmly. "Thanks for coming. Get some rest before that baby makes his grand entrance."

"I will," Tessa promises, waving goodbye to everyone as Lake ushers her toward the exit.

Kaenan approaches next, wrapping an arm around Isla. "My mom texted. Berkeley refuses to go to sleep until you sing her a song goodnight, and the baby's running a little warm from teething. We need to head out too," he tells her, pressing a kiss to the top of Isla's head.

I glance at my phone. Sure enough, it's creeping close to midnight. The night is officially winding down, but I'm not leaving without answers. Not this time.

The other girls begin gathering their jackets, their respective partners filtering in to claim them. Shawnie, now renting a room in the penthouse since it's mostly vacant anyway, will likely walk home with Ryker and Juliet. I'm the only one leaving solo, but that's fine—I'm not going anywhere until I know what Bex would have wished for.

Bex, standing near the bar, is deep in conversation with Seven and Brynn. I know he won't tell me anything with an audience, so I make my way to Aaron at the bar, pulling out my card. "Can you add Shawnie's tab to mine?"

Aaron shakes his head, refusing my card. "Bex already covered it."

I blink in surprise. "Oh, okay. Well, here's my card for my tab, then."

Aaron pushes it back toward me. "He covered yours too."

My brows knit together. "He paid for mine?"

Aaron nods, filling a pint for another patron.

"Did he cover anyone else's drinks tonight?" I press.

Reeve steps up beside me, handing his card to Aaron. "Hey, can you run this for Keely and me?"

"Sure," Aaron says.

So Bex didn't pay for Reeve or Keely. Just Shawnie and me. Now it makes even less sense.

Reeve glances my way, offering a quick smile. "Nice shot earlier tonight on that corner pocket shot. I think you almost got Bex to smile."

I try not to let his comment bring me any hope. Bex doesn't know how to smile.

"I wouldn't count on it," I mutter.

"He's warming up to you. I can see it," Reeve says with a nod to Aaron after he, signs his receipt.

"Much good that's doing me when I'm dealing with an arctic glacier. I'll be dead by the time he defrosts at this rate."

Keely steps forward as Reeve helps her into her jacket. "Do you have a ride home tonight? You can crash in our guest room. We just got into a bigger apartment at The Commons," she offers.

"No, thanks. I'll take a rideshare home. I have a lot of work to do tomorrow anyway," I tell them.

We say our goodbyes and then I turn back to Aaron once Keely and Reeve head for the door. "Why did he pay for mine?" I ask.

Aaron raises his hands in mock surrender. "Whatever this is between you two, I'm staying out of it."

Between us? What does that mean?

I let out a huff. If I want a real answer, I'll have to go straight to the source.

As I walk up, Ryker, Juliet, and Shawnie are saying their goodbyes to Bex.

"Thanks for buying my drinks, birthday twin. Next year, we're celebrating together," Shawnie tells him, her words slightly slurred. She had a good birthday, the drinks were flowing and the conversation and friendship in this group of women is always a good time.

"I don't do birthdays, but we can celebrate yours," Bex replies.

"Psht. You're aging like fine wine, Coach Bex. Embrace it."

He nods at Juliet, Shawnie and Ryker as they leave, then turns to see me approaching.

"You paid for Shawnie's drinks?" I ask, crossing my arms.

He stares back at me, his eyes squinting at me for a second and he pushes his hands into his pockets. "It's customary on someone's birthday,"

"Okay, but it's not my birthday, and you paid for mine too. Did you pay for anyone else?"

"No." he says simply, his jaw tightening and his hands sinking deeper into his pockets. He doesn't like this line of questioning. Too bad.

"So why did you pay for me?"

"It's time to go," he says, breezing past me.

"Time to go—" I sputter, grabbing my jacket and chasing after him. "Where are you going? You still owe me a birthday wish."

"I'm taking you home first," he says, holding the door open for me. "Let's go."

"Taking me home?" I ask, but do as he instructs.

"Yes. It's late, and you live further out than everyone else. You shouldn't be taking a rideshare alone at this hour. I'm going to ride with you to make sure you get there safely."

"I do it all the time," I counter.

"Well, not tonight. I'm delivering you to your doorstep myself."

I roll my eyes, falling into step beside him. "I suppose there's no point in arguing with you. Plus, you still owe me your wish."

He smirks, leading me to the car idling at the curb. "If you're a good girl and get in the car, I'll tell you what it would've been... if I celebrated birthdays, which I don't."

"This isn't a bargaining chip," I argue. "I already won the wish with my wicked pool shot. Even if I'm a bad girl on the way home, you still have to tell me. A deal is a deal."

"You're right. A deal is a deal," he concedes, opening the door for me. "And I never doubted you'd make it."

We climb into the car, and the driver, an enthusiastic Bex fan, launches into a lively conversation about his hockey career. I steal glances at Bex throughout the ride, marveling at the way he patiently answers every question.

When we pull up to my building, Bex steps out, opening my door and offering his hand to help me out. I take it, the contact sparking something in my chest.

"I'll walk her up," he tells the driver. "Keep the fare running. I won't be long."

I shouldn't let him trouble himself walking me up, but I don't stop him either. Part of me wants to experience this moment—to have Bex walk me to my door, like something out of a movie. And he still owes me a secret anyway.

Inside, as we wait for the elevator, I glance at him. "Just a warning. If my neighbor Hans comes out griping about the noise, just smile, okay? I like his dog."

"You like his dog?"

"Yeah, and he lets me watch him sometimes. Don't ruin a good thing for me."

He raises a brow. "Is this the neighbor you said I have a lot in common with?"

"Yep."

The elevator dings, and we step inside. For a moment, the air feels charged, like something unsaid is hanging between us. But I let it go, focusing on the sound of our steps echoing down the hallway.

Chapter Nineteen

Bex

Riding up the lift car with Rowan to her apartment, there's an anticipated silence between us. We stand close enough that I feel the faintest brush of her shoulder every now and then, but I keep my hands firmly in my pockets.

What am I even doing here? Walking her to her door like this is some kind of date. I've never been one for romantic gestures, but there's something about Rowan that makes me want to... linger. Maybe it's her laugh. Or the way she looked at me earlier tonight, like she saw straight through the layers I've built around myself.

When the elevator dings, she steps out first, leading the way down the hall to her door. She fumbles with her keys, muttering something under her breath that I don't quite catch, and I can't help the small smile that tugs at my lips. She's nervous. It's endearing.

The door opens, and I follow her inside, immediately hit with the unmistakable sense of *her*. The space feels warm and lived-in—a mix of cozy clutter and deliberate placement. Framed prints hang on the walls, alongside what looks like magazine articles. Her work.

I linger near the door as she drops her keys on a small table, watching as she straightens a stack of books almost out of habit. There's something intimate about this, stepping into her world.

"Nice place," I say, my attention caught by a framed article on the wall. I step closer, scanning the title.

She follows my gaze, a small, proud smile playing on her lips. "That was my first big break after college," she says. "I won a contest for an art piece I wrote about. My sister framed it and sent it to me. Guess I'm a little sentimental."

I nod, studying the piece again. "It's an accomplishment. Not many get to frame it on their wall. You should be proud of it."

"I suppose you're right," she agrees, leaning against the wall as I take in the rest of the space. My eyes drift over her small collection of art and prints, noting the way they're thoughtfully arranged but somehow incomplete.

"You could use something big on this wall," I say. "A proper statement piece—something that grabs attention, takes up the space it deserves."

She quirks a brow, a small grin tugging at her lips. "I thought you didn't care about art."

"I don't care much for it but I grew up attending art galleries with my mum. Turns out some of it stuck."

She crosses her arms, tilting her head and stares at the blank space I'm referring to. "Hmmm. You might be right, but I can't afford something like that right now."

She turns and heads for the small kitchen that opens up to the living room.

"You're doing alright though I assume? Living alone in a one-bedroom apartment close to downtown isn't cheap."

She reaches for two glasses in the cupboard and fills them with water and then walks back over to hand me one.

"I'm lucky, I didn't mean to suggest that I don't make enough. Getting this promotion has a small pay increase, but my salary is no Head Coach for the Seattle Hawkeyes contract," she smirks with a glint in her eye and then takes a sip of her water. "But don't change the subject, you're here for one reason only. You have a secret birthday wish to spill and I haven't forgotten."

"I've noticed." The humor fades slightly as I lower my voice, suddenly aware of the weight of what I'm about to say. "Alright. My wish..." I hesitate, both of us turning from staring at the wall and face each other. I glance at her lips before locking eyes with her again. "If I were the type to make wishes, Rowan, mine would've been for a chance. Just one good, proper chance. No interruptions, no other people involved. Just you and me, to see what it could be like. Maybe more than once."

Her eyes widen slightly, and for a second, I worry I've overstepped. But then her expression softens, a flicker of something vulnerable and open crossing her face.

"A chance for what?" she whispers, her voice barely audible.

"To do this without all the distractions," I admit. "To see what you and I could be without anyone or, in my case, hockey, getting in the way. No Drew, no games, no one else... just us."

The air between us thickens, her gaze locking on mine like she's trying to read every unspoken word beneath the surface. My heart pounds in my chest, louder than the quiet hum of the building around us.

"And you were just going to keep that little wish all to yourself?" she asks, stepping closer.

"I thought you were too stubborn to wait 'til midnight to find out," I say, a smirk tugging at the corner of my mouth despite the nerves gnawing at me.

"Guilty as charged," she murmurs, taking another step. She's close enough now that I can feel the warmth radiating off her, her eyes searching mine. "Well, now that you've made your wish, Coach... what's next?"

I don't answer immediately. Instead, I reach for her hand, tracing her fingers lightly before letting my thumb rest over the back of her hand. "This," I whisper, leaning down slowly.

Our lips meet softly at first, a tentative kiss that feels like a question, an offering. Her hand slides up to my shoulder, pulling me closer as I deepen the kiss, pressing her gently against the wall.

Time seems to slow, the world narrowing to the quiet rhythm of her breath, the soft press of her body against mine. For the first time in my life, hockey's place in my world might have a true contender.

Chapter Twenty

Rowan

It's been a week since Bex kissed me in my apartment and tonight the Hawkeyes are playing another home game. I make my way to my seat watching the crowd light up with anticipation for the game. My breath catches when I see it—a large Hawkeyes jacket draped over the back of my chair. The bold, embroidered name *Coach Bex* on the front chest pocket leaves no doubt as to who left it. On the seat itself is a heated blanket powered by a small battery pack and a Stanley thermos, still steaming with what smells like hot apple cider.

I sink into the chair, pulling the blanket over my lap and immediately slipping into the oversized jacket. The warmth surrounds me, and so does his presence, as if he's here with me despite being on the other side of the rink. I cradle the thermos between my hands, sipping the cider, letting its heat soothe me. This is the warmest I've ever been at a game. I'm usually concerned with my professionalism, but tonight, just this once, I can't deny my heart beating a little more rapidly for the premeditated thought that Bex put into making sure I'm comfortable.

This wasn't a spur of the moment decision. This took planning—it was intentional and meaningful, and also, one hundred percent practical.

He didn't leave flowers and chocolates.

He left a blanket with batteries he probably brought from home. The jacket isn't one I've ever seen him wear which means he probably brought that from home too. And the cider? Well, the stadium doesn't sell it, and this has a spice and caramel added like the spiced cider down the street at Serendipity's.

"Don't look now," the woman next to me whispers conspiratorially, leaning closer. "But Coach Bex hasn't stopped staring at you since you walked into the aisle."

I glance up instinctively, and there he is. His hazel eyes lock onto mine even as Ezra leans toward him, pointing at something on the clipboard he's holding. Bex doesn't even glance at what Ezra's saying. He's staring right at me, his gaze steady and unmistakable.

My breath hitches. I mouth, *Thank you*, hoping he understands. The corner of his mouth twitches, the smallest acknowledgment before he shifts his attention back to the clipboard, but I can feel the weight of his gaze linger even as I look away.

The game starts strong. The Hawkeyes dominate the first period, scoring twice. The crowd erupts with every goal, a wave of cheers and chants rolling through the stadium. I lose myself in the rhythm of the game, texting Hans during the break to let him know I won't be around to help with Sherlock next week since I'll be traveling with the team.

As the second period approaches, I notice a movement beside me. Someone slides into the previously empty seat, but I'm too focused on the rink to pay much attention. The coaches file back into their box in front of me, and my eyes naturally drift to Bex.

Except Bex isn't looking at me. His eyes are fixed on whoever is now sitting beside me, and the sharpness in his expression sends a chill down my spine. He looks... furious.

"Bex doesn't seem happy to see me," a familiar voice says, pulling my attention to my left.

I snap my head around to find Drew sitting next to me, a smug grin on his face.

"I suppose he doesn't," I reply flatly, the warm glow I'd been feeling moments ago now dimmed. "You haven't exactly been on his good side lately."

Drew shrugs, unbothered. "That might be true, but he seems to like you just fine. You've written enough digs at him to deserve the same hostility, but maybe your defense of him at the gala changed his tune." He eyes the oversized jacket I'm wrapped in, his smirk widening. "His jacket looks warm. Makes me wonder if he's warming you up for a biased article—or if you're just making it personal to attack a fellow journalist and friend."

The jacket suddenly feels heavier, as if it's a spotlight shining directly on me. I shift uncomfortably, the soft comfort of it now tangled with Drew's implications.

"Drew," I snap, lowering my voice to keep the conversation between us. "Whose jacket I wear has nothing to do with you, and Charles and the readers of *The Seattle Sunrise* are the only ones who matter when it comes to my writing."

For a moment, Drew is silent, but I can feel the tension radiating off him. Then, to my dismay, he leans closer. "I didn't know Clare was going to mention the baby. We agreed to wait until she was further along—"

"Stop." I cut him off sharply. "I don't care, Drew. I hope you and Clare have a healthy pregnancy, but you need to get this through your head. I don't think about you, or your future. Not anymore."

He follows my gaze, which has shifted back to Bex. Drew sighs, leaning forward in his seat. "I see. I wish you luck with that. You're going to need it."

Without another word, he stands and walks away, leaving me to process the awkward exchange.

The game is well underway, but there's a new tension in Bex's tight shoulders and locked jaw. He's trading players, barking instructions, shouting at the refs with the intensity of someone fighting a losing battle but the Hawkeyes are ahead. It doesn't make sense.

Then, chaos erupts on the ice. A late hit on Briggs Conley sends Lake Powers and Kaenan Altman into retaliation mode. The ref misses the initial hit and calls the penalties on the retaliation instead, sending Powers and Altman to the penalty box.

Bex loses it.

I'm on my feet before I realize it, the blanket tumbling to the sticky floor beneath me. Bex is yelling at the ref, his face red with frustration. When the ref refuses to acknowledge him, Bex jumps over the sideboards, landing on the ice with a determination that makes my heart race.

The crowd roars as Bex confronts the ref, his voice booming across the rink. Ezra rushes to pull him back while Seven steps between Bex and the ref. The second official charges into the altercation, and within moments, the call is made.

Bex is ejected from the game.

I watch helplessly as he storms through the tunnel, disappearing from sight. My heart pounds in my chest, and before I know it, I'm weaving through the crowd, muttering apologies as I push past fans with beers and hot dogs. I flash my badge to get past security and I don't stop until I'm standing in front of his door.

I knock once before pushing the door open.

"Rowan?" His voice is rough, his eyes widening in surprise before narrowing. "You shouldn't be here. And if you're planning on writing this in your next article."

Of course he'd jump to conclusions about my intentions. "I'm not writing about this and I'm not going anywhere," I say firmly, closing the door behind me. "What happened out there? You almost got in a fistfight with the ref. What were you thinking?"

"Rowan," he says, his voice low, "I'm warning you. You should leave now before I do something I'll regret."

I take a step forward. "You wouldn't hurt me. And I'm not leaving until you talk to me and tell me what happened out there," I say.

He turns around, taking heavy long strides towards me until he's standing in front of me, and I do everything I can not to fidget or step away from him.

"Of course I'd never hurt you. That's not what I meant," he says

"Then why are you so mad? Hits like that happen out there. It's not unusual."

"You." he says.

"Me?"

"You think I can just stand there while he sits that close to you, a thick sheet of plexiglass keeping me for telling him to stay the fuck away from you. That you don't belong to him anymore? That he doesn't deserve to breathe the same air as you?"

My eyes widen, where is this coming from?

"Bex..." I say.

"Leave, I'm too worked up for you to be this close to me." His voice is raw, and I feel the weight of his words settle between us.

"Drew means nothing to me."

"Leave," he says again, but this time his voice cracks.

"If you're that worked up, then use me," I say softly, stepping closer.

His breath hitches, and I know I've stepped over the line we've been playing with for months. "Use you?" he asks.

"All that build-up. It's burning in you, isn't it? You need a release. Release it on me," I tell him, my body already tingling at the idea of Bex unloading all his build-up inside of me.

His expression is almost pained at the idea of it.

"Seeing Drew that close to you... I don't just want to fuck you. I want to ruin that pussy for anyone else but me, do you understand? The way I want you should scare you--it scares me. And nothing more will happen after we leave my office. Even if I had it in me to choose anything over hockey, which I don't, I'm retiring to England and your career and life is here."

I step forward, placing my hand on his chest. He might be right, he might only be capable of these stolen moments we've had together, and our lives might not be headed in the same direction but I'm too selfish not to take the little he has left to offer.

"Take me however you need it. I want to know what it feels like to be ruined by you. Even if it's just once."

He sucks in his lower lip. I can see it in his eyes that he knows he should turn me away, but I'm too wet for him to hurt me. I'm too turned on not to come as soon as he enters me.

His eyes darken again and hood with arousal. We both need this, not just him and he sees it in my eyes too.

"Hands flat on my desk, Rowan. Nothing on but your panties. I want to take those off myself." He waits for me to signal that I understand his instructions and then sidesteps to let me pass.

He watches me walk to his desk, stripping off the jacket he left me on my seat, and beginning to quickly unbutton my blouse.

I turn back to watch him pull his polo up over his head as he walks to the door, twisting the lock until it engages, the sound building more anticipation, an agreement on both our parts that neither of us leave until we both get what we came for.

I stand there as he sheds off the last of his clothes, his hard cock bobbing in front of him with me bent over his desk in only a beige thong. He steps behind me, his hands caressing my ass until his fingers twist into the material of my panties, tugging up tight, causing delicious pain that makes more arousal seep into the material. He bends over me, his erection sliding between my bare thighs, his chest flat against my back, pulling my thong tighter.

I moan out in a mixture of pain and pleasure, my center squeezing at the need for more of him.

"Do you know how long I've thought about fucking you like this? Bent over my desk, all mine to claim, this perfect pussy waiting for me? Do you know how long I've wanted to make you scream loud enough that a packed stadium of fans hears you beg me to let you come?" he asks, his free hand sliding around the front of me, his fingers moving the thong out of his way as he works my clit, sliding to my entrance but not giving me the penetration I need. Instead, his fingers move away just as I think he's going to press into me.

"How long?" I ask, knowing that up until a few weeks ago, he hasn't wanted me anywhere near this stadium.

"Since the first day I saw you sitting in the front row of the press box two years ago. Those prim little trouser suits, that slicked back perfect hair. A good little journalist—too smart to get mixed up with the likes of me," he says against my ear as he works me to a sopping wet mess for him. "I wanted to know what you'd look like, properly messy and feral, begging for every inch of my cock as I fed it into you," he says, my fingers digging into his desk, my body humming with need. "I was a good lad, did my best to keep my distance, and then you went and let him sit next to you, making me properly jealous enough that I picked a fight with a ref."

His words hit me harder than they should. Was he really thinking about me all this time? Watching me, wanting me? My mind flashes to every moment we've shared these last few months, every argument, every stolen glance, and now I understand—it was never just the tension between a coach and a reporter. It was this, always this, building and burning until it finally exploded. And now, I'm his fire, and he's mine.

His fingers slide out of my folds and hook on either side of my panties, pulling them slowly down my legs, until I step out of them and then he tosses them onto his desk. "Those are mine now. You don't get those back. After you leave my office thoroughly fucked, I want to know that you're out there in the stadium for the rest of the game and interviews tonight with no panties on because they're in my desk."

I should keep my smart mouth to myself, but I can't—not with him. "If I had known that Drew would make you jealous, I would have had him sit next to me sooner," I admit.

The sound of a slap and the sting of Bex's hand against my ass makes me jump and squirm, but my center clenches tighter and more heat pools low in my belly.

"You want this, don't you?" he asks, a soothing hand rubbing the spot he spanked.

I nod, and I hear the sound of a groan rumble through his chest.

"No condom. I want to coat every inch inside of you with me," he says, but I know it's a question. He's asking for permission.

"Yes," I whisper, my voice trembling with a mixture of anticipation and need, knowing full well that a baby can't come from this, even if, somehow, we both wanted it. "No barriers between us."

A feral sound escapes his throat, his grip tightening on my hips, his control slipping, and then he's there, the blunt head of his cock pressing against my entrance. He pauses for a heartbeat, his hand splaying across my lower back to hold me steady. "You're not leaving this office without my mark on you," he mutters, and then he thrusts forward, filling me completely.

I cry out at the intensity of it, the sensation of him stretching me, claiming me and putting me back together, being wanted like this—by him. It's overwhelming in the most exquisite way. My nails dig into the desk, anchoring me as he pulls out just enough to drive back in, setting a pace that's rough and relentless, just like him—just like he promised he would take me.

"Fuck," he groans, his hands gripping my hips hard enough to leave marks, but I don't care. Every thrust sends sparks of pleasure shooting through me, building with an intensity that borders on too much.

"More," I plead, pushing back against him, meeting his thrusts with my own desperate need. "Don't hold back."

"God, you're perfect," he groans. He takes my hand and presses it to my belly, pushing into the low of my stomach. "You feel that? That's me, driving deep into you."

The sensation is almost too much, and I moan, my body tightening around him. His other hand tangles in my hair, pulling my head back so he can murmur against my ear, "No one else will ever fuck you like I do. And no one has ever or will ever feel as good wrapped around my cock as you do."

His words tip me over the edge, and my orgasm rips through me, my body clenching around him as I scream his name. He follows moments later, his grip tightening as he buries himself as deep as he can go, his release hot and claiming, filling me to the brim with his cum.

For a long moment, the only sounds in the room are our ragged breaths and the faint hum of the arena outside the office, and the smell of what we just did. He doesn't pull away immediately, his hands sliding over my body, grounding me, as if he's reluctant to let go. As if wanting one more touch.

Finally, he eases out of me, leaving me feeling both sated and empty. I straighten slowly, turning to face him. His eyes are dark, his expression unreadable as he reaches for his discarded shirt to clean us both up.

"This doesn't change anything," he says quietly, his voice rough. "It can't."

"I know," I say, though my heart twists at the finality in his tone.

He grabs my panties off his desk and balls them up in his hand, squeezing them as if he likes the feeling of their dampness in his hand and then he places them in his bottom drawer. I guess he's serious about keeping them.

"You can use my bathroom to clean up." He points to the door in the corner of his office. I guess I never noticed it before. "Take your time, there's a shower in there if you want. The second period is over by now and I need to check on the team and the coaches in the locker room."

I nod and then gather my things. I'm not ready to wash him away so quickly, but a shower is necessary since he stole my panties. As I gather my clothes and straighten my hair, I can't help but think that no matter what he says, something between us has already shifted. And neither of us can undo it now.

Chapter Twenty-One

Rowan

The sound of my phone buzzing against the nightstand snaps me out of the fog I've been in for the last hour. It's been a few days since the home game where I ended up bent over his desk in his office.

And now I'm here, laying on top of my neatly made bed like a starfish, staring at the ceiling with an open suitcase on the floor that still has nothing inside of it. I reach over, grabbing my phone, and the subject line of the email catches my eye immediately.

"Bexley Townsend Piece – Urgent Follow-up"

I tap the screen and read through it quickly, my stomach twisting more with every line.

Rowan,

This is my last warning on the Bex story. If you can't deliver, I'm pulling you from the project. Bex is hot right now, and we can't wait any longer to run a piece that gets readers more insight into his life off the ice. You've spent enough time with him. There's got to be something juicy under that hard shell of his. Fans want to know what makes him tick. Dig deeper. This could be huge for your career... or it could end it.

Best, Charles

I drop the phone onto my bed, letting it bounce onto the pile of clothes that I have yet to organize into my suitcase. My chest feels tight, like I can't get a full breath in. Writing a story on Bex without him knowing, after everything that's happened between us? No. That's a line I'm not willing to cross. Not now.

The problem is, I can already feel the deadline breathing down my neck. Charles will want a draft soon, and the last thing I need is him pressuring me for "exclusive content." But the thought of betraying Bex's trust, what little of it I have, makes me feel sick. How am I supposed to do my job when it feels like every move I make with Bex pushes us further apart?

What would a future with him look like? He's already said that he missed his chance for a wife and kids. Maybe the eighteen years between us is too big of a gap. He's looking to retire someday in England and my career is just starting.

And then there's babies. I can't have any of my own. He already said he won't have a family but does he mean that? Or would he resent me later when the reality of not having children sets in like it would have with Drew?

I flop onto the bed and stare up at the ceiling, trying to shove down the anxiety building inside me. Why did things have to get so complicated?

"Okay, what's with the heavy sighing in here?" Jordan's voice cuts through my spiral of thoughts. She pokes her head around the doorway, eyebrows raised in that knowing way only sisters can manage.

I groan and cover my face with my arm. "It's nothing. I'm just... packing."

Jordan steps into the room, holding a bag of chips in one hand and some sort of green juice in the other. She gives me a skeptical look before flopping down next to me on the bed, narrowly avoiding my phone.

"Uh-huh, sure. Because you always sigh dramatically when you're packing," she says, crunching on a chip.

I peek at her from under my arm, but of course, she's already got me figured out. "Fine. It's not *just* packing. I got an email from my boss. He wants a story on Bex."

Jordan chews thoughtfully for a moment, then offers, "That sounds... like your job, though? And you've been salivating at the idea of getting the dirty scoop on the sexy as sin Coach since you started covering the Hawkeyes. What seems to be the problem?"

I sit up, grabbing my phone again, and scroll through the email until I find the part that makes my stomach flip. "He wants more insight into his life. Personal stuff. I don't think he's looking for a puff piece. He wants me to dig deep."

Jordan's face softens with understanding. "Ah. That's a tricky spot to be in."

"Tell me about it," I mumble, dropping my phone back onto the bed.

Jordan doesn't say anything for a second, then she nudges me with her shoulder, a mischievous grin starting to spread across her face. "Okay, so... you and Bex. You wanna talk about the fact that you've been spending an *awful* lot of time together?"

My cheeks instantly flame. "I don't know what you're talking about."

Jordan rolls her eyes. "Oh, come on, Ro. You can't fool me. I can see it. The 'I slept with a hot hockey player twice and don't know how to act' look."

I stare at her, my mouth opening and closing like a fish before I finally let out a strangled, "How do you even *know* that?"

"Because I'm your sister, and I know everything," she says, her grin widening as she nudges me again. "So spill. How was it?"

I groan, dropping my face into my hands thinking about how he almost took out a ref on the ice because of how jealous he was of Drew sitting next to me. "I shouldn't even be telling you this. I should forget it happened and get back to work."

"Nope, no hiding from me. We're in too deep now," she teases, yanking my arm away so I can't hide. "I need details. Was it good? Where did you do it?"

I feel like my face is about to catch fire. "Yes, it was good, okay? I'm not telling you where. I'm not sure if we could get in trouble for it."

Jordan cackles, clearly enjoying my embarrassment way too much. "Oh my God, did you do it in the locker room showers?

"Eww gross, no! I don't even want to know what's on the floors in those showers."

"Okay fine," she says crunching down on another chip. "Big gloves, big stick, though, right?"

"Stop!" I smack her with a pillow, laughing despite myself. "But seriously, Jordan, it's complicated. He's...complicated."

Jordan sobers up just a little, still smiling but with more curiosity now. "Complicated how? I mean, you like him, right? What's stopping you?"

I hesitate. I like him—there's no denying that—but it's more than that. The way Bex looks at me, like he's constantly battling himself. And then there's everything he said the night in the limo, accusing me of using him. And... There's something I haven't told Jordan yet.

"We didn't use protection," I blurt out before I could stop myself.

Jordan's grin falters, and her brows shoot up to her hairline. "Wait, hold up. You mean—"

"I *can't* get pregnant," I interrupt quickly. "I know that. And Bex knows that, too, but... it also feels like the act is reckless for other reasons."

Jordan stares at me for a moment, and then she shakes her head. "Okay, so... he's an ex hockey player with baggage. Big deal. Guys are idiots sometimes, especially when they've been burned before."

I nod, but the knot in my chest doesn't loosen. "He's been hurt by reporters before. That's why he doesn't trust me. He thinks I'm just like the others—only interested in a story. It's like, no matter what I do, he won't let his guard down."

"Yeah, well, maybe if he stopped being such a block of ice..." Jordan teases, but then she softens her tone. "Listen, Ro. Bex isn't some regular guy. He's a pro athlete, and he's probably used to keeping people at a distance. The money and the shiny lights have a way of bringing in the vultures but that doesn't mean you can't break through. But if you want anything more with him, you're going to have to trust him, too. That means being honest."

I bite my lip. "If I catch real feelings for him and can't write the article that Charles wants, it could cost me my job."

Jordan shrugs. "Then I guess you have to ask yourself if a future with him is worth it."

I roll my lips together as I think over her words. "He doesn't want kids."

"Maybe that's what you need. For someone to take the pressure off of you, and for you to take the pressure off yourself. You could be happy together, without all the stuff that hurt you before."

Her words hit me like a punch to the gut. Is that what Bex would be for me? Someone who wouldn't leave because I can't give him a family? There's something incredibly appealing about that, about the idea of being with someone who won't resent me for not being able to have kids. But there's also a tiny, painful part of me that hates the idea of closing that door forever.

"I don't know," I say, quieter this time. "I always thought maybe I could adopt one day... or meet someone who already had kids. Being with Bex means giving that up."

Jordan leans in and bumps her shoulder against mine, her smile softening. "Well, you don't have to decide that right now. But if you do really like him—and it sounds like you do—you owe it to both of you to be upfront. No more dancing around each other. Just talk to him."

She might be right but Bex told me that he doesn't have any more to give and I have to respect that. Besides, I have a job to do too, and my boss is about to have an aneurysm if I don't give him a story.

"There will be time after the Hawkeyes win the Stanley Cup. I have a job to do and a promotion to earn."

Jordan wrinkles her nose and scrunches up her lips. She doesn't like that answer but it's all I have. Bex isn't exactly offering me a relationship. In fact, he already said that he's incapable of it.

"Then you'd better get packing. And take some normal clothes will you? If you get time, you should go see some sights. You said the last away game is in Vancouver and I've heard it is beautiful there."

"Smart thinking," I agree. "Juliet will be in town and her sister-in-law is the one that put on the art auction at the gala a while back. I was thinking about asking her if she'd be interested in co-hosting a show with The Painted Easel sometime. Bex's brother Leo is wanting to branch out with the magazine."

"Ugg," she groans, "that's work. I meant for fun."

"It is fun."

She rolls her eyes. "Fine well I have to leave and check on the new assistant manager I just hired at the hotel. I'll see you later," she says. "Oh, and Ro?"

"Yeah?" I say, turning up to look at her.

"Next time you sleep with the 'hot coach', I strongly suggest you use protection. I think that man is subconsciously trying to knock you up."

I groan, chucking a sock at her as she cackles down the hall.

As soon as she's gone, I flop back onto the bed, staring at the ceiling once more. She might be right that I need to be honest with Bex about how I'm feeling but I can't do it now. I need to stay on task just like he is. We both have a job to do, and I for one, am going to do mine.

Chapter Twenty-Two

Rowan

The last few days on the road with the team have been busy, jumping from city to city, the Hawkeyes fighting for each win and coming out victorious. And each place we go, Bex finds out where I'll be and leaves his jacket for me.

We share glances here and there but we both have teams relying on us to do our jobs. And with Charles on me about this story, I feel the guilt creeping up my neck. There's no story that I could tell that Bex would approve of, I already know that. There's no piece puffy enough to get away Scot-free from his scowl. Any article I write could be the end of anything that was starting to grow between us.

Yet, my notebook keeps filling with more and more pages of little tidbits that I learn about him.

At the team's usual dinner after the game, I overhear Bex talking to Seven about staying another night in Vancouver

"I won't be on the flight tonight morning with the team. I'm staying overnight."

Seven raises his eyebrows, his eyes glinting with curiosity. "Got yourself some plans, Coach?"

Bex only shakes his head, a barely-there smile on his face at what Seven is insinuating. Whatever his plans are, he isn't sharing them with the rest of us.

And it shouldn't matter to me. I mean, it doesn't matter to me. I have no claim over his plans, his whereabouts, or his decisions. But somehow, knowing he's staying—unexpected, unplanned—has me curious.

Just then, my phone buzzes in my lap. I check the screen—Charles.

I excuse myself from the table and step outside, where the crisp Vancouver air nips at my bare arms in only a shirt. It's April and thus hard to predict the weather. I left my jacket inside the restaurant but hopefully this won't take long.

I swipe to answer. "Hi, Charles, I'm still working on it, I promise."

"Working on it?" His voice is a mix of impatience and authority. "Rowan, I need that interview with Townsend—tomorrow. And before you say he won't be in town, I already know he's staying overnight."

I'm speechless. "He didn't tell me..."

"Hold on," he snaps, cutting me off, and I hear him bark some commands to his assistant before he returns to me. "Check your email."

The notification dings just as he says it, and my stomach sinks as I read the message on my screen. A new hotel reservation, extended flight, all arranged by Charles.

"My new itinerary?" I ask.

"Get the interview, Rowan. Give him whatever he wants. Shouldn't be hard... from what I can see, Townsend has an obvious interest in you."

I balk, my grip on the phone tightening. "Excuse me?"

"Townsend hasn't done an interview with a reporter in nearly twenty-five years since he became a rookie. This would be a huge story for us, and you owe me this one. That magazine article that just came out about Keely Woods and her father being the front man for the mob— don't tell me you didn't know that your new best friend didn't have ties to Barrett Humphries. You knew and you gave the story to a magazine instead," he says, his voice gruff—he's not happy and I don't blame him.

That was click bait at its best and *The Seattle Sunrise* would have made a good profit and tons of new subscribers. And yes, if Keely wasn't turning into one of my best friends, and I didn't feel a loyalty to the Hawkeyes, I would have busted that story wide open.

I bet Charles would have given me the promotion right then.

"Charles–" I start, but he cuts me off.

"The only reason that you're not fired already for pulling that stunt is because you're in good with the Hawkeyes and I know you can pull this off. Make it happen," he says.. "If you want to be considered for the head sports journalist position, I need to know you can rise to the occasion. Don't let me down." And with that, he hangs up.

I stand in the cold for a second, trying to catch my breath, processing the conversation as frustration and disbelief mingle. As if Bex's interest in me could be casually exchanged for some exclusive interview. The audacity of it—it's demeaning, both to me and Bex. I almost want to march right up to Charles's office back in Seattle and let him know exactly where he can shove his "head journalist" position.

When I finally walk back inside, I catch Bex's gaze as I return to my seat. There's a quiet warmth there, a curiosity, and I force my gaze away, hoping the frustration on my face isn't obvious.

With Bex nowhere to be seen this morning around the lobby, I decided to take Jordan's suggestion and take a little time for myself.

I slept in, found a great breakfast place that makes strawberry crepes to die for, and caught up on a few emails from Leo.

Working on things for The Painted Easel isn't work for me. It's more like a reward that I treat myself with after I complete a requirement for *The Seattle Sunrise*, and I'm beginning to wonder what my life would have been like if I would have taken a different path in my career and not taken the one dropped in my lap—the one that led me into sports journalism.

It's early afternoon when I decide to take a break from The Painted Easel project and head downstairs to the cafe for a caramel latte.

I'm sitting in the hotel lobby, my coffee in hand, trying to figure out how to manage the situation with Charles. I don't want to be here, playing into his assumptions and bending over backward for a job I suddenly realize I'm not sure I want. But when Bex spots me, he crosses over, a look of surprise mingling with intrigue.

"You're still here?" he asks, hands shoved into his pockets as he steps closer.

I could lie and say that I'm here for the scenery, but I know better than to think Bex will believe it. Honesty is the best policy with Bex even though I know it might have him on alert. If I don't tell him and he finds out later, he'll have a real excuse not to trust me, and with our history, it's likely he'll hear it from someone.

"Charles booked me a flight tomorrow morning. He thinks I'll convince you to give me an exclusive by... well..." I hesitate, but there's a smirk on my face I can't help. "By sleeping with you."

His face darkens. "What a fucking asshole—Did you tell him to go to hell?"

Charles has heard worse insults than that. He sells people's secrets for a living. "I almost told him we've already slept together twice, and that it hasn't helped to loosen your lips in the least, but I didn't think that would help my situation," I tease, hoping to lighten the mood.

A grin lights his face, his eyes narrowing with that familiar glint of humor. "And here I was, thinking you'd be mortified at using me for career-advancing sex."

I take a sip of my latte and shake my head. "Oh, my career isn't worth *that* much." Though that's half a tease and half a truth. "But if the sex were for recreational purposes, I might be persuaded."

I hear a gasp, and turn to find a mother covering her child's ears while running in the opposite direction, sending me a low brow scolding.

She's welcome to do her worst. Her scolding has nothing on the man standing in front of me.

His head is turned to watch the woman running from us too. He chuckles low, shaking his head as if he can't quite believe me, but I can tell he's more amused than annoyed. There's a glint in his eyes as he folds his arms and leans slightly toward me.

"So, if you're not planning on advancing your career with me in my hotel room, what are you doing until our flight home?"

I lift a finger to my chin, pretending to think. "Maybe I'll do some sightseeing? Or head back upstairs to check over a new social media campaign that Leo sent me."

His face shifts, his eyes darkening slightly. "If Leo's taking up too much of your time, I'll tell him to knock it off—"

"No, please don't!" I wave my hands to emphasize. "I'm loving it. Getting to be part of the magazine, even if it's small, is a dream. Your brother is brilliant, and it's a chance to see how your family built this legacy from the ground up. I'm learning a lot."

He pauses, studying me, and I get the feeling he's seeing something in my expression he hasn't before.

"Fine," he says, relenting. "But if he starts crossing a line, tell me."

"Don't spoil it, Townsend. I'm living out my girlhood fantasy working with an art and travel magazine—even if it's pro bono."

His brow lifts, but he doesn't push further. Instead, he checks the clock and glances back at me. "So, how about something a little more in-person?"

"Oh? Out in search of Vancouver's best English pub?"

He's already pulling out his phone, firing off a quick text before I can even finish. "Got a better idea. Come with me.

CHAPTER TWENTY-THREE

Bex

Twenty minutes later, we're standing in front of a small art gallery on a quiet street. The sign above reads "Harbor Art Collective," and the look on Rowan's face as she takes it in—it's something I'll hold onto.

"Bex! An art exhibit? We're grossly under dressed for this event. Leo would be appalled," she says, glancing down at her trousers and puffy jacket.

"You look good to me," I say, letting my gaze sweep over her deliberately.

Rowan's dressed casually—denim trousers, a puffy jacket, and her hair loose around her shoulders. There's something about the way she carries it all that makes her look effortlessly beautiful. For once, it feels like we're together for something other than work. There's something relaxed and easy about being out with her this afternoon.

The taxi pulls to a stop, and I step out first, turning to offer my hand to help her out. Her eyes flicker to mine, a slight hesitation in the curve of her lips before she places her hand in mine.

"Thank you," she says, her voice soft, and her hand warm.

I'm in no rush to let go, as I help her out, but as soon as her feet are firmly planted on the ground, she breaks the connection.

"Ready?" I ask, my voice steady despite the way my pulse seems to quicken every time she glances at me.

"To drool over art? Always." She beams. "I didn't know you cared much for galleries," she says, her voice laced with surprise and that curiosity I've come to crave.

"Didn't say I don't care," I tell her, opening the door and gesturing for her to go ahead. "I just don't take art as seriously as my family does."

Inside, the gallery is filled with bright canvases, bold sculptures, and photographs that seem to freeze time. There's a quietness in the room that feels like reverence, and I slow my pace as I watch her take it all in. We start at the first painting and I stand to her left as a constant companion, craning my neck left to right when she does, trying to see the painting the way that she does, shifting from one painting to the next as we work down the row of well lit canvas.

There's something almost magical about seeing Rowan here, a place where she's in her element. As she steps closer to one of the pieces, I watch the way her eyes light up, taking in every brushstroke, every shade and shadow. It's different from how she watches a game—this is softer, like she's connecting with something personal.

We get to another piece, the largest one in the collection and based on the additional lighting and the fact that it's displayed proudly by itself without any other painting near it, I venture to guess that it's the most expensive piece here.

Rowan lights up the moment she sees it.

"See, this is the kind of painting I hope to hang in that spot in my apartment, except my apartment wouldn't do this masterpiece justice. It should be in some beautiful home somewhere being admired daily," she says, taking in the painting with wonderment.

The painting is called Effervescent Embrace and it already sold for a low six figures, but that doesn't stop Rowan from admiring it. Her crystal blue eyes gaze over every inch of the colorful landscape, as if she doesn't want to miss a single brush stroke.

"It's like you can feel the wind in it," I murmur, realizing the words fall out of my mouth on their own. I clear my throat, a bit embarrassed, but she only nods, a soft smile tugging at her lips.

"You can always tell when an artist poured themselves into their work," she says, her eyes not parting with the canvas for even a second. "It's like it's alive."

I glance at her, at the way she seems almost part of the painting herself. She has that same energy, that same kind of passion, and it pulls me in, stirs something deep in me I'm not sure I'm ready for.

"You're not looking at the painting," she says, catching me.

"I can admire it better through your eyes," I say, and it's true. Seeing her here, seeing her like this—it's like I'm discovering something I didn't know I was searching for.

She turns to look at me, searching my face for a joke, but there's no teasing smirk on my face. I meant what I said.

"Have you ever thought about going into art journalism? Leave *The Seattle Sunrise* behind?" I ask, remembering our conversation back at the gala.

Her face softens, and she laughs quietly. "My career path chose me and I'm not mad about it. It works for me. I'm carving out a piece of that world for myself. And one day I'll have a piece like this in a home where I can appreciate it everyday. That will be my reward, and it will be enough," She shrugs, as if it wasn't a big decision to give up her dreams, but I can see that it was. "And to think, you could have had my dream job, but I think hockey chose you."

I huff out a laugh. "Hockey didn't leave much choice, no."

We fall into a comfortable silence, our shoulders nearly touching as we move from piece to piece. The air around us feels thick with something unspoken, an understanding that feels natural but new. I find myself looking at her more than the art, watching how each piece affects her, how her eyes glint with inspiration or soften with appreciation.

Movement from across the room catches my attention. Harper's face lights up as she and I lock eyes. She strides over, eyes flicking between the two of us with a smile that says she's up to something. "Rowan," she says brightly, "have you met the artist yet?"

Rowan's face lights up, "Oh, I couldn't... I mean, I'd love to, but—"

She looks over to me, seeking some kind of sign that this is okay. I nod, keeping it casual, but inside, there's nothing casual about how I feel seeing her this excited.

"Come on!" Harper says, already tugging her along before Rowan can finish the sentence, guiding her to where the artist is standing, chatting with a few patrons. I watch as Rowan disappears into a small group clustered around the artist, her eyes shining with admiration.

Just watching her, I feel... well, I don't know if there's even a word for it. It's a mix of pride and longing, something deep and unrelenting, like being caught in a rip current I don't want to escape. She's utterly unaware of the spell she's cast, but it's got me tangled, pulled under, and sinking fast.

I turn back to Harper, catching her just as she's about to drift off to check on other patrons. "Harper, that piece that Rowan likes—the Effervescent Embrace" I say, pointing at it. "Who did you sell it to?"

There's a glint in her eye. We don't know each other well except for a few times we've met when she came down to Seattle to watch Ryker play, yet still, I have a feeling she knows why

I'm asking. "You know I can't give out names of the buyers, Mr Townsend."

"Fine, I don't need a name, just offer the buyer double. Tell them that the recipient will appreciate it more than they will. I'm sure they're collectors that won't even hang it up. It'll stay locked in some walk-in safe somewhere," I say, my voice firm, leaving no room for negotiation.

Her eyes widen in surprise. "Double?" she asks and then her eyes shoot over in Rowan's direction.

"Triple if you have to. Whatever it takes to make it happen. in season tickets and my private box at the Hawkeyes stadium. I never use it anyway," I tell her. "Just get me that painting."

Harper's lips curl into a knowing smile, and she pulls out her phone, taking down my details and nodding as I give her Rowan's address—the one I've memorized from the times I dropped her off in the limo and the rideshare after Shawnie's party. Just in case. "All right, Coach Townsend," she says, nodding with a grin, "I'll see what I can do."

Harper heads off as someone waves her over to a painting, but she stops briefly to her assistant, telling him something and then points at me quickly. He nods and starts dialing a phone number and disappears into the back. I turn my gaze back to Rowan. She's still conversing with the artist, hanging onto her every word. For a moment, I just stand there, watching her face light up with every new thing she learns. It's strange; I'd always thought that being happy in hockey, and chasing a dream that big, was enough. But now, the idea of bringing Rowan this kind of happiness is a high that hockey hasn't brought me in a long time.

It's not that I don't still love the sport. And there are few things that feel as good as holding a Stanley Cup over your head in a stadium full of fans going wild, but I'm beginning to realize that hockey isn't enough anymore.

A few minutes later, Rowan breaks away from the conversation, her eyes darting around until they land on me. She walks over, a content smile on her lips.

"Ready?" she asks.

I shake my head, glancing back at the gallery around us. "We can stay as long as you want."

She beams up at me, and that's it. It's like she doesn't even know the hold she has over me. I'd stay here forever if it meant seeing her happy like this. And that's when I feel it—that realization I hadn't expected. Rowan's the one. And I don't know if she's looking at me the same way, but hell, I want her to. I want her to see me as the man who'd do anything for her.

When we make it back to the hotel, I know this is my shot to tell her how things have changed for me, before we get back to Seattle and a world of distraction hits us again. I'm walking her to her room, rehearsing the question in my head—Can we make this work? Do you want to be with me? Seattle—Liverpool—The Hawkeyes. All of that is still up in the air. And maybe she'll say no. I've given her enough reason to.

She turns to me, a gentle smile on her face, and I take a breath, ready to ask if I can come in so we can talk for a minute.

But then her phone rings. She glances at it, her sister's name lighting up the screen. With an apologetic look, she picks up, giving me a soft smile as she holds the phone away from her mouth. "Thank you for tonight. Really," she says, her eyes holding mine for a moment longer, and opening for me to interrupt her phone conversation but I stall too long. "See you tomorrow, Bex."

With that, she turns, stepping into her room as she chats with her sister, her voice fading as the door clicks shut behind her.

I stand there, staring at the closed door, feeling something in my chest tighten.

Chapter Twenty-Four

Rowan

"Earth to Rowan, are you even listening?" Jordan asks, interrupting my daydream.

I shake myself back to attention. "Yes! Girls' weekend... right? Sounds great—I'm in."

"Good," she says, laughing. "Because you sound like you could use a break. You're distracted."

Before I can answer, another call flashes across my screen. It's a Vancouver number and for all I know, it could be the hotel calling about moving my room or a leak in the bathroom. "Hey, can I call you back? I've got another call coming in."

She lets out an annoyed sister sigh. "Fine. But I'm you to that weekend!"

"Great, I can't wait."

I click over to the new call, hoping it's no bad news about my hotel reservation for the flight tomorrow. "Hello?"

"Hi, Ms. Summers. This is Harper's assistant from Harbor Art Collective," a cheery male's voice says on the other end. "I just wanted to double-check the shipping address for the painting Mr. Townsend purchased for you."

"The painting he purchased for me?" I ask, replaying the entire evening in my head, trying to remember a time when Bex would have purchased a painting–and for me no less.

"That's right. The Effervescent Embrace. It turns out that the collector who originally purchased the painting is a good friend of the artist and agreed to Mr. Townsend's extravagant offer of triple the purchase price. We'll have it shipped directly to your home as soon as we process the transaction."

I'm caught out at the thought of Bex paying that much money. "I'm sorry, did you just say triple?"

"Yes, but as I understand it, the collectors are only keeping their original purchase price and are donating the rest to a cause that they say Townsend is a big contributor to. A Kids With Cancer fund. I guess they were at the gala this year and are big Hawkeyes fans. They did say they are keeping the box seats though."

I just about swallow my tongue at the thought of what Bex just did for me.

"Ma'am, are you still there?" he asks.

"Yes," I say, clearing my throat, "I'm here."

Harper's assistant lists off my address and I barely hear the address. Only enough to confirm and then he thanks me and hangs up the phone.

Bex bought the painting. For me.

I knew tonight had felt different, that there was something between us that wasn't just friendly, wasn't just casual, but this? This is beyond anything I expected.

The second the call ends, I toss my phone on the bed and bolt for the door, needing to confront him about this. I make my way down the hall to his room and knock, my pulse hammering as I wait. It only takes a moment before the door opens, and there he is—looking a little surprised to see me standing here, especially at this hour.

"Summers?" His voice is soft, cautious.

I take a breath, but it does nothing to steady me. "You bought that painting for me?"

A flicker of surprise flashes across his face. "How did you know that?"

"They called me asking to confirm my address. I don't understand."

He opens the door to his hotel room to allow me to enter. I take quick steps with so many questions on my mind. So many that my brain feels cloudy and disorganized. I never feel like this.

"Why?" I turn around as he shuts the door behind me. "Why would you do that, Bex? It's more than I'll make over the next four years working for *The Seattle Sunrise*. And that's with a promotion."

He turns to me running a hand over his jaw, clearly searching for the right words. When he finally speaks, his voice is low, almost vulnerable. "Because the moment I saw you light up looking at that painting, I knew I'd do anything to make you smile like that again. Even if you never smile at me that way. I'm tired of bringing you pain, I don't want to do it anymore. I want to make you happy."

I don't know if he understands the effect of his words, but they hit me deep. Without thinking, I cross the small space between us and throw my arms around his neck, pressing my mouth to his in a fierce, grateful kiss.

His arms wrap around me instantly, pulling me closer, and I feel myself being lifted as he tightens his hold around my waist. My fingers dig into his hair, and I can't get close enough—I need him, need all of him. It's as if something's snapped, something we've both held back for far too long, and there's no going back.

He carries me to the bed, his lips moving over mine in a way that steals every coherent thought. We tumble onto the sheets together, his body covering me as he begins stripping away every barrier between us, piece by piece. I gasp when his hands reach my skin, his touch setting me on fire while also soothing the burn. My shirt, his pants, the rush of hands and heat, all of it discarded in our frantic need to be closer.

When there's nothing left between us, I run my hands over his bare shoulders, savoring the solid strength of him, how he feels above me, strong and steady, as if he's exactly where he's supposed to be. He pauses, his breath coming hard, his gaze fixed on me, searching, as if needing my permission to continue.

"You make me happy," I breathe, answering his unspoken question, pulling him to me, "It's only you that I want."

With a growl that sends a thrill down my spine, he moves against me, and I feel every inch of him, feel how he holds nothing back now. This is real, raw, a connection I can't deny, and I realize at this moment that I don't want to. I let go, giving in to everything I feel, every ounce of passion and need I've been holding back.

Our rhythm builds, the tension between us igniting into something almost desperate. And when we finally shatter together, his name is on my lips, and I know, deep down, we were meant to find each other.

Afterward, we lay tangled together, his arm wrapped around me as if he can't bear to let me go. I rest my head on his chest, listening to his heartbeat, my finger tracing the scar on his shoulder from the surgery on his arms years ago. The injury that cost him his career.

He and I each have scars, some physical, some internal, but laying in his arms, I feel more at peace than I have in a long time.

Bex shifts, pressing a tender kiss to the top of my head, pulling the covers up over my bare hip to keep me warm, and then murmurs, "I want to give this... us... a try."

I can't keep the dumb grin off my face or stop the giggle that's begging to bubble out of me. I stare up at him finding no hint of hesitation—just that same determined focus he brings to everything he does.

"You do?" I ask.

"Yeah," he says, his lips curving into a small smile. "We'll tell the Hawkeyes and your boss. I don't see why it would be a problem. Half the Hawkeyes players are dating women who work for the team. This isn't any different."

My mouth opens, then closes. Bexley Townsend, notoriously private and fiercely protective of his personal life, is suggesting we go public—now? He's diving in, fully committed, as if he's thought it all through and made a decision. And I realize that... of course he has. Bex doesn't do things halfway. He's deliberate, and when he goes after something, he's all in. He's choosing me, and he's ready to let the world know it.

I can't help the rush of excitement, but I doubt Charles will feel the same. In fact, this is a conflict of interest, even though he did just tell me to sleep with Bex for the story. "Charles might see this as an issue since I'm supposed to be unbiased with my articles about the team. I need some time to find a way to tell him. Are you okay with waiting to tell everyone?"

He stares back at me for a moment, debating it. "I need to tell Sam, and I can explain to him the situation that you're in. He'll keep it to himself. But don't make me wait long, yeah? You're the first thing in my life that I don't want to keep a secret. I want everyone to know."

I nod, feeling like I'm in a dream to be having this conversation with Bexley Townsend while laying naked against him in his hotel bed.

He reaches for my hand, tangling our fingers together over his chest.

"My age isn't an issue for you?" he asks.

"No," I say. "Though I'd prefer it if you were a little older. That guy at the gala was really doing it for me before you scared him off."

"Is that right?" he asks, reaching over, tickling my side.

I squeal and push his hand away. I'm ticklish and he doesn't need to know that he can use that against me. Besides, I have my own question to ask, and it's not one that comes easy.

"Does the fact that I can't have kids bother you?" I ask, tracing a line with my finger down his chest, not allowing myself to meet his gaze.

He pulls me impossibly close. I thought I couldn't be any closer to him but he proves that's not true. He slides a finger under my chin and lifts my head to meet his eyes.

"I want *you* Rowan, nothing else matters. I'm not Drew," he says.

"I know you're not," I say because I know it's true. He and Drew couldn't be any more different.

"Since we're doing this, I need you to promise me something. It's important," he says, staring up at the hotel ceiling.

"What is it?" I ask, watching him from my spot tucked into his side.

He lets out a breath, and I brace for whatever it is he's about to tell me. "Lily left after our first two years of marriage. When I got drafted, we decided to get married. It was either that or break up and we'd been together for four years, it seemed like the next logical step."

"That makes sense. A long-distance relationship would have been hard," I tell him, encouraging him to continue.

"She moved away from her family and friends to live with me in the states when I started in the NHL. My rookie year was hard on her. I practiced every waking hour and traveled a lot during that year. The second year, I didn't ease up. It seemed like I had more to prove to my team than ever, and my hard work paid off. We won our first Stanley Cup," he smiles for a second at the thought of winning the Stanley Cup, but then his smile falters. "But Lily was feeling more like a fan than a wife. I picked hockey over her every chance that mattered. I didn't love her the way I should have. When the tabloids heard that Lily filed for divorce, they loved the narrative that I was unfaithful to her. That infidelity got between us while I was out on the road. But the truth is, I was always married to hockey, there wasn't room for Lily."

I didn't know the inner workings of his marriage to his first wife and their divorce, but his hate for the media now makes more sense as to why he stopped taking interviews. I can't blame him for that.

"That's why you stopped taking interviews with the media," I say, putting more of the pieces together for why Bex doesn't play nice with the press and why he was quick to paint me out to be after gossip.

He nods. "She left divorce papers on the kitchen table and when I showed up from an out-of-town game, she was already packed. It was our anniversary... I didn't even remember. I signed the papers and after she left, I went straight back to the stadium to practice."

"You were young, and the pressure was high," I say, trying to offer some kind of excuse for him.

He shakes his head, his eyes still on the ceiling. "That wasn't it. You know... she used to knit back in the UK—nothing big, just little animals or a hat for her gran's cats," he says with a snicker. "And she used to sing when she did the dishes. There were just all these small things, and it took me years after our divorce to realize that she stopped doing all of those things during our last year of marriage. I killed her spirit, Rowan. And that's why I've stayed away from you all this time."

"You won't kill my spirit. You said it yourself, I need a man who can handle my fiery personality."

A small smile stretched over his lips. "That's true."

"So why after all these months are you willing to try something with me?"

He turns to look at me. "Because you are the first thing in my life that I want more than I want a career in hockey. If the choice is between you or hockey, then I'll retire from coaching. It took me until recently to realize that."

My heart gallops at his proclamation, my whole body tingling, and my body warming for him again.

"So," I whisper, my voice shaky but steady enough to meet his gaze, "what did you want me to promise you, then?" At this moment, I'd agree to just about anything, desperate to close the space between us.

His eyes soften, his need for reassurance blazing in them. "Promise me," he says, his voice low. "That you'll tell me before you stop knitting, before you stop singing while you do the dishes. Tell me before you pack your things and leave the divorce papers on the kitchen table," His breath hitches and his eyes lock on mine. "Because you're the one thing I'd give up everything to keep."

"I promise," I tell him.

A grin spreads across his face, and before I can take another breath, his lips are on mine, capturing me in a kiss that makes my head spin. It's long and deep, charged with all the emotions we've kept at bay. Then, with a growl that sends heat sparking through me, he pulls me back under him, his body pressing into mine, his intentions clear.

"Is this a bad time to ask what happened to Lily?" I say.

He lets out a chuckle. "It's not great timing, no. But I'll tell you that she's happily remarried to a nice dentist. He doesn't leave town much."

"Good for her," I say, happy to see that in fact Bex didn't crush her. She got back up and found love again.

And as he lowers his mouth to my neck, trailing kisses along my skin and down between my breasts, taking time on each one before sinking further down my body, past my belly button, I know this isn't just *trying*. It's the beginning of something real, something powerful.

Chapter Twenty-Five

Rowan

The elevator dings as I step out onto the floor of *The Seattle Sunrise*, the usual bustling sound of a busy newsroom with reporters typing furiously, making calls, and piecing together stories for tomorrow's edition. But none of that matters right now. Not when I'm headed straight to Charles Albright's office with one goal in mind—to set boundaries about my story on Bex Townsend.

As I approach his door, I clutch my notebook, stuffed with notes, though I haven't gotten to write down anything in it about Sam's retirement and "love after hockey". As of right now, it's still all in my head. This might be the first time I won't need notes to write an article. It's also full of all my usual scribblings. It's my lifeline on the job and has been for years. I use it to write down everything that comes to mind. Lately, it's been overflowing with insights about Bex, some professional, some not.

I take a deep breath and knock, determined to stay calm and stick to my decision.

"Come in!" Charles's voice booms from the other side, already anticipating a conversation that, judging by his tone, he thinks he's won.

I push open the door and step inside, my notebook held firmly in my hand. Charles is leaning back in his chair, looking like the cat that just swallowed the canary. "Rowan! Glad to see you're back. How was Vancouver?"

The memory of Bex, with that serious glint in his eyes when he said he wants us to try, makes my stomach flutter, but I push the thought aside. "It was productive. The team did well, and the readers are eating up the player highlights that I've been writing. Our social media accounts are growing like crazy. I think we're building something here."

He nods, pleased. "Good, good. Keep your readers hooked—especially with all those juicy details about Townsend. The readership is going to pour in with us publishing the first exclusive of Bexley Townsend in years," he says, his eyes gleaming with dollar signs and bragging rights among with news outlet colleagues.

I grip my notebook a little tighter, but I don't let my discomfort show. "That's actually why I wanted to talk to you," I say, my voice as steady as I can manage. "There's something you should know."

His brow arches in curiosity, and he gestures to the chair across from him. "Go on."

I take a seat, my grip on my notebook firm. "I can't write the article that you want me to write." Confusion covers his face. He's not sure where I'm going with this, "I still have a story, it's just going to be different than you expect."

Charles' jaw tightens. He's not happy but he's listening. "What do you mean, different than what I expect?"

I lean back into my chair, settling my boundary. "I mean, I'm not digging up dirt on him. There's a reason he's kept his life private," I clarify, my voice firm but calm. "I'll write a good story, Charles. An honest one. But I'm not crossing the line."

His eyes narrow slightly, and he leans forward, elbows on his desk. "Come on, Rowan. You're telling me you're sitting on a gold mine of a story—getting up close and personal with Bex Townsend, inside access to the team—and you're not going to use it?"

I clench my notebook even tighter, feeling its familiar edges press into my palm. I shake my head. "I'm going to give you a great story, Charles. But it'll be one I can stand behind. One that respects his trust."

He lets out a dry laugh, shaking his head in disbelief. "Rowan, you're missing the big picture here. You have a once-in-a-lifetime chance. The readers want more than stats and game highlights. They want the real Bex. His divorce, his love life, his family overseas that he never talks about. You've got the inside scoop—so let's use it."

"I'm going to give them the real Bex," I reply, setting my notebook on his desk and patting it in front of him. "It's all here. I have the story, I'm just not giving up his closely guarded privacy. I'll find a way to balance both."

Charles stares back at my notebook and then reclined back in his chair, his fingers lacing together in front of him.

"I let the story about Keely's father go... I would have fired anyone else for keeping that under wraps. That cost this newspaper missed revenue, Rowan. Just ask yourself if Townsend is worth your job," he says.

"Are you threatening to fire me?" I ask, standing my ground.

With the head sports journalist still out from his surgery a few months ago and milking his time off, Charles still needs me to finish out with the Hawkeyes. Besides, I have too much he wants to use and I've been bringing in more subscribers with my articles about the team that most of the reporters at *The Seattle Sunrise* combined.

"No, I'm not going to fire you. I'm going to make this very clear. I hired you because I know you're good. But I also know you're ambitious, which is why I'm offering you this opportunity. Don't waste it. I need the story, and your job depends on it."

The words hang between us, cold and unyielding. I know he means it. *Your job depends on it.* The weight of that promise—the tension between my professional life and my future relationship with Bex—settles heavily over me. But I can't back down.

"I'll get you a good story," I promise, my voice unwavering. "But it'll be on my terms."

He studies me for a moment, eyes hard. Then, with a dismissive nod, he says, "Fine. But don't let me down, Rowan."

I stand out of my chair and head for the door. "I won't."

Without another word, I turn and head out of his office, feeling the tension unwind just a little with each step I take.

A few hours later, I'm typing up Sam's story with a feverish speed on my laptop, the story spilling out of me, guided only by the memory of my conversation with the GM. Details about Sam's legacy, the chance at rekindling a love almost lost. Once Charles sees what I have for him instead, he'll see that I still have a headliner—a scoop that no one else does.

I write into the early morning hours and then pass out on my bed, fully clothed.

A chime sounds, another message, waking me from my sleep. Autumn again, this time with a frantic question.

> Autumn: Rowan, are you okay? Please tell me if the article you posted this morning is some kind of mistake?

Another text pings through, this time from Tessa:

> Tessa: I had no idea that Bex's wife left him without any notice. That's really sad.

I blink at the text messages in shock, my fingers flying over my screen, until I make it to the post Autumn and Tessa are talking about. The newest post first thing this morning on *The Seattle Sunrise's* social media account. It's already hit a million views with thousands of likes. I scroll through the influx of comments flooding *The Seattle Sunrise's* latest post. My vision is a blur, and the pounding of my heart almost drowns out the words in front of me, but the truth is glaringly clear. Somehow, the details—the raw, personal moments Bex shared with me—are all there in black and white, printed under my byline.

"No, no, no..." I whisper, my mind reeling. I'd never planned to share any of that. Those were his secrets, his stories, entrusted to me in vulnerable moments I never intended to use.

I can barely breathe. How could this have happened? My mind races, piecing together fragments of the last few days. Then, an icy chill spreads through me as a memory clicks into place—my notebook, the one with every intimate detail about Bex. I left it on Charles' desk when I left.

Oh my god. Charles.

I read through the article again, each line gutting me as I read things I never meant to publish. The story has everything Charles would have wanted—Bex's journey, the well-to-do family in England, the years of struggling in hockey, the regret of the missed last years of his father's life, the discarded ex-wife who left him to marry a dentist. And all of it—*all of it*—under my name.

Panic fills my chest, twisting tight. It's still early in the morning. Maybe I can get to him before Bex sees this—-before the team sees this.

I close my eyes, dread washing over me like a wave. And then I jump off my bed, grab my car keys and race out the door of my apartment, nearly running into Hans and Sherlock as I weave past them in the hallway from their morning walk.

Bex trusted me, believed me when I said I wouldn't dig for a story about him. And now, it looks like I've broken every promise I made to him.

The thought of facing him, the pain I'll see in his eyes if I can't get to him first, is almost unbearable. But no matter what, I have to talk to him. I have to make him understand that this was never supposed to happen.

My fingers fumble across my phone screen, dialing Bex's number before I can second-guess myself. But as it rings, I realize I have no idea what to say to him. How do I even begin to explain?

The call goes to voicemail.

"Bex, please... Please call me back. Don't look at your phone, okay? I'm on my way to the stadium and then I can explain. I didn't know he would—" My voice cracks, and I can't finish the message. I hang up, panic threatening to consume me.

I feel like I'm falling, spinning in a nightmare I can't wake up from. He's going to think I betrayed him for a headline, just like every other reporter he's tried to shut out. And maybe worse, he's going to think that this entire time, I was using him for information, for an exclusive.

I need to get to him, to make him understand that I would never... But even as I think it, a cold realization settles over me. How will I make him believe that when the proof is staring him in the face?

I can still hear Charles's voice from that last conversation, *"Your job depends on it."* And maybe it does—but I never thought he would take my notes and turn them into this. My stomach turns, a sick feeling bubbling within me.

I call Bex again, but it goes straight to voicemail again. I have no idea if he's already seen it. Autumn and Tessa have, does that mean he has too?

I press the phone to my chest, drawing in a shaky breath as I fight to keep my composure. One step at a time, Rowan. First, I'll get to the stadium, and then... well, I don't know what comes after. But somehow, I'll find a way to make him believe me.

Chapter Twenty-Six

Bex

Walking into the locker room for practice bright and early, I see a similar scene— every guy on the team is staring down at their screens, an eerie silence filling the room. It's strange—the tension. This isn't the usual pre-skate banter, and Seven's expression just cements it.

"What's this now?" I try to cut through the tension with a joke. "One of your favorite pop groups went and broke up, did they?"

"Not quite, Coach." Seven's voice is flat, as he flats his phone to my chest. "Might want to read this."

I don't know what to make of it until I see the title: *The Man Behind the Team: Coach Bexley Townsend.* And there it is, Rowan's name in neat, clean print, right under the title. My stomach drops, a sour twist forming as I scroll down and see the first few lines—lines I've said to her in confidence, in private, as raw as it gets.

There it all is, laid bare for anyone with an internet connection to see. Details I've never shared, even with my own damn teammates. Lily leaving, the divorce papers on the kitchen table, my dad's funeral, the regrets I buried along with him. But somehow, Rowan managed to dig up all of it, slap it down in print with a tone so detached, it's as if she never knew me at all.

The guys go back to getting ready, but the atmosphere is thick. No one says a word, but I can feel the weight of their concern, the unspoken questions. I clench Seven's phone tighter before handing it back to him, breathing through the rage clawing at my insides.

I'm the idiot who gave her everything she needed to write this. I fed into her charms, let myself believe she was someone I could trust, someone who'd understand. She had every chance to tell me what she was planning. Instead, she let me open up to her, promising she'd never write a piece like this.

I feel the weight of betrayal settle heavily on my chest. As much as I tried to keep my guard up, it's clear now I didn't do nearly enough. And she's proven exactly why I should have.

I don't waste any more time standing around, gripping my stick so hard my knuckles turn white. I storm out of the locker room, into my office, suiting up in my gear. There's only one thing that's going to get this out of my system—skating, hitting, anything that lets me burn through this anger before it eats me alive.

Scrimmage is on the agenda this morning, and I'm out there, practically skating holes into the ice. Every hit, every slam against the boards, I imagine the betrayal slipping away but no matter how hard I hit, or how many goals I make, it doesn't do anything to lighten the weight. I need to focus on the team, on keeping us moving toward the playoffs. This is just a distraction—a painful one, but a distraction nonetheless.

The guys give me space as I push myself harder, skating until my legs burn, my breath coming in heavy gasps. But nothing is enough. Even after the team clears off the ice, I'm still there, trying to burn out the anger clinging to every cell in my body.

It's then that I spot her. Rowan, out of breath, running toward me down the tunnel. And the sight of her here, in this space that's supposed to be mine, feels like a slap in the face.

She looks like hell—hair messy, face flushed—but I'm in no mood for her excuses.

"Bex!" Her voice echoes in the empty arena, raw with desperation. "I'm so sorry! I can't even tell you—"

I cut her off with a raised hand. "Save it, Summers."

She stops short, stunned, but I can't muster a single shred of sympathy. I need to say this now, lay it all out so there's no question left for either of us.

"I blame myself for this, you know," I say, forcing the words past the lump in my throat. "I knew who you were the moment I met you, but I wanted to believe you were someone else. I made a bad judgment call... that's on me. It won't happen again."

"You knew who I was?" Her eyes flash with something that almost looks like pain. "Bex, you know me better than that. I would never—"

"But you did," I snap. "You used every single piece of leverage you could to get what you wanted from me. Just like Lily. Hell, at least she had a reason. She had every right to leave, and now I wonder if I even loved her like I..." I bite back the words, forcing them down like bile.

She flinches, her eyes going wide, and for a moment, I see something raw, something vulnerable. But I can't let myself get drawn back in. I tap my stick against the ice, the sound echoing in the empty rink.

"Please, just listen," she pleads, taking a hesitant step forward. "I can explain everything. Just give me a chance to—"

"I don't care anymore." I skate toward her, each step a reminder to myself of why I have to cut her out now, before I let her hurt me even more. "This was always how it was going to end, wasn't it? If anything, you proved me right. You're just like the rest."

The words taste bitter, but they're true. I step off the ice, every fiber of my being telling me to get as far from her as possible. I don't need her, and I sure as hell don't want to give her another chance to hurt me.

As I pass her, I notice the jacket she's still wearing, the one I gave her, the one that's become some kind of symbol of whatever we've had. "Keep the jacket, or better yet," I say, my voice cold, "burn it. I don't want it back."

Because all it will ever do is remind me of her. Of the life I almost had.

Chapter Twenty-Seven

Rowan

It's been a week of raw emotions and sleepless nights since Bex stormed past me in the stadium and Charles' office sent me an email to let me know that *The Seattle Sunrise* was letting me go. Charles still hasn't taken any of my calls and he's told security to escort me out if I ever so much as touch the building that houses his office.

Jordan practically dragged me out of the house this afternoon, insisting I need groceries to feel human again. I'm a mess, and I feel like I haven't eaten anything with substance in days.

As we wander through the aisles, Jordan casually opens a bag of popcorn she grabbed off the shelf and holds it out to me.

"Want some?" she offers, already crunching a handful.

I recoil instantly, the buttery smell hitting my nose and making my stomach twist. "Ugh, no." The reaction catches even me off guard—I usually love that stuff.

She pauses, frowning. "This is your favorite popcorn, Ro. What's up?"

"Nothing." I wave her off, trying to ignore the nausea creeping up. "I'm just not feeling great. You could try being a little more sensitive, you know. My entire life just imploded." I shoot her a pointed glare. "Plus, my period is due any day now. That's probably it."

Jordan eyes me skeptically, crunching another handful. I try to ignore her intense scrutiny, but as she sets a bundle of bananas in her cart, I find myself gagging again. Her gaze sharpens as she watches me turn away, trying not to dry heave.

"That's it." She storms off, leaving me standing in the aisle with our cart.

"Where are you going?" I call out for her.

"Wait here," she calls over her shoulder, marching toward the front of the store.

Three minutes later, I'm still standing there, brows knit, trying to figure out what on earth she's up to. Then she returns, a receipt in one hand and a small, pink cardboard box in the other. Without a word, she presses it into my hands.

I glance down, and my heart stops. Pregnancy test.

"Are you serious, Jordan? Why would I need one of these?"

She crosses her arms. "Rowan, you missed your period. I had mine almost three weeks ago and I just realized that you didn't call me over for CSI and ice cream like you usually do when you're on your cycle," she says, giving me a meaningful look.

My heart sinks as I shake my head. "That doesn't mean anything. I can't get pregnant, Jordan. I mean, Drew and I tried everything and nothing took. And Bex and I have only been together a few times," I scoff, trying to convince myself as much as her. "It's impossible."

"Okay, but... did you have your period and just decided not to invite me over for our moon party? We usually don't miss one." Her voice softens, and her brows lift.

Her words sink in, reminding me of the cycle I've built around disappointment. But I push it down, shaking my head. "I've missed it plenty of times. It's not unusual. It doesn't mean..." I trail off, my voice fading.

She doesn't let up. "Look, I already bought it, so you might as well take it. And if you're not pregnant, we'll know right now, and you can stop freaking me out over here." Her voice is gentle but firm. "Do you want me to come with you?"

I want to argue, to push back and insist it's pointless. The idea that I could be pregnant with Bex's child feels... impossible, and yet my heart aches with a longing I can't explain. I'm almost as terrified of a negative result as a positive one. A part of me—a part I'm ashamed to acknowledge—wants it to be positive, while another part of me doesn't want to face Bex with the news. What will he think since I promised him I can't conceive.

I swallow hard, clutching the test. "No, it's fine. It'll just be a minute and then we'll move on and pretend this didn't happen."

My feet feel like lead as I walk toward the bathroom at the back of the store. My hands are shaking as I unwrap the box, the crinkling of the cellophane cutting through the silence. I shut myself in the stall, and for a second, I'm frozen. Memories of tests just like this flash through my mind, each one bringing nothing but disappointment and heartache. But I take a deep breath and follow the steps I know by heart.

I take both tests, just to be sure, and set them on the box, glancing at my phone to time the wait. But the results start to appear almost instantly, the plus signs turning vivid and undeniable right before my eyes.

My breath catches, and I stare, unable to process what I'm seeing.

I'm... pregnant?

Tears well up, blurring my vision as I sit there, gripping the tests as if they're the most precious thing I've ever held. Joy, disbelief, and overwhelming love flood me all at once, filling the space where doubt and fear once lived.

Suddenly, I hear a soft voice. "Rowan? Are you still in here?" Jordan's voice is cautious, as if she's afraid of what my answer might be.

I swallow hard, struggling to find my voice. "Yes," I squeak, my throat tight with emotion.

I hear her footsteps inch closer until her white sneakers come into view just outside the stall door. "Are you okay?" she asks, her voice soft and supportive.

Wordlessly, I slide the box under the door, the two positive tests perched on top of the box for her to see. I'm relieved she's here with me as I flush the toilet and stand, pulling my sweats back into place.

I hear her gasp and then open the stall door to see her hands flying to her mouth. "You're pregnant!" Her voice is barely a whisper, filled with awe and joy, and somehow hearing it aloud makes it more real.

And that's the moment it hits me too. I'm pregnant. After years of thinking I couldn't have kids, of resigning myself to a different life... I'm pregnant. And not just with anyone's baby—with Bex's baby.

My hand goes to my belly, tentative, as if I'm afraid to believe it. I smile, tears slipping down my cheeks, and Jordan's excitement echoes in the background as I sit there, basking in the incredible, unexpected wonder of this new life.

My next thought?

I need to make an appointment with my OBGYN, immediately.

Chapter Twenty-Eight

Rowan

My phone buzzes with Leo's name flashing on the screen. My stomach twists, half from excitement, half from dread. I have a million things I want to tell him, but I'm not even sure where to start.

"Leo!" I answer, trying to keep my voice steady.

"Rowan, darling," Leo's British accent is as chipper as ever. "Just wanted to check in on you and see if you received the file I sent over?"

"Oh, uh... yeah, I got it. Looks amazing," I say, trying to focus on his words and not the mess my life has become over the last few days.

"Good, good," he says, and I can practically hear the smile in his voice. "How are things with the team? Are you traveling with Bex this week?"

My heart stumbles at the mention of Bex. Leo must not have talked to Bex recently. "I... um..." I fumble for words, biting down the rising knot of emotion. "Things are... complicated, Leo."

Leo lets out a soft chuckle. "Is Bex being a twat, or is he treating you alright?"

It takes all my strength not to burst into tears right then and there. My hand tightens around my phone as I try to keep my voice steady. "Actually... I got fired, Leo."

Silence hangs heavy for a moment, and when he speaks again, his tone is serious, soft. "Fired? Bloody hell, Rowan. That's... I'm sorry. That's a damn shame, and those fools don't know what they've lost."

"Thanks," I whisper, swallowing hard. "It's alright, though. I'll figure something out."

"Well, that's one of the reasons I'm calling. I wanted to talk to you about joining us at the magazine. Officially," Leo says, his voice warming. "What do you say?"

I open my mouth to respond, but a knock at my door interrupts. "Hold on, Leo," I say, getting up and crossing to the door. When I pull it open, my breath catches.

There, wrapped in protective coverings and handled with extreme care by two white-gloved delivery personnel, is the painting. *The painting.* I had almost forgotten about it with everything else going on.

"The painting," I breathe, wide-eyed and in awe. How could I forget? How could I forget the way Bex watched me look at it, his eyes softer than I'd ever seen them?

"What painting?" Leo's voice comes through my phone, slightly confused.

"It's, um... a painting I really loved from a gallery. The Effervescent Embrace. Bex bought it for me," I tell him, still staring at the canvas like it's a mirage.

Leo's surprised laugh filters through. "Bex bought you a painting worth over a hundred thousand euro?"

I manage a shaky laugh. "Actually... he paid triple. The original owners only took what they paid and donated the rest to a non-profit that Bex gives to every year."

There's a pause, and then Leo's voice drops to something close to awe. "What did you do to my brother?"

"Nothing," I whisper, tears welling up in my eyes, a mix of gratitude and heartbreak. This painting... it's proof of a side of Bex that I didn't just imagine, proof that he cared... once, before I screwed it all up.

"Doesn't sound like nothing, love. Sounds like my brother's in love with you."

A sharp breath escapes me, and I grip the phone tighter. *In love?* Is that even possible after everything? But before I can process that thought, one of the delivery personnel interrupts gently, "Where would you like us to set it, ma'am?"

I wave them in, pointing to a spot across from the couch where I'll be able to see it every day. "Just... right there, thank you," I manage, barely holding it together as they carefully unwrap the canvas and set it against the wall. The moment they step back and I see it fully revealed in my space, the tears I've been holding back spill over.

"Thank you," I choke out as the delivery team offers a polite nod and exits, leaving me alone in the silent room with Leo still on the line.

"Rowan?" His voice pulls me back, soft and kind. "Think about my offer, alright? Whether something happens between you and my brother or not, you're what this magazine needs. You could work remotely to start, but ultimately, we'll want you here to manage your own team in Liverpool. Your own staff."

I wipe my face, trying to pull myself together. "My own staff?" I murmur, the prospect is almost too big to process.

"Yes. Your talent is bigger than anything *The Seattle Sunrise* could ever deserve," Leo says, sounding confident. "And I spoke with Harper. We're going to do some big things in the years to come. We need you on board for this. I'll send over a complete benefits package and a sign-on bonus I think might persuade you."

A part of me swells with excitement, and I feel the temptation tugging me in, drawing me toward this incredible opportunity, one I've only dreamed of. But another part of me feels trapped, torn between my future and the growing secret that I'm carrying Bex's child. I can't just take a job halfway across the world without telling him about the baby.

But what if he doesn't want this child? Or worse, what if he thinks this is just another angle, I've taken to trap him? There's no easy answer, no simple solution, and I feel the weight of it pressing down on me, heavy and unrelenting.

"I'll... think about it," I finally whisper to Leo, my voice shaky.

"Good," he replies, clearly pleased. "I'll send over everything to your email, and you can take a look when you're ready."

We say our goodbyes, and as I hang up, the room feels quiet, almost hollow. The painting catches my eye again, and I stare at it, the vibrant colors a stark contrast to the gray uncertainty clouding my mind.

I press a hand to my stomach, the weight of the baby inside me more real now than ever. How can I bring a child into this? How can I leave Bex, take this job, and move halfway across the world without giving him the chance to know? And yet, how can I stay here, jobless and directionless, when I have a chance to build a life for myself and this child?

The offer is everything I've wanted professionally... but now my life feels more complicated than ever. The idea of working for Leo, managing a team, building something entirely my own—it's thrilling. But it's not just about me anymore.

My heart aches as I gaze back at the painting, its brushstrokes capturing more than just a beautiful image. It holds a piece of Bex too, of the man he is beneath the walls and gruff exterior. Maybe, just maybe, there's a chance he'd understand. Maybe he'd even want to be part of this, part of us.

But there's only one way to find out. And whatever comes next, I owe it to both of us—and to this tiny life growing inside me—to tell him the truth.

I have to shake this off because I need to head to my OBGYN appointment.

CHAPTER TWENTY-NINE

Bex

I can hear it in Leo's voice over the phone. He's been dying to give me hell since he heard about the painting I bought for Rowan and what I paid. I believed it when Harper said that she doesn't share the buyer information of purchased pieces, but the art world is tight knit and not shocking to find out that the information got back to Leo.

"Word around town is that some rich hockey bloke bought the Effervescent Embrace for three times what it sold for only a few hours before, yeah? Can you believe that?" I can hear the smug sound in his voice and the chair in his study groaning as he leans back into it.

"Don't start, Leo." I say, scooping protein shake powder into a plastic tumbler to take with me to the stadium gym.

Leo doesn't heed my warning, a throaty chuckle escapes instead. "Just admit that you have it bad for this girl. She's special, I already know that. So when are you bringing her home to meet Mum?"

The question hits me harder than I'd like to admit. "There's nothing to bring home, alright?" I growl, the words tasting bitter. "It's done. Finished." The pain of it still throbs, like a chunk of my heart got ripped out and left to freeze over on the rink.

His voice turns serious. "Done?" he asks, as if annoyed by my answer. "And all because of that story she ran about you on *The Seattle Sunrise's* social media page? Just a clean cut then?"

I exhale sharply while twisting the lid on my tumbler. "More like a jagged one," I mutter. "She didn't just write a story, Leo. She laid out my life, like she was peeling it open for the world to see. Lily, Dad, every goddamn private moment she could dig up. And for what? A promotion for a job she didn't even want?"

"Now hold on, that doesn't sound like Rowan at all," he says, the sound of concern in his voice.

I snap back, frustration bubbling up. "How do you know what 'sounds like Rowan'?"

I hear his chair move again like he is preparing for battle. "She's been helping me get the magazine fully online. I offered her a full-time job, thinking she'd jump at it. I also know that her talents are wasted in sports media—no offense. But she turned it down. Wouldn't take it, and now I think I understand why."

"How is that supposed to mean anything to me?" I ask, trying not to let him needle me. "You're telling me that makes her a saint? I gave her everything, Leo. Every part of me she wanted, she got."

Leo shakes his head, undeterred. "What journalist, who supposedly sabotaged her personal life to get ahead, would turn down the job she's always dreamed of—one that pays double, includes a living stipend, and her own bloody corner office—just to avoid stepping on your toes?"

He has a point and it has me questioning her motives. If Rowan was hell-bent on advancing her career at any cost, she would've taken that job with Leo in a heartbeat. But she didn't. She turned it down, and there's a crack in the certainty I had before.

I clench my jaw. "You're right, none of it makes sense. But the article had her name on it. She must've done it. And she's one of the only people that knows over half that stuff in the article."

He's thinking over what I just told him and then speaks. "You're sure it was her? Because I know her work. I've been following her stuff for awhile, and that article... that wasn't her voice. I don't know who wrote it, but it wasn't Rowan."

"What are you trying to say?" I demand, though his words dig under my skin.

"Bex, listen to me," he says. "I've got contacts in the industry, and I heard from a friend of a friend in the IT department at *The Seattle Sunrise* that Rowan left a notebook behind when she went to talk to Charles after the Hawkeyes got back from Vancouver. Charles had access to it."

I straighten, my grip tightening on the phone. The notebook. My mind flashes back to the notebook she always has on her, taking constant notes, the one she clutched like it held her entire career—because it did. And if I knew what that notebook contained, I bet Charles knew too. A chill runs through me.

"Charles used her notebook?" My voice is low, but the weight of the revelation presses against my chest.

"That's what I've heard," Leo admits hesitantly. "He either wrote the article himself or had someone else do it using her notes. But from everything I've seen and heard, Rowan didn't write it."

The crack in my resolve widens. If that's true, she didn't betray me. But she still left the notebook behind, didn't she? Still gave Charles the ammunition to tear me apart.

"Why didn't she tell me about the notebook?" I ask, though the question is as much for myself as it is for Leo.

"She might not have known," Leo offers. "Or maybe she thought you'd never believe her. I don't know, Bex. All I know is that the Rowan I've been working with isn't someone who'd do this to you."

Something about what he's saying feels right. I'd convinced myself that Rowan charmed me—that she was just another person trying to take something from me, even though I knew better than to think that about her.

"Even if you're right," I say slowly, "How the hell do I fix this?" I admit quietly.

"You start by talking to her," Leo says simply. "Find out the truth before it's too late."

We say our goodbyes, but his words linger long after the call ends. I sit there, staring at the floor, the weight of the conversation pressing down on me. If Rowan didn't write that article, then I've been wrong about her—about everything.

I need to see her, but we leave to head back on the road for the second round in the playoffs. I need to get my team past the next few days and then I can think about how to address this with Rowan.

Because if there's even a chance that I've been wrong, I don't know if I can live with myself for pushing her away.

Chapter Thirty

Rowan

The moment I step into Penelope's apartment, the sound of excited chatter from the usual crew of friends fills the space. Penelope invited us all over to her place to watch the game. A tradition, as I've been told, that's been around since before I started coming around. And though I no longer work with the Hawkeyes as the journalist on the exclusive, the girls have continued inviting me to all the usual events.

The moment I enter the living room I notice Tessa, Autumn and Cammy are already sitting in the large section discussing the new sushi restaurant that opened down the street, while the pre-game excitement heats up on the T.V. Popular retired hockey players are guest commentators giving their opinions for game seven of the second round. Whoever wins tonight goes head to head for the final round and the Stanley Cup.

Tonight is the night that we find out if the Hawkeyes will have another shot at the championship. It stings a little that I'm not out-of-town with the team but I'm happy to be gathered on her massive sectional with my friends, everyone in various states of excitement, anticipation, and, in my case, nerves.

Tessa tosses me a pillow to tuck behind my back as I settle deeper into the corner of the couch. "So," she says, narrowing her eyes playfully, "how's life after Charles Albright?" she asks, her tone light, but I know she's curious.

I let out a small laugh, shaking my head. "Honestly, being unemployed is busier than I expected. Leo has been emailing me constantly, I'm helping with a collaboration between The Painted Easel and Harper's art exhibits, and I've been getting a crash course in what it actually takes to run a magazine. Turns out, it's more than just editing articles and picking out pretty pictures," I tease. Of course I knew it would be a lot of work.

"When will the job offer come? He can't expect to keep you for free," Penelope smirks, giving my arm a nudge.

I rub my lips together, unsure of how to admit this part. Once I tell them the truth, they're all going to wonder why I haven't packed my bags and moved to Liverpool. "Actually, Leo already made me an official offer last week. Full-time. Senior editorial position. It's the kind of job you don't turn down. Not to mention, it's based in Liverpool, and they're willing to work with me remotely in the short term."

I can feel all of my friends stare back at me, dumbfounded by the offer, and probably all wondering why I'm not jumping with joy.

"Oh my God, Rowan, that's incredible!" Brynn exclaims, leaning forward with wide eyes. "Are you going to take it?"

The room falls quiet, all eyes on me as I feel the weight of their question settle over me. I can almost see them waiting for me to declare my future, to know if I'm staying or packing up for the other side of the Atlantic.

I hesitate, fiddling with the pillow behind my back to distract myself. "I don't know yet," I say, and nibble down on my lower lip. "Things have gotten a little more complicated than I expected."

Zoey glances over from the far end of the couch, her dark eyes sympathetic. "It sounds like you love what you're doing with The Painted Easel and this new opportunity with Harper. What's complicated about that?"

I open my mouth, the words lingering on the edge, but before I can answer, Isla appears, holding up a bottle of wine. "Does anyone need a top-off?" She looks around, her gaze pausing on me with a knowing smile. "Rowan? Do you need a glass?"

I swallow, shaking my head. "No, thanks. I can't drink for a while."

There's a moment of silence as the words sink in. Then, as if on cue, all heads whip toward me again, eyes widening, mouths dropping. Tessa raises an eyebrow, a sly smile curving her lips.

"Rowan, you can't drink?" she asks, tilting her head, "And exactly how long are we talking here?"

My heart races as I realize this is it—no more hiding, no more hesitation. These are the women who I know will also catch me if I fall, or if I just need a hug and a good laugh. This, here with them, is my safe place. I clear my throat, feeling a mix of nerves and excitement bubbling up. "Nine months."

The room erupts. There are squeals, gasps, and shouts of "Oh my God!" as they all rush to hug me, laughing and congratulating, hands covering their mouths in pure shock and joy.

"It's Bex's, isn't it?" Penelope asks, voice soft but laced with excitement. She's looking at me with an expression that's both thrilled and tender, as if she's seeing this future unfold for me, one she's clearly rooting for.

I nod, my heart pounding. "Yes... it's his."

The room falls silent again, but this time it's different. There's an understanding there, a weight, as each of them processes the news. They know what happened between us, the whole franchise knows, really.

News travels fast, especially when Bex practically bit my head off over the article in the middle of the players tunnel. The stadium echoes and I doubt anyone without the walls of the building missed him telling me off.

He didn't believe me, and now I've lost him and my career. But in its place, the hope of a new life with a baby and maybe, if I can find a way to tell Leo that I'm carrying his nephew or niece, a new world overseas.

A very pregnant Tessa breaks the silence first, her tone serious but warm. "So... why not take the job then? This could be the perfect solution. The job is flexible, right? You can work remotely for a while, and then, when you're ready, move closer to his family. I'd think Bex would agree with that, especially if it means you'll be around people who care about you both."

And this is where the shit hits the fan, as they say.

"Bex doesn't know about the baby yet," I admit quietly, feeling a familiar weight settle in my chest. "I haven't told him. I just had my first ultrasound and I'm ten weeks along."

"The gala?" Autumn asks, and I nod back in response.

"You're almost out of your first trimester!" Isla beams. "What did the doctor say?" she asks, knowing about my struggles with conceiving in the first place.

"She's really happy with the baby's growth. She says that she doesn't have any concerns right now but that she'll see me for an official ultrasound in a few weeks."

"Oh, honey," Isla says, reaching over to take my hand with sad eyes. "You should tell him. He deserves to know. I was scared to tell Kaenan at first too. We hadn't planned to get pregnant last year but it happened and he was so happy when he found out. Give Bex a chance to be excited too."

I swallow, my gaze drifting to the game on the screen. Bex is there, stoic and focused as ever, his eyes locked on the ice as he goes over last-minute plans with the assistant coach. "I know. It's just... complicated. I don't want to tell him and have him think I'm using it to fix what's broken between us. He deserves to know, yes, but not if he feels trapped. I didn't think that I could get pregnant and now, I am."

"Look," Brynn interjects, her tone more confident than I feel. "This is Bex we're talking about. He's not the kind of guy to feel trapped by anything. And if he didn't use a rubber, then he's just as responsible for this sweet little baby. Besides, it's not like he doesn't already care about you, Ro. Anyone with half a brain could see how he felt about you before everything went sideways. This isn't just about you anymore. He's going to want to know he's going to be a father."

The girls all nod in agreement, each of them staring at me with that same fierce determination, the same certainty. They've become my family here, each one of them, and I can feel the strength in their combined support, the certainty that they want this for me, for Bex, for the little life growing inside me.

Their words resonate deep inside me, touching that part of me that's been so afraid, so conflicted. The truth is, I want him to know. I want him to be a part of this, to share in every joy, every milestone. I'm terrified, but maybe that's okay. Maybe that's what happens when you're about to embark on something truly meaningful.

The game kicks off, and the room explodes with cheers, our attention snapping to the screen as the puck drops. Each one of us holding our breath as the players skate down the ice, a dance of speed, skill, and grit. The Hawkeyes have made it this far, and every goal, every near miss feels like a heartbeat, pounding in time with the tension in the room.

The minutes slip by, each one an eternity, until finally, with a minute left on the clock and the score tied, the Hawkeyes manage a final, breathtaking goal. The room erupts in screams, laughter, and clapping as the buzzer sounds, and the Hawkeyes are officially on their way to the Stanley Cup finals.

For a moment, I'm swept up in the joy, the excitement of it all, but then my eyes land on Bex. He's on the screen, arms thrown around his players, a grin splitting his face in a way I've rarely seen before, the last time was lying in his arms in the hotel room in Vancouver. He's radiant, triumphant, his joy unfiltered as he celebrates with the team, the players, and the city that loves him.

The camera shifts, zooming in on him just as he turns to scan the stands, and my heart skips a beat. His eyes search the crowd, as if he's searching for someone... as if he's looking for me. And when his gaze meets the camera, there's something in his expression that fills me with a warmth so intense I almost can't breathe.

In that moment, it's like a weight lifts from my shoulders, and everything clicks into place. This isn't just his story. It's ours. And it's no longer just about us—it's about the life we've created, the future we have waiting. I press a hand against my belly, the tiniest flutter stirring within, and though I know it's too early to feel the baby move, I swear there's a connection there, a knowing that bridges the gap between us.

The girls notice my silence, each of them glancing over with wide eyes, and Tessa nudges me with a knowing smile. "You know what you have to do, don't you?"

I nod, a small smile playing on my lips as I tear my gaze from the screen. "Yeah," I say softly, my voice filled with a newfound certainty. "Yeah, I know."

Penelope grins, wrapping her arms around me in a tight hug. "Good. Because this is your story, Rowan. And you deserve to live it fully."

The rest of the night passes in a blur of laughter, hugs, and excitement, each of us basking in the afterglow of the Hawkeyes' victory. But as I sit there, my hand resting protectively over my belly, I know that this is only the beginning. Tomorrow, I'll tell him. Tomorrow, I'll let him know about the life we've created, the future that awaits us both.

And for the first time in a long time, I feel at peace. I'm ready. And no matter what comes next, I know I'm not alone.

Chapter Thirty-One

Bex

Rowan walks through the door, and it's the first time since I left her standing in the stadium that my world starts spinning again. My breathing stalls and my chest tightens, being this close to her. I haven't seen her since... well, since I'd let my own insecurities get the best of me, accusing her of doing exactly what every other reporter I'd ever known would've done.

The article.

I was so damn sure she'd betrayed me, and without a second thought, I'd thrown words at her that still haunt me. But I know better now, don't I?

I've replayed every conversation, every look she's ever given me, trying to figure out how I could've been so wrong. I should have known she was different. Hell, I *did* know. I was just too blind, too scared to see it. And now, here she is, standing in my office, and the look in her eyes, the determination shadowed by something else, something that cuts right through me says that this isn't easy for her either.

She steps forward, and my mind races with how to begin. An apology? It feels so damn inadequate, but it's all I've got.

"Rowan, I'm sorry—"

She cuts me off with two words that flip my world on its head. "I'm pregnant."

The room stills. It's as if those words have halted time itself. I feel heat rising up the back of my neck, that's not what I thought she was about to say. I thought she was here to curse me out, to tell me that I'm right to believe that I should stick to hockey. That all I ever do is hurt people who care about me, put everyone second to hockey, too stuck in the game to notice that the article sounded nothing like Rowan at all.

I should have seen it like Leo did. For Christ's sake, I should know her writing better than he does. I've read every article she's ever written since the first time I saw her two years ago sitting front row during a post game interview with the press,

But that's not what she said. And now I can't seem to find my voice.

"You're... pregnant?" I manage, my voice thick with disbelief, hope, and something like awe.

"Yes. And I promise, I didn't know this could happen. My doctor told me it was impossible—at least, that's what I thought. We tried... Drew and I tried... and nothing worked. I accepted it." She pauses, her eyes dropping to the floor. "I didn't think this was possible."

I step closer, watching as she stares down, clearly wrestling with her own emotions. The sadness, the guilt—it's all there. But there's something else too, something softer, hopeful. I reach out, hooking a finger under her chin, gently tilting her face up to meet my gaze.

When her eyes meet mine, there's a sheen to them, like she's on the verge of tears, but she is one of the strongest women I've ever met and I know it would take a lot to break her down. Still, I can see it in her eyes, the same fears and uncertainty mirrored in my own. She's pleading with me to be kind, to understand. If she only knew how hard the time apart has been for me too.

"Aren't you going to ask if it's yours?" she asks, her lips trembling.

"No. I don't need to. I already know it's mine," I say gently, trying to show her that she shouldn't be afraid of what she has to tell me.

"How could you know that?" she asks, searching my eyes for truth.

"Because I wanted you pregnant in that limo. It was subconscious—I didn't know it then, but I know it now. I wanted to give you something that Drew never could. And I think there's been a part of me that's wanted to tether us together for a long time."

She has no idea that ever since the gala, her and this baby are the only things I've been sure of anymore. My heart is pounding in a way I've never felt before. I swallow, letting that truth settle deep inside, the reality of it all finally taking hold. She's carrying my child. *Our* child.

She nods but her eyes don't soften with relief the way I expected them to. "Then you should know that I'm keeping it," she says, lifting her chin just a fraction, a flicker of defiance there despite the tears brimming in her eyes. "I'm keeping this baby."

"Are you happy about it?" The words are out before I can stop them, and I realize, shamefully, that a part of me needs her answer more than I can admit.

She nods, a small, trembling smile appearing on her lips. "I'm happier than I've ever been."

In that instant, I'm overwhelmed by a tidal wave of emotions. Regret, pride, longing—all tangled up in the thought of her carrying my child. And seeing her here, willing to bring this life into the world, even after everything I put her through... it's humbling and I can't help but want to make her dreams a reality in return. I take another step closer, reaching for her hand.

"Are you happy it's mine?" I ask, needing to hear it, needing to know that she's as certain as I am.

She studies my face, and I hope she can see it in my eyes how much she means to me, how sorry I am for not believing her. Her gaze softens, and her eyes well with tears, a soft, grateful smile spreads across her lips.

"I wouldn't want it to be anyone else's," she says, her voice thick with emotion.

That's all I need. In one swift movement, I pull her into my arms, my lips crashing against hers as if it's the only way to tell her everything I've been holding back. She clings to me, her hands pressing against my jaw, her lips answering my unspoken question...Do you forgive me?

"I have to confess something about my birthday wish," I say.

She giggles against our kiss, her arms snaking around the back of my neck to pull me closer. "Okay, what is it?"

"My birthday wish was a little different than what I told you. This is what I really wished for, to make something with you, something that's half of both of us. And I promise you, I gave you my best half."

Her laughter bubbles up again, but it's softer this time, her gaze brimming with warmth. "Every part of you is the best, Bex. I hope our baby has all of you, not just the parts you think are good enough."

I brush my thumb over her cheek, a grin spreading across my face. "I love you, Rowan," I whisper, letting each word linger. "And I want us to be a family. I want to be by your side, through every step of this. I love you."

She nods, her hands siding up the back of my neck, her forehead resting against mine. "I love you too. And there's no one else I'd rather live this next chapter of my life with than you."

In one movement, I lift her, her legs wrapping around my waist as I carry her to my desk, swiping everything to the floor in one big sweep—everything crashing down onto the floor. She lets out a surprised laugh, her fingers already working the zipper on my jacket.

I press my lips to her neck, savoring the soft sigh that escapes her. "Do you think I can get another baby in there?" I tease, reaching for the hem of her shirt.

"Twins?" she says with a raised brow. "Nice try, you're potent swimmers are potent but I think that only works for cats. You'll have to try again in nine months," she teases. "But then again, I didn't think you could get me pregnant once."

"Didn't I tell you that I never miss a goal?" I tell her with a grin.

She hums with approval. "That's some hell of a slap shot you've got there Townsend."

Her fingers trace down my chest, while my hands move to her hips, pulling her closer, notching against her wet entrance with my tip, our bodies fitting together perfectly.

As we find our rhythm, our movements fall into place, her hands gripping the edge of my desk while I press into her, savoring each soft gasp, each desperate whimper, until she's clawing at my back as she comes, muffling her sounds against my shoulder.

And then I come right after, spilling every drop I have inside of her, loving the way her eyes dilate when she knows I filled her full of me.

I stay buried in her as we both breathe through the aftermath of our climax, keeping her wrapped tight in my arms, her head resting on my shoulder, she tilts her head up, eyes shining with a mischievous light.

"You know," she says, her voice light, "I might just take Leo up on his offer to work remotely until June of next year."

My brow arches. "Next June? The end of my contract," I murmur, recognizing the implication.

She nods, her smile widening. "It would put you in the perfect position for the daddy position I have open in Liverpool."

I chuckle, kissing her gently. "Is the daddy position for you, or for the baby?"

Her face softens, her hand sliding over my cheek, her thumb brushing my jawline. "Both."

Her answer floods me with a sense of relief, fulfillment and purpose. Something that hockey always gave me. But now my purpose of supporting Rowan as she navigates through a new career and a move across the ocean, as well as becoming a father, is bigger than anything before it. She's thought this through, imagining a future that stretches beyond Seattle, beyond hockey, beyond anything I've ever dared to envision—and she wants to do it with me.

"If you're moving across the pond," I say, voice thick with emotion, "then that's where I'll be too. Hockey or not, all I want... all I'll ever want from this day on... is to be with you."

She smiles, reaching up to cup my face, her thumb brushing the corner of my mouth. "Are you sure you're ready to give up the game?"

I nod, a peace settling over me that I've never felt before. "For you, Rowan? For you and our baby? I'd give up the world."

She presses her lips to mine, sealing a promise that needs no words. And as I hold her in my arms, our future unfolding in front of us, I know that for the first time in my life, I've found the home I'd always been searching for. And it's not an arena, or a stadium, or even a city. It's her. It's us. It's this new life we're building together.

Chapter Thirty-Two

Rowan

It's been two weeks since I told Bex that I'm pregnant, and I've stayed every night at his penthouse since then. Each morning, when I wake up wrapped in his arms and he tells me, half-asleep, that this is the only way he ever wants to wake up. That his penthouse never felt like home until now that I'm in it. And that tells me that I'm right where I need to be.

After the first night that I stayed in his penthouse, he didn't just clear out the spare room, he transformed it for me. The office, which used to be cluttered with playbooks and old equipment, is now filled with color and light, with art pieces chosen by Harper. She found these breathtaking abstract pieces, full of vibrant swirls and delicate brushstrokes, adding life and energy to the room. And there's a special piece from a local artist in Liverpool that Leo sent me as a "Welcome to the team" present for my new temporary office until we make our move overseas. The painting that Bex bought me hangs in the large living room where I can admire it everyday.

There's a brand new desk by the window, a corner chair for reading, and enough storage space to hold every document Leo could throw at me in this new role as Editor-in-Chief.

Every time I walk into that room, I feel like I'm in a dream. Not just because it's beautiful, but because it was Bex's idea, his way of making his home mine too. I'm starting to realize that everything about this life—Bex, the baby, the work with Leo's magazine—it's bigger and better than I'd ever dared to imagine for myself.

I accepted the life that was handed to me, not realizing that I'm capable of building my own dreams from scratch. Having Bex to do it with is the dream I never saw coming.

Tonight, I pull out something special from the back of the closet—one of Bex's old jerseys, number #14 from his days playing for the Hawkeyes. I have no idea how he'll react, but if it's anything like the way he looked at the barely there baby bump just starting to show into my second trimester, I know it'll be worth it.

Dressed in thermal gear from head-to-toe and a set of warm Faux fur boots that Bex bought me for the games, I make my way to the locker room, slipping through the familiar corridors that I used to travel through as a reporter, but tonight, I'm here as something entirely different—as his. I spot Bex talking with some players, his face lighting up the moment he sees me standing there in his jersey. He freezes mid-sentence, his eyes locking on me, then slowly raking over every inch of me.

"Fuck... you're wearing my jersey," he growls, his voice low as he steps forward, gently taking my hand and spinning me around to take in the full effect. "And for once, you don't look like you're freezing. You look like a proper hockey girlfriend."

A giggle escapes my lips; I thought he might like it, but this is more than I hoped for.

He wraps an arm around my waist and leans down, his breath hot against my ear. "I'm so goddamn hard right now seeing you with my name and number on your back."

I smirk, unable to resist a little teasing. "It does something for you, huh?"

His eyes flash, and he murmurs, "What do you say we find a broom closet and we'll do a reenactment of how I put that baby in you?"

I laugh, wrapping my hands around his face, pulling him close. "Tonight... after you win. You can put as many babies in me as you want."

He shakes his head, muttering curse words to himself, his eyes darken and hood with arousal. "You promise?"

"Bex?" Coach Ezra calls, poking his head in through the door. "You ready?"

Bex reluctantly lets go of me, giving me a look that promises this isn't over, then nods at Ezra. As the door closes, he turns back to me, and for a moment, I think he's going to kiss me right here in front of everyone. Instead, he hands me a small ticket.

I glance down at it. Row 3, Seat 7. My usual spot from back when I came to watch practices, back before I'd ever met him.

"Wasn't this seat already booked? I couldn't get anything online since everything was sold out. The girls said I could watch in the owner's box with them."

His face softens, as if he's a bit embarrassed by the sentiment. "If you'd rather sit with the girls—"

"Bexley Townsend," I interrupt, giving him a firm glare. "All you have to do is tell me where you want me to sit, and that's where I'll be."

He nods, a flicker of relief in his eyes. "It's where I always look for you. It feels off when you're not there, and tonight... I'll need you close."

I bite my lip, feeling a warmth spread through me that has nothing to do with the heating in the stadium. "Where you always look for me?" I ask.

"Ever since you got that exclusive and started showing up to the stadium." His voice is rough, like he's admitting something he never planned to say.

My heart flutters, and I reach up, brushing my fingers over his temple and through his hair. "I'll be right there, Bex. Every second of tonight."

He gives me a soft smile and a nod, and I feel like he's just said something more profound than anything I could've asked for.

As I settle into my seat in Row 3, Seat 7, the energy in the stadium is electric. This is it. Game four of the Stanley Cup. The crowd around me pulses with excitement, chanting and clapping, a sea of turquoise and white stretching across the stands. My hands rest on my belly, and I give a small, comforting pat, whispering, "You're about to witness history, little one. You're daddy is about to win his third Stanley Cup."

The game is intense from the start, both teams moving with an urgency that has the fans on the edge of their seats. Every minute that passes feels like an hour, the tension building with each play. The Hawkeyes score the first goal, and the crowd erupts, the sound echoing in my bones. But the other team isn't backing down. They score twice, and my heart drops, my hands clutching the thermos of apple cider Bex left me so hard that I think I might actually dent the stainless steel.

It's tied 2-2 when we hit the third period, with only minutes left on the clock. The players look exhausted, dripping sweat from their faces, steam practically radiating off their helmets, their skates carving deep lines into the ice as they fight for control. Bex is at the bench, shouting orders, his eyes fierce and unyielding. I know how much this means to him—how much he's poured into this team, into this game. It's not just a Stanley Cup, it's the culmination of years of sweat, sacrifice, and resilience.

The puck flies down the ice, Powers shoots the puck to Matthews as he charges across the ice, dodging defenders with impossible speed. My heart pounds as he takes the shot, and the whole stadium holds its breath. The puck slips just under the goalie's glove, sliding into the net with a loud thunk that seems to echo through every single person in the arena.

The crowd goes insane. People jump out of their seats, strangers hugging strangers, a wave of excitement for the home team and crushed faces from the opposition, roll through the stands. My own scream mingles with the noise, my hands flying to my mouth, my heart racing like I'm the one who scored.

And then I see him.

Bex turns, eyes sweeping the crowd, and he finds me almost instantly. Our gazes lock, and his face splits into a smile so full of pride, so raw and vulnerable, that my breath catches. It's a smile that says everything—every word he's never been able to say out loud. In this moment, I know, beyond a doubt, that no one has ever looked at me like this before. No one has ever seen me the way Bex sees me.

My heart thuds hard against my ribcage, the enormity of this moment showing me what the future will hold with Bex. Every victory, every defeat, every little piece of life in between, from this day on, we get to do together.

As the final buzzer sounds, sealing the Hawkeyes' victory, Bex jumps out onto the ice with the rest of the team. It's a sea of Turquoise, black and white. Helmets getting tossed into the air and stuffed animal Hawkeye birds getting tossed onto the ice.

The celebration is chaotic, everyone jumping, crying, shouting. And yet, as Bex finally breaks away from the team, he makes his way straight toward me, cutting through to the players tunnel, jumping up and over the railing, pushing through the row of people between us who are all slapping his shoulder for a job well done. But he doesn't take his eyes off of me.

I reach out for him as soon as he gets close and he pulls me in to him, slamming a kiss against my mouth. I pull him tight as if he's not close enough.

"You did it," I whisper, against our kiss.

He pulls back but stays close, staring down at me with those warm hazel eyes. "No," he says, his voice thick with emotion. "*We* did it."

And I know exactly what he means. Because this is more than a game, more than a championship. This is our life, our future, built one moment at a time, together.

He pulls me close, pressing a gentle kiss to my knuckles, and I feel tears sting my eyes. I've spent so much time chasing stories, searching for meaning, but here it is, right in front of me.

As the cheers continue to roar around us, drowning out everything else, Bex and I just stand there, caught in our own world, and for the first time in my life, I feel truly, perfectly whole.

Chapter Thirty-Three

Bex

Tonight, I can say that I have reached the pinnacle of this chapter in my life and the one that has defined me for decades. It's the Stanley Cup win, the crowning glory of a long, brutal career on the ice, and behind me, I can feel Rowan's gaze, steady and confident in me, a reminder of everything good that's come to me since she's been by my side.

I take a deep breath as I settle into the seat at the press table, the bright lights from the media room flashing in my face, intensifying the heat of the moment. Press conferences have never been my favorite, but tonight isn't about me, and for once, that makes sitting here almost bearable.

Next to me, Sam leans forward in his chair, resting his hands on the table. To his right sits Penelope Roberts, her poised expression masking what I can only imagine are nerves at the weight of the announcement we're about to make. This moment is monumental—not just for Sam or Penelope but for the entire Hawkeyes organization.

Rowan stands at the back of the room, just beyond the reach of the cameras. My eyes flick to her briefly as she exchanges a reassuring smile with Penelope. That's Rowan—always the first to support the people she believes in. It's a quality I've come to depend on and exactly what we all need right now.

Reporters call out questions, and cameras flash, but Sam waits until the noise dies down. Sam clears his throat, and the room falls silent. The flashes stop for a breath as every reporter waits, ready to catch the first words.

"Thank you all for coming," Sam begins, his commanding voice filling the room. "This season has been one for the books. Watching this team fight their way to another Stanley Cup win, and being able to watch from my spot in this stadium has been the kind of moment a GM dreams about in this business," He pauses, glancing at Penelope with a proud nod. "But as all of you know, nothing in hockey—or life—is permanent. And though it doesn't always feel like it for the players and coaching staff that make this great sport their life, there is life after hockey," he says, glancing over back at Rowan who smiles at him and then turns her eyes to me, her hand resting on her growing belly.

Curious chatter starts around the room, reporters reaching their mics out further to make sure they catch every word that

Sam has to say. Sam's always had a way of commanding respect without trying.

"After much thought and consideration," he continues, "I've decided that this season will be my last season as the General Manager of the Hawkeyes."

The chatter from reporters turn to gasps, and the clicking of cameras starts anew. Sam holds up his hands to settle everyone.

"It's been an honor to be a part of this organization, to help shape it into what it is today. I will stay on next year in a support position to ensure a seamless year. And as I step away, I'm proud to announce that Penelope Roberts will be stepping into the role of General Manager starting next season." He gestures toward Penelope, whose steady confidence doesn't falter, even as the press surges forward, desperate for a better angle.

Penelope leans into the microphone, her voice calm and assured. "I'm deeply honored to take on this role, and I want to thank Sam, Mr. Carlton, Coach Townsend, and the entire Hawkeyes team for their unwavering support. This organization has always been like a family to me and my father, and I promise to continue building on the legacy that all the great GM's before me have created."

Sam speaks again, cutting through questions as reporters try to sneak them in. "This decision wasn't made lightly. But I leave this team in the best hands, knowing that the players, staff, and fans will thrive under Penelope's leadership. And I want to thank Coach Bex Townsend and Phil Carlton, who have both been instrumental in making this transition as seamless as possible."

All eyes shift to me, and I lean into the microphone, my voice calm but firm. "Penelope knows this team better than almost anyone in this franchise. She's been behind the scenes for many years and there are few people who want the best for this franchise more than she does. She's got the full backing of the team and the staff, and I look forward to next season, working together to make the Hawkeyes organization stronger than ever."

Sam gives the room a nod as if to signal the questions and the room erupts with questions, flashing lights and camera shutters firing off in a frenzy. Reporters shout, trying to get details, and Tessa moves forward to settle them down, but Autumn takes over since Tessa is about due with her baby. Autumn does her best to hold the press at bay.

I stand, pushing back my chair, ignoring the barrage of voices calling for more. The noise doesn't matter now. All I care about is getting to Rowan, about pulling her into this moment. I step to the side, gesturing for her to walk in front of me, shielding her from the frenzy.

We exit the media room together, and I can hear Autumn's calm, commanding voice, trying to redirect the press, herding them back as they try to snap photos and shout questions.

"Big day," she says softly, her hand brushing mine as we fall into step together, heading toward the corridor.

"Bigger for Penelope," I reply, though my voice betrays a hint of relief. The transition feels like the start of something new—not just for the Hawkeyes but for me, too. A chance to reassess, to figure out what comes next. And for once, I know it's not just hockey that's on my mind.

As we move through the throng of people, Drew steps into our path, his smirk firmly in place. For a brief second, my old irritation flares, but I push it aside. Tonight isn't the night for old grudges.

"Townsend, Congratulations. Big changes ahead. Hope you're ready." he says, holding up a pen and a Hawkeyes jersey with my name on the back. "Mind signing a jersey for a fan?"

I glance at him, then at the small line forming nearby, true fans who've been waiting with jerseys and memorabilia of their own.

Maybe he plans to sell it, or give it away, I have no idea. I doubt he plans to display it on the wall in his office, or godforbid, wear it, but there are too many witnesses to blow him off like I would like to.

"Right, didn't realize you were such a fan," I say, barely able to contain the sarcasm in my voice.

His gaze shifts to Rowan, standing beside me, her hand resting protectively on her belly. His eyes glide over the old jersey she's wearing. Drew's brows furrow, clearly surprised.

"You're still on this side of the media line, Rowan?" He smirks, arching a brow. "They know you're not with *The Seattle Sunrise* anymore, right?"

His attempt to insinuate that Rowan doesn't belong here doesn't sit well with me, and I pull Rowan in closer, wrapping my arm protectively around her waist. "She's not here to work, Drew. She's here so our baby can have a front-row seat to watch the Hawkeyes win the Stanley Cup."

I catch his shocked expression as he glances between us, his mouth hanging open. "Your baby?" His voice wavers, and I can see him trying to process what I just said.

I reach for a marker, ready to add my autograph to Rowan's jersey in the most obvious spot I can think of. Rowan's eyes widen, her hand catching my wrist, a quiet question in her gaze.

"What are you doing?" she whispers, her face flush with surprise. "You don't like people knowing your personal business."

"That doesn't apply when it comes to you," I say, giving her a soft smile. "I want everyone to know the baby you're carrying is mine and that you're coming home to me every night." I pause, letting my words sink in. "That is what you want, isn't it?"

A smile blooms across her face as she nods, her hand releasing mine. I bend down, resting one hand on her belly, my thumb brushing the fabric over our growing baby as I sign my name right across her belly. I want everyone to see that Rowan, and the life we're building, is more important than any title or career milestone.

As I straighten, Drew stammers, glancing from Rowan to me. "Wait—you're pregnant?" His voice is thick with disbelief.

Rowan glances at me, a beautiful, proud smile on her face. "Sixteen weeks," she says, glowing with happiness.

Drew's jaw practically hits the floor, his gaze darting to her stomach as he stumbles over his words. "But... I thought... the doctors said..."

I pull Rowan closer to my side. "It's not your fault, Mate. Your shit isn't top-grade baby batter. Don't beat yourself up about it. She had to bring in the ringer."

Rowan chuckles, leaning into me, and I feel her hand slide down my back, an unspoken message of thanks. It's clear now, in this moment, that we're moving forward, leaving the past behind and starting fresh with the family we're building.

I dip down, planting a kiss on her belly for good measure. Rowan's hand slips to the back of my head, her fingers warm and gentle as I press a kiss against the fabric covering our child. I love how she finds little ways to reassure me, to remind me that we're in this together, no matter what.

Drew stands there, floundering, unable to mask his shock. But his reaction is irrelevant now. As I straighten, there's a sparkle in Rowan's eyes for me.

She doesn't need words to tell me what I already know. This moment is ours, and together, we're unstoppable.

Epilogue

Five Months Later

Bex

I stare down at the baby in my arms, wrapped in a pink blanket, and fast asleep in only a diaper, laying against my bare chest as I rock her in the corner of the hospital room.

Skin-to-skin, the nurse called it. A way to bond with the baby. I didn't need convincing—this little girl already has me wrapped tightly around her finger. Her heartbeat is steady against mine, and I marvel at how something so small can fill every corner of a space I didn't even know was empty.

She's only six hours old, but she's already taken over my world.

I shift slightly in the rocking chair, careful not to disturb her. She doesn't even stir, her little body warm against mine, her soft breath rising and falling in perfect rhythm.

It's hard to imagine something so perfect and innocent came from what happened in the back of a limo.

Everything about her is so tiny—her fingers, toes, the little wisps of dark hair like mine currently hidden under her yellow infant beanie. I'm told that her hair might all fall out and new hair will grow. There's no saying what part of her will look like me or which parts she'll take after Rowan. If I had my choice, she'd look just like Rowan. Blonde hair, blue eyes, and that smile—the one that's been the undoing of me since the moment I first saw it.

God, that smile.

The memory makes me chuckle softly, careful not to wake the baby. For nine months, that smile had me doing things I never thought I'd do. Midnight runs to the grocery store for ice cream and popcorn, assembling cribs and rocking chairs with instructions that might as well have been written in a lost language, and countless foot rubs because "the baby" demanded them.

My daughter—Keira, a soft, weighty bundle in my arms—is sleeping, her little fingers curled into fists. I stroke my thumb across her back, reveling in the fact that I'm her safe place. I feel something within me shift, deep and irrevocable. The small tag around her foot reads *Townsend*, and the sight of it nearly knocks the wind out of me. It's a name she'll carry, a name I'll make sure means safety, love, and family.

And it's the name that her mother should be carrying too.

Rowan stirs from her short nap. She needed a break after a long labor, getting the hang of breastfeeding, lactation specialists, and nurses coming in constantly to do their checks on her and Keira.

Her eyes flutter open with that quiet smile that's always been just for me. How she can find the strength to smile like that, after everything she's gone through to bring our daughter into this world, is beyond me. I look back down at our little girl, hoping she inherits her mother's resilience, her fire, her tenderness.

"You're a natural," she whispers low to not wake the baby. "She looks like she's always belonged there, in your arms."

I meet her gaze, feeling a grin pull at my lips. "I think she always has," I say, taking in each tiny, perfect feature again.

Rowan shifts on the bed, and I can see a hint of discomfort in her eyes, quickly replaced with a content grin watching us rock back and forth together. I feel a newfound admiration for her.

I've always known she was strong, resilient—but to witness the love and grit it took for her to bring our child into this world… I'll never feel for anyone what I feel for her.

In my pocket, I can feel the square box digging against my thigh, a small weight I've carried since after the Stanley Cup win. I've waited for the right moment, finding excuse after excuse, too caught up in the whirlwind of Rowan's new career and me working with Sam, Penelope and Phil to make sure that the transition for Penelope is as smooth as possible before the new season, and my last one, starts up.

Not to mention house shopping in Liverpool remotely with Leo and his wife doing the physical walk through for us. We've been busy, but I've never considered not asking her. Not since she told me she was pregnant. That was when I knew we were in this life together, for worse or for better, in sickness or in health.

Now, sitting in the room, just the three of us, I knew what I was waiting for— Keira.

With our daughter cradled in my arms, I know this is it. This is the moment.

I glance down at our daughter once more, then carefully hand her back to Rowan. She settles against her mother's chest, and Rowan lets out a soft, contented sigh, her hand cupping the back of our daughter's head.

"Rowan..." I begin, feeling my heart pound with anticipation as I reach for the ring in my pocket.

She looks up at me, her eyes tired but happy, and a glint of curiosity. Her eyes dart down to my pocket as I fumble with it.

"I've been trying to find the perfect moment," I say, my voice low. "But something kept telling me to wait. I didn't know why until now."

Rowan's eyes widen, and she lets out a soft, breathy gasp as she sees the unmistakable box in my hand.

"This moment—seeing you here with her, knowing everything we've gone through to get here... I've never been more certain about anything in my life." I sink down to one knee beside her hospital bed, holding up the small velvet box. "Rowan, you and our daughter... you're my family, my heart. I was empty before you showed up, and I know now that I'll never be whole without you. Will you do me the honor of spending the rest of your days with me? Will you be my wife?"

She stares at me, her hand flying to her mouth as tears fill her eyes. She glances down at our daughter, then back up at me, her lips parting in a smile that's equal parts joy and surprise.

"Yes, Bex," she whispers, and nods, "Yes, I'll marry you."

"It's time that both of my girls were Townsend's," I say, and then I slide the ring onto her finger, a promise that feels as sure as anything I've ever known. Rowan reaches for my hand, holding it tight, and I press a kiss to her lips and then a kiss, gently, on our daughter's head.

Together, we sit there in the stillness of the morning, a family in love, stronger than anything I've ever known, I know that I've found exactly where I'm meant to be.

THE END

Thank you so much for reading!
I am currently working on a BONUS chapter – "WHERE ARE THEY NOW? THREE YEARS LATER", which will give an update to every couple in this series and where their lives have taken them.

Keep an eye out for this Bonus Chapter by subscribing to my newsletter by visiting **www.kennaking.com**
Or by joining my reader Facebook group here **Kenna King's MVPs**

NEED MORE HAWKEYES BOYS?!
You won't have to wait long!
Pre-order Cammy Wrenley's story, Book #1 of the **Rookie Hawkeyes Series**
Enemies to Lovers
Coach's Daughter
Second Chance